Joseph C. Sweeney

The
Lambert Revels

The
Lambert Revels

by *Terence de Vere White*

An Atlantic Monthly Press Book
Little, Brown and Company - Boston - Toronto

LIBRARY OF CONGRESS CATALOG CARD NO. 75-91233

Third Printing

Published in England under the title
THE LAMBERT MILE

ATLANTIC—LITTLE, BROWN BOOKS
ARE PUBLISHED BY
LITTLE, BROWN AND COMPANY
IN ASSOCIATION WITH
THE ATLANTIC MONTHLY PRESS

PRINTED IN THE UNITED STATES OF AMERICA

For Osbert Lancaster

PART I

CHAPTER I

On an April morning in the early days of the atomic age, the postman appeared in the kitchen of Cumberland Lodge, as his habit was, to pass the time of day with ageing Angela who, in cold weather, fortified him with a cup of tea before he proceeded on his way. He put the letters down one by one, sharing Angela's curiosity over each.

"That's from Miss Elizabeth," Angela said. Then she and the postman stared at the envelope addressed in an impulsive feminine hand to the Canon. It bore two foreign stamps.

"She must be thinking of paying them a visit," the postman said, and Angela nodded her head with becoming gravity.

Thus was the message securely attached to the grape-vine, and it would run now with the speed of light down the Lambert Mile.

When Angela came up to the dining-room with the post she found the Canon alone at the table. He knew from the barking of the poodle that the postman had arrived at least ten minutes before. Even so he could not bring himself to reprove her. She had to deduce from certain signs that he was displeased. He thanked her for the letters, but refrained from enquiring after her health or how she had passed the night. More pointedly, instead of saying 'Ah!' and beaming with anticipation when she put the letters beside him, he asked her to bring them into the study, thereby conveying that the morning programme was running behind schedule on account of her inconsiderate gossiping.

She carried the letters into the study and put them on the little table beside the fire, which had been slacked so as to keep it in for the morning. On the table was a book of memoirs, which the Canon was reading. In due course it would be passed up the road to Miss Beddington.

Angela looked round the study to see if everything was in order. Napoleon, the Siamese cat, lay in the hearth waiting for his master, who would appear at any moment carrying the newspaper in one hand, a saucer of milk in the other. On one occasion he had put down the paper for the cat and poured the milk over his own waistcoat. The post had been more than usually absorbing that morning.

Angela lingered hoping to be forgiven.

"Is the sun too much for your eyes? Will I pull the curtains over a bit?"

"No thank you. Napoleon enjoys the sun."

He sat down rather heavily; and the cat, which had never taken its eyes off him, leaped into his lap, rolling itself into a comfortable position.

The Canon gave the slightest inclination of his head towards Angela and said: "If anyone telephones take the message and say I am busy."

This was as always; and Angela was satisfied. She closed the door behind her.

The morning had now entered its final phase. The Canon was, by implication, busy in the study. Angela would return to the kitchen and heat up the kettle for another cup of tea. Her mistress would be employed upstairs. The Ormsbys had only Angela now and Michael to help outside. Servants were never easy to get on the Mile; and the Ormsbys were counted lucky.

The Canon was never cross, but he had a rare talent for getting hurt, which was universally respected. He had conveyed to Angela that she had hurt him by her thoughtlessness, and she would not be perfectly happy until he 'joked with her' again, and thus conveyed that she was completely forgiven. It was a tribute to him that he could keep her so attuned to his moods and still pay her half the current wage. True, she was past her best, and even when at it was never a very efficient cook; but she would only have worked for Barbara Beddington for the same wages, knowing perfectly well what was being paid by the Perrys to their staff at Sussex. Major Paul, known as 'the Count', had an Italian couple, to whom he was known to pay a king's ransom.

The Canon was able to get away with it for some occult reason. It was the same in his relation with Michael Molloy. Michael's devotion to the Lamberts was a local legend. His father had been the coachman, and he haunted the place like a banshee; but he would not have anything to do with the steward, Bradshaw; and the services which he gave to the Canon, at an absurdly nominal wage, were a sort of feudal due, which he paid him as the true representative of the family interest, the friend and relative to whom he knew the fortunes of Mount Lambert were a matter of deepest concern.

The third willing slave in the Canon's household was his wife. Her fortune relieved him of the necessity of parish work. Mrs Ormsby worked like a black, but spent her time concealing this from her husband whom the knowledge would have distressed.

The Canon lived in clover; but there was something gently plaintive in his manner which suggested a sensitivity of organisation that could not exist with anything less.

No sound was accustomed to come from, much less penetrate, the Canon's study when he was 'busy'; but this morning the door was thrown open and, in a voice singularly free from the slightly mincing tone that his customary precision imparted, he roared into the void.

"Penny come down here out of that. A letter from Elizabeth."

When Mrs Ormsby, slightly ruffled, carrying a duster, came in, her lord was sitting up in his chair with a letter in his hand, poised, like the conductor of a symphony orchestra, ready to begin.

A tiny furrow, indicative of discontent, appeared between his large, melancholy eyes, and he paused as the conductor might if he observed that the second violin was blowing his nose.

"Sit down, dear."

There is nothing more annoying than to deliver weighty news to someone who gives the impression of taking it on the wing. Mrs Ormsby sat down. The furrow disappeared.

"Listen to this:

Dearest Uncle Silverpenny
(She never forgets that. Bless her!)
I owe you a letter for ever so long, and I don't believe that I ever thanked you and Aunt Pen for your perfectly marvellous Christmas presents. But I shall explain when I see you why I neglected everyone and everything during the so-called festive season. It's all over now (the trouble, I mean).

I have been trying to persuade my parents to come over to Mount Lambert this summer; but they won't. Pa still insists that he was so unhappy there he swore that he would never go back; and Ma hates to leave this awful Majorca for more than a day. I'll be 21 in October, as you know, and Pa's idea is that the place should be sold; but I know that he has had it on the books for years and he never gets an offer, so that it won't be so easy, and he doesn't want to give it away. He says that it costs him £5,000 a year to keep up, and even if we halve that, which in Pa's case I always do, it's still a terrible drain on the family income.

Unless I can get a rich American to marry me, the prospect looks rather dreary; but I half suspect that the place could be run much more economically. Ritzy has been writing Ma such hair-raising letters about the present set-up. He wants to take it over himself; but as he has twice gone bankrupt and left here owing millions all round, I doubt if that would be wise. However, his powers of persuasion are fabulous.

I've decided to come over and see for myself. Now

12

that Ralph has gone into the office it will be much easier for me to find out what I want to know. Mr Fox always put the wind up me; and I can never hope to persuade him that I am a consenting adult.

This means, of course, that I'm going to land myself on you again. Can you put up with me or, rather, put me up? And when would it be best to come? I'd like to get something fixed up before my birthday. When I hear from you I'll write to Mr Fox for politeness sake. He can tell Bradshaw. I don't want to write to him.

Give my love to Aunt Pen, Ralph, Angela, Napoleon, Ritzy—if you ever see him—Barbara and your old dear self.

Your affectionate god-child,
Elizabeth.

"Well!"

The Canon looked at his wife as if he had emptied a cornucopia of ripe blessings into her lap.

"Who's Ritzy?" she asked, without relaxing the little frown of strain that never left her forehead.

"Major Paul, of course."

"The name rather suits him. I always told you he looked a blackguard."

"An over-optimistic attitude towards his income hardly justifies such an epithet."

"Fiddles! You will never face up to realities. The man has cast a spell over you, and I only hope that he won't lead you into some folly. He's quite capable of it."

The sunshine drained out of the Canon's face. Penelope was the best of women; but every now and then she tore open the cocoon in which he was at such pains to wind himself, and left him naked to his enemies. She always took care to wrap him up again and, to be fair, carried out these operations in private and under her own steam. Her loyalty outside the walls of Cumberland Lodge was unwavering; and even the slightest attempt to prick his balloon of pretension aroused the tiger in her. But she had seen him in his

13

shirt and even less. She knew the man under the cloak. She had been his partner in moments when his feelings got the better even of his syntax. She supplied him with all her money. She was privileged occasionally—very occasionally—to speak her mind; and it had probably a therapeutic effect on the Canon, a salutary change from a diet overloaded with sugar.

"Well, go on, dear. What were you going to say?"

Mrs Ormsby's tone had become conciliatory. The Canon fought back his disappointment—he had expected her to share his instant enthusiasm—but he was not going to let a vessel with such a cargo go aground at this stage if by an effort he could refloat it.

"I must write to Elizabeth at once. When do you think it would be most convenient to have her? There will be a certain amount of gaiety in August. I wonder if Ralph could take some of his leave then."

"He was planning to go to winter sports."

"But even so. He didn't know Elizabeth was coming. I'm sure Mr Fox will give him as much liberty as he wants, in any event. This decision about Mount Lambert's future will require a lot of thought."

"I hope she won't expect us to provide her with much entertainment."

"I'm sure Elizabeth will not be at a loss. There's Barbara Beddington who is quite devoted to her."

"Barbara is not in a position to give her a very riotous time."

"And she knows Major Paul."

"Do you think those mysterious parties of his are quite the thing for Elizabeth? Although I suppose she is a pretty up-to-date piece herself."

The Canon frowned.

"We must get up some entertainment for her. A ball perhaps..."

"Where could we hold a ball?"

"These rooms are quite large. We have entertained fifty

people without moving furniture. They could dance in the drawing-room. I'm sure it could be arranged. Ralph will have to be consulted."

"I don't know that I could face . . ."

"Or—I tell you what—" the Canon's sad eyes suddenly radiated pure joy. "We will give it at Mount Lambert. I'll write to Julian as we must get his permission. Elizabeth ought to have a coming-out dance in any case. Perhaps Julian and May will take up the idea themselves. They do precious little for their daughter. It will be the first big party Mount Lambert has seen for half a century. Do the house good, too. Air it. We can engage a good band and hand all the arrangements over to a caterer. What would it cost nowadays—if we have to pay for it, I mean? I don't suppose we could expect less than a pound a head. And would that include champagne? We must do it properly. Say 200 guests at . . . Oh! my dear, it will certainly run us into money. I wonder could we manage to do it ourselves? Barbara would help; and she would lend us Mrs Bartholomew for the occasion. We might get out of it for a hundred pounds. I shouldn't mind spending that. After all, she is my god-daughter and we owe everything to the Lamberts."

Mrs Ormsby's expression passed from one degree of perturbation to another as she listened to her husband. But she knew that it would be fatal to deflate him in his present mood. The letter induced euphoria. It would pass off. She had only to bide her time.

"It will cost much more than a hundred; and where would we collect the guests from? We hardly know any young people."

"Ralph will produce them. And everyone round here will want to come : Barbara and the Perrys and Captain Loftus and the Brownes, and I suppose Ritzy, as we may call him, will expect to take part. I am a little bit afraid he may incline to disparage our arrangements. He does everything so *en prince* himself, he will find our efforts rather homely."

"I should certainly not allow that to worry you. But do

you think it's necessary to go to so much trouble? Elizabeth won't expect it. We aren't in the way of that sort of entertaining. And Ralph is always complaining that he knows practically nobody because you insisted on sending him to England for all his education. He is not the sort of boy who picks up friends easily."

"The Misses Tottenham would not like to be left out, and we must make out a list of the families that knew the Lamberts when they lived here. There are not many of them left, I fear—the Sarsfield-Emmets, the Ponsonby-Crowes, the Cunningham-Dawsons, the Pooles, the Porridges and the Worralls. I'll think of more if I'm given time. Wherever I preach in the county, there is always someone who introduces himself and makes a link with the past."

"Are you thinking now, dear, of a dance to be given by us or by the Lamberts?"

The Canon waved away the distinction with a beautiful movement of a long white hand. He hated the intrusion of niggling detail on any of his grand designs.

"Miss Charteris is still around. We must get in touch with her. And the Jasper-Halls! I declare that I was almost forgetting them. They were living at Lough Corrib when I last heard of them."

"They would be well over eighty if they were still alive."

"There would be a problem about putting people up for the night. We could take two. Barbara, I am sure, would row in; and I expect the Perrys will help. Loftus is incalculable; but I expect that he would oblige us if Elizabeth was involved. God knows he owes the Lamberts a lot. He has Wales for what wouldn't hire a mousetrap nowadays. The Brownes will want whoever is the grandest guest. Nothing less than a lord for them. And then we may be able to open some of the rooms in Mount Lambert. It can be managed, I have no doubt, if we lay our plans in time."

As the Canon went on spinning his fantasy of a ball composed of octogenarians, invalids and eccentrics, his wife made more sober calculations. Angela gave her very little help; and the prospect of a month of unending festivities oppressed her. She suffered from anaemia and a weak heart, neither of which she had brought to her husband's notice in case it would disturb his equanimity. Moreover, she was beginning to worry about money. Her income had not grown; and what was ample when she married for both of them on the scale they lived was now beginning to wear thin. The Canon, who had been brought up with only family pride to sustain him on 'the smell of a rag', had never recovered from the first experience of opulence.

It was she who consulted bank managers in private and paid calls on Mr Fox, the solicitor, and bore the burden and heat of the day. She could just make do if the Canon would forego the rôle of Maecenas; and a campaign such as he planned for Elizabeth was quite out of the question unless they were to run into debt.

"The band might be expensive. I don't know what that sort of thing costs nowadays. Ralph will be able to tell us."

"A proper band will cost you a small fortune, coming out all this way. I would not nourish any illusions about that."

"Perhaps we could muster one among ourselves. What a pity we got rid of the piano. When I was young everybody had a piano. In a decent house there was a Grand; a baby Grand if your drawing-room was small; and the meanest habitation boasted a cottage piano, an upright one, you know. Where have they all gone to? Somewhere there must be a vast store of discarded pianos, in some elephants' burying place. Let me see: Barbara hasn't got one, has she? I'm sure there was one at Clarence in her mother's time. Nobody ever gets inside Wales, so that we don't know whether Loftus mightn't have one tucked away. Ask him about it, will you, dear? The Brownes went all modern and got rid of theirs with the standard lamp and the outdoor larder. I don't recall a piano at the Perrys', do you? The Major hasn't got one; he said something about getting an original harpsichord, but that was more by way of show. I don't think he had any intention of playing it. Isn't it a curious reflection on the times that nobody makes music now? It was delightful to have a little Chopin on tap, Beethoven, Mozart . . . Bach was always a little beyond me. Not that I could ever play myself. We hadn't a note of music in us as a family."

"Wireless and television. Nobody could stand the sort of strumming we had to put up with."

"Still. I can remember very enjoyable evenings round a piano, singing some chorus everybody knew. Something from *The Gondoliers* or the musical comedies. All that sort of thing has gone. People are not so pleasant as they were. I remember a chap who was in college with me—Atkinson—I can't recall his first name; very long and thin he was; didn't wash much. He had a beautiful tenor voice; really remarkable. It took some time to warm him up; the great thing was to get him to sing *Angels Guard Thee*. He got more and more difficult to persuade, and drunk quite a lot in the process. My poor mother enjoyed his visits until one evening when he was sick surreptitiously behind the sofa. We never heard *Angels Guard Thee* in our house after that. He was a very clever fellow in a disorganised sort of way. His rooms were smelly—quite offensive, in summer especially. Always borrowing small sums of money; capable of pinching things, too—nothing really valuable, needless to say—razor blades and that sort of thing. He had aunts up north from whom he had expectations, which he decided eventually to anticipate by going to live on them. I believe he died quite early on. Pity."

"Darling, I must go back to the laundry list. The van will be calling at any moment."

The Canon's benevolence suffered a further inroad. He had quite lost himself in pleasant reminiscence, and as always delighted in sharing it. But the pace of modern life invariably encroached on these happy occasions. It literally drove the Canon out of his house. When interrupted by some importunate tradesman or discouraged by the whirl of domestic activity—as now—he would ask Angela to ask Michael to catch the horse and harness him.

Driving his dog-cart—the sort of conveyance he preferred—around the neighbourhood, he stopped to greet everyone he met on the way. Robinson, as the horse was called, became so used to this method of progress that when he was lent during the hunting season to any friend who needed a quiet mount he came to a dead halt even in the midst of a gallop if he saw any man, woman or child approaching. The clop of Robinson's hooves on the tarmacadam brought many a householder to his door. At this time of day it was usually a female; but whoever it was the Canon pulled up at the gate and exchanged a few non-contentious words. He knew everybody's business, and there was usually a sick child, an aged relative, or a dog to be enquired after.

"I think I'll drop over to Doctor Lawlor's and ask him for that prescription for my throat."

"I'll see if Michael is outside. He was in rather a hurry this morning. His mother is ill again, poor dear. I'm afraid she will not be with us for much longer."

"I could call on my way and enquire. Have you a pot of jam or something? I don't like to go empty-handed."

"I don't think Mrs Molloy is up to a visit. Michael was talking of sending for the priest."

"She might still like a pot of jam. I don't suppose Michael is able to supply her with many delicacies of that nature."

Mrs Ormsby concealed a sigh. Jam-making was one of her annual chores; but as fast as she made it her husband gave it away, pressing it, as in this instance, on the most unlikely people.

"That's the last pot of marmalade," she said later, coming into the hall to see the Canon off. He no more liked to go out than to come in without the household in attendance.

"I am very sorry to hear about your mother," he said to

19

Michael, who was standing at Robinson's head. "I shall pray for her. I hope she will like this marmalade. She was very appreciative of the last pot."

"I'm afraid she's past taking nourishment now, Canon."

"I am really sorry to hear that. We must only put our trust in God. I'll just pop my head in as I'm passing, and I'll leave the pot down in case she picks up later on and feels like a little nourishment."

"You're very good," Michael said.

The Canon took up the reins; Robinson, acting on the signal, moved forward with the slight reluctance which always marked his first steps away from home (he came back at a spanking trot). The Canon waved to his wife, waved to Angela, waved to Michael. Mrs Ormsby waved to the Canon. Angela waved to the Canon. Michael waved to the Canon. He flourished his whip in the air in a gesture of farewell to all assembled. Robinson quickened his pace. At the gate, the Canon reined in and halted. Michael ran forward.

"Have you forgotten something, Canon?"

"Something has just occurred to me. Haven't you got a piano, Michael? I'm sure I remember one in the cottage, an upright one, with photographs on it?"

"I suppose you might call it that, Canon, but I never knew anyone to play on it in my time. You'd be welcome to try it if ever you had a mind to; but at the moment, I'm afraid it might distract my poor mother."

"That wasn't what I was thinking of at all. It just struck me that you had a piano. I wanted to make sure."

He nodded and drove on.

CHAPTER II

MAJOR PAUL, IN a braided silk dressing-gown, sat in
front of a plate of peaches. He knew the ways of the world
too well to allow any communications by mail to obtrude
upon his early morning thoughts. Upstairs, Benito, his Italian servant, was laying out his clothes; he had had a delicious bath; the peaches were first rate. He rang the bell for
the Italian's wife, Maria, to come and fetch him more
coffee.

Seated, the Major looked a big man. He had a powerful
head, on which the hair brushed closely back was only
faintly speckled with grey, and becomingly at that, behind
the ears. His complexion was sallow and his expression self-
indulgent. But the remarkable feature of his face was the
eyes: the pupils were large, and the impression of vivid
black against staring white was unforgettable, and could be
terrifying. For this reason—or perhaps to heighten their
effect when he used them to the full—he kept his eyes
hooded. Sitting there, he reminded the housekeeper, when
she came in with the coffee, of a bird of prey resting after
his sanguinary meal in the Zoo of her native Milan. She
crossed herself.

His moods were incalculable; but she was quick to see
that he had not yet opened his post, and his temper was
probably—if the seat of the passions may be likened to a
gear-box—in neutral; besides he was a good master. Better
to servants and to animals than to any beings who might
obstruct or thwart him. He expected loyal service and
rewarded it. His standards were almost impossibly high.

In spite of his reputation and his bachelor state, he was
never familiar with her. He had a code of his own. Bills ran
in shops, but wages were paid. His horses and his dogs

would never go without. All he demanded was implicit obedience. The rest of the world did not lend itself so readily to the dictates of his code; but he had long ago determined that the world would meet him on his own terms. Take the post, for instance, which lay on the table, asking to be opened and read. He was not going to allow himself to be made the tool of the writers with their requests and demands. When the last peach was eaten, and he had rubbed his hands in the lawn napkin, he sorted the letters out as if he was arranging a game of cards, with royals and trumps at the top. He knew at once to what category each letter belonged. Holograph took precedence over typewritten; open envelopes were put into the fire at once. He was too cautious to use waste-paper baskets. Where the writing was a woman's, and there were several examples, he opened the more unfamiliar first, glancing very quickly over the pages. If he knew the hand-writing he usually put the letter into the pocket of his dressing-gown to read it at his pleasure.

If the lady was a bore or inclined to be intense, he might carry the letter round for days before he read it. As this sometimes led to practical inconvenience (for himself) he tended as a rule to glance quickly at the beginning and end of the letters which he lacked the energy to tackle at once to see if immediate action was necessary.

He rarely wrote letters himself, but sometimes sent telegrams for effect, and was a compulsive user of the telephone. He knew that properly used a telephone is an offensive weapon. One sprang propositions on people when they were unaware; and the Count was difficult at any time to resist. His voice was blandishment itself. The inflections sent a ripple of pleasure down the spine; and the contrast between this mellifluous persuader and the formidable presence at the other end of the line usually did the trick.

Everyone felt they needed his approval : and in order to gain it were prepared to make considerable sacrifices. The pictures on his walls, all by artists of the first water, were

evidently propitiatory offerings. The carpets, the furniture—
almost all had the same origin—presents from people who
wanted a permanent place in a museum for which the
exhibits were chosen with such relentless fastidiousness.

When he needed money—and he was in continual need
of it—he usually got it from women. They lent it, touched
by the thought that he needed their help, taking the security
which he never failed to offer in order to save his pride;
sometimes they gave from gratitude, sometimes to streng-
then a chain, sometimes to open a door; but they seldom
wanted it back. With men, his approach was different. To
them he held out a prospect of a fabulous return on investment. Usually the transaction had to do with horses, about
which he knew a great deal; and it was alluring to think
you had bought a stake in the Derby winner, two years
hence, or the yearling which would make a record price at
the Newmarket sales, or were to share the fees of a prodigious sire. In retrospect it always seemed as if the lender
had pressed the money on the reluctant Count from sheer
covetousness and in spite of warnings that horses were not
gilt-edged investments. One individual (who got nasty) was
treated to the fullest measure of the Count's contempt; and
to restore himself in his good books doubled his stake and
saw the new loan pocketed with a shrug.

This morning, after the usual shuffle of the letters took
place, the Count decided to open May Lambert's letter
from Majorca. He made an exception in her case, and
wrote to her occasionally about Mount Lambert, having
determined to take it over and seeking the means to put his
plan into operation. He could not at the moment raise the
money to buy it. His tenancy of Kent Lodge was a private
arrangement with May which involved a complicated and
highly private series of transactions. No money passed. He
had gone over the lands and interviewed Bradshaw, the
steward, and had no difficulty in coming to the conclusion
that the place would make a good stud farm when it had
about £50,000 spent on it. He also decided that Bradshaw

23

was robbing the Lamberts. As always he was right—in both suppositions in the present instance—but the carrying out of his plan would necessarily involve a large investment by somebody else; and that somebody might be difficult to find because nobody ever came out of a financial partnership with the Count salvaging a penny.

His scheme was to sack Bradshaw, put the place in order, and have himself installed as stud manager at a salary of £5,000 a year with a free hand to buy suitable mares. About a quarter of a million was his idea of the amount of capital required. Needless to say he would have to look beyond the Lamberts for this. But he had put it to May that any part in a decent scheme of this kind was more in keeping with the family honour than letting the place run down while a fraudulent steward milked whatever profit there was to be got from it during its decline and fall.

As well as a salary the Count looked forward to a substantial share in the profits from the stud in return for his own contribution, a yearling filly whose own sister had bred the fastest two-year-old in Italy in the previous season. Lady Lambert had not jumped at the proposition; and the Count was anxious to know what the latest bulletin disclosed.

Opening the envelope, his face wore the *blasé* expression he reserved for women's letters. He had May's measure; and her caperings were a sheer waste of time. His eye behind the monocle lightly skimmed the page. She was dodging the issue. Silly bitch. Trying to put him off and keep him on a string at the same time. Then he came to a passage which made him start. May dropped out that Elizabeth was coming over to stay with the Canon; and she made a coy reference to the impossibility of her staying at Kent Lodge, and in a cryptic phrase seemed to ask him to be at the same time nice to her and to leave her alone. There was something pitiful always about a *femme fatale* with a daughter growing up, especially when, as in Elizabeth's case, the daughter was incontestably attractive.

He pushed his plate away, and sat with his head buried in his hands staring at the end of May's letter.

For once, he did not see his way clearly. His code, of which only he knew the rules, was being put to a severe test. He wanted to get hold of Mount Lambert and had failed to get round May. Julian refused point blank to discuss any schemes; he had no doubts in his mind; his sole desire was to sell. Elizabeth's coming was like an answer to prayer. It was extraordinarily foolish of May (and Julian) to let her come while he was formulating his plans. Of course, he would use her to the fullest extent possible; and he had no doubt whatever that he would be able to bend her to his wishes. But in the process—he thought of May's rather pathetic and secret appeal—the girl would undoubtedly fall in love with him. She was a woman, her mother's daughter; she had had two rather unsatisfactory and, presumably, inconclusive affairs; she was ripe. And how could he exercise his powers so as to make her his accomplice in securing the place for his purposes and escape an emotional involvement? It had never happened to him in his life. To young women in particular he was irresistible, an Othello without the colour bar. He was not a scalp-hunter where women were concerned; he had always found them easy prey, and he did not want to seduce May's daughter. The only obstacle was the law of his code that if he got involved with a woman at all he must go through with it, as when out riding he would never let a horse refuse a fence, however often he had to put him at it.

An instinct made him open one other of the letters—a typewritten one but with a certain air of authority about the envelope. The letter came from a London firm of lawyers inquiring after the welfare of the horses at Kent Lodge upon which the Count had borrowed £8,000 to be repayed after the Doncaster sales.

Now the man of action was called into being—the problem of Elizabeth was shelved—the Count rang the bell for his clothes. Always dressed for the part, he put on his best riding outfit, giving himself the appearance of a retired cavalry officer turned horse trainer.

He had completed his toilet when he heard the clop of Robinson's feet at the top of the Lambert Mile. The Canon was coming. Now the Canon was the only person in the district for whom the Count had any respect. Like called to like in a mysterious manner; for no two people could have been superficially less alike. Yet, deep down there was an affinity, and each recognised it. The Canon was the only person who could have understood the Count's code. The difference between them in the Count's eyes was merely one of size. The Canon was content to put on a perfect performance at a small out-of-the-way theatre before a strictly limited audience; the Count's nature demanded a grandiose display, and this necessitated an effort on a totally different scale. The Count might use anyone for his schemes; but when he needed friendship—admitting equality—he would turn only to the Canon. He needed a friend now.

He was at the gate when the dog-cart drove up—it had stopped outside Miss Beddington's.

"Good morning, Major."

"Your horse is not quite right on the near fore. Let me look. I thought so. A little pebble in the shoe. I noticed the fault in his action coming down the hill."

"I am very much obliged to you, Major. I stopped to tell you that we had great news today. Elizabeth is coming to stay. She sent her love to you. We have found out a secret. She has a pet name for you."

"Ritzy. She calls me that. It is very cheeky of her. But, then, I have a very rude name for her. When is she coming?"

"She leaves that to us. August, I was going to suggest. There will be more entertainment for her then. What do you think? How are two old people to make life gay for a young woman?"

"What about that son of yours? When we were his age, Canon . . ."

"We will have to rely on Ralph. They were like brother and sister when they were young. It's hard to believe she is just twenty-one."

A film came over the Count's eyes as if a squid's protective ink had been ejected from the dark pupils. It meant that he was busy with his own thoughts.

"May I beg the hospitality of one of your stables, Canon? I have been informed that a racing tout is in the neighbourhood, and I am particularly anxious that he shan't see one of my small string. It is unlikely that his curiosity will bring him as far as Cumberland Lodge; you haven't a reputation as a breeder of thoroughbreds."

"With pleasure. I'll send Michael down this evening to fetch it. But shouldn't you inform the Guards? That is the worst of horses, they attract undesirables. Wherever they are, there is always fighting and fornication. And what noble beasts they are, putting to shame the low types that use them for gaming."

"The yahoo exploiting the houyhnhnm. Exactly. If you don't mind, Canon, I would as soon that you say nothing to Michael about the matter. I shall drop the filly over in your place after lunch. The walk will do me good. I don't want you to be a party to any deception; but I wonder if we could agree on some formula which without compromising the truth would lull Michael's suspicions. Suppose I were to go through the motions of selling the filly to you for a nominal sum. You could truthfully say that she was yours. Then, when the coast is clear, I can buy her back. Odd, but perfectly in order. I am relying on your good-will to sell her to me after she has become your property."

"Very ingenious. Worthy of Mr Fox. Indeed, I sometimes think that he does not exercise all the ingenuity he might to rescue me from the ravages of the income tax people. But why the complication? If I explain the state of the case to Michael he will perfectly understand."

"I don't like my business to be known to servants. They talk."

"Michael's the soul of discretion."

"Still he might let something fall. I have to be careful. I have enemies, Canon, powerful enemies."

"Enemies! Major. Surely, you exaggerate."

"You don't know the world as I do."

"You distress me. You distress me very much. I won't tell Michael the horse is yours; but I shall have to tell him not to talk about it, otherwise he will see no reason why he shouldn't."

"That is why I want you to buy her. Then you can say that you want the matter kept a secret. Michael will understand. You might say that you had got it for Elizabeth, or does Michael know enough to see that an unbroken yearling would make an unsuitable hack for a young lady?"

"I won't attempt untruths. My memory is not good enough. But leave the matter to me. I shall keep your secret. I had no idea that racing touts were such villains."

The Canon, abruptly for him, broke off the conversation and resumed his drive. The incident disturbed him. Because it was unpleasant, he put it out of his mind at once. Someone was approaching, he could not see who, but Robinson had slowed down and was preparing to halt.

"Ah! Mrs Perry."

But the Canon was not so pleased to see her as he sounded. She had only one topic these days—the Coppingers who had bought Cambridge Lodge. Now the Canon wished he had stayed at home.

CHAPTER III

THERE WERE NO cottages and no shops on the Mile, and as the land was rather poor nobody coveted it. The survival of the character of the settlement was not really so extraordinary. In point of time, three long-lived generations spanned it, and because the houses were planned on a fairly modest scale they never became a drug on the market as Mount Lambert and mansions of that size had been ever since the end of the first World War.

But the painstaking historian would note a subtle change in the original character of the neighbourhood: to begin with, the apex of the triangle was Mount Lambert and the presidency of the reigning baronet; the present holder of the title had never been there since he inherited, although there was a fiction that he kept closely in touch and exercised a remote control; but it had no basis in fact. Mr Fox, his lawyer, who lived in the city, collected the rents and was rarely seen on the estate. The Canon was believed to be the link between the Mile and its master, but he had not seen Julian since boyhood, and rarely got a letter from him. The Christmas card last year had no signature on it. That was the measure of the baronet's involvement in his hereditary estate.

In this condition of affairs the Canon acted as a sort of Viceroy; but he, if he could be persuaded to commit himself, would have agreed that only Barbara Beddington was *vintage* Mile. The Brownes by virtue of a remote relationship with a distant peer regarded themselves as born Milers; but they were newcomers without any connection with the place or the family. They bought York when they sold their larger place in the country. Mrs Browne was a pushing woman who never let her husband's slender connection with the peerage lie. Her restless ambition was wholly out of keeping with the essentially backwater character of the neighbourhood. Old Milers would never have accepted her, whatever they might have thought about her husband, whom she brought round on a figurative leash.

Captain Loftus owed his place—the humblest—to the Lamberts; but he, too, was something of a transplant. He might have passed had he not introduced the Perrys. Herbert Perry was a connection of some kind who chanced to hear that Loftus had fallen on his feet in the sort of neighbourhood that he (Perry) was looking for. He had worked in Ghana but did not wish to remain when that country was given its independence. Perry, keener on exploiting than being exploited, looked around for some place to settle where he could get domestic service and good value for money.

While observing rigid economies which the grape-vine spread about, the Perrys gave expensive entertainments, at which he always appeared to be slightly drunk. Nobody enjoyed their parties much except Captain Loftus, who blossomed in a vicarious rôle, plied the guests with drink, and at intervals, or when there was a lull, greeted his 'cousin' Herbert loudly across the room. Perry never resented this cashing in on the relationship, because he needed support; and he returned his 'cousin's' call with equal bonhomie and in a voice that carried so far as the road. At these entertainments Miss Beddington would instinctively take shelter under the Ormsbys' wing, rather subdued, clinging to glasses of sherry and resisting the Captain's noisy exhortations to 'drink up' and 'let me fill your glass'.

The Ormsbys and Miss Beddington invited all their neighbours to their own modest entertainments, but the Count summed up the situation at once, made it clear that he would have nothing to do with the Perrys or the Captain (whom he declared were 'not up to snuff'), laughed in Mrs Browne's face and treated only the Ormsbys as allies. With Miss Beddington he established a special relationship; he approached her with a stylised gallantry which might have misfired, but found its target with exquisite precision. The conquest of Queen Victoria by that battered amorist, Napoleon III, was an historical parallel which occurred to the Canon, whose range of reading was wide and unpredictable. Needless to say, he kept the observation to himself.

The Canon's catalystic efforts were undermined by the Count's recklessness. The harmony of the Mile was disturbed; the hatred of the Perrys for the Count was almost pathological; the Brownes were fascinated and terrified; Loftus, on his own would have suffered in silence, but his 'cousin' enlisted him in his campaign to 'show the fellow up and send him packing'. The trouble with Perry was that nobody liked him and consequently his attacks were apt to boomerang. Most of his time, therefore, was spent with his 'cousin' into whose ears he poured the content of his reservoirs of malice. The position, it need hardly be said, could have changed in an instant. Had the Count asked the Perrys to one of his legendary weekend parties, he would have been elected 'best friend' on the spot. But the Count had his code; and open contempt for tenth-rate persons unlikely to be of any use to him was one of its articles.

The threatened advent of Bernard Coppinger, full of money, who had recently bought Cambridge Lodge, might have been expected to thrill Perry; and again it required special knowledge to understand why he had enlisted Loftus to keep Coppinger out. Perry was a man who passionately wanted to be accepted by the gods he worshipped.

It was a desperate effort to prove himself an insider on the Lambert Mile that prompted him to resist the coming of the wealthy Coppinger. He was opposing everything that he enjoyed in life for the sake of winning the good opinion of people with whom he had nothing in common, whose company bored him to an extreme. If he succeeded in keeping Coppinger out, he nourished the hope that he would become in local legend like Horatio who kept the bridge in the brave days of old.

31

It was the Captain's own idea to call on Ralph Ormsby. As the Canon's son and Mr Fox's assistant, Ralph should have known better than to let the Coppingers in. Perry was not sanguine about the result. He had considerable business capacity and the wretched Loftus had none; but he let him carry out his plan, for what it was worth. He would not himself have undertaken, an expedition of such a forlorn nature, but he had agreed to play golf with his 'cousin' to hear his report.

Loftus was taking practice swings on the tee when the Jaguar's tyres crunched on the club-house gravel. The caddies emerged from their hiding-places at the opulent sound, but as hastily withdrew when they identified the driver. Perry's disillusionment about local labour costs were not confined to the golf links, but he had had a nasty shock there as well. Now he pulled a caddy-car behind him with his gorgeous set of clubs gleaming on it. Loftus had a light cheap bag and the minimum of ancient implements. He carried them himself.

Perry took a long time in the club-house preparing himself, and this added to his opponent's ill-humour. Loftus resented having to come by bicycle and wait on his 'cousin's' pleasure. In due course Perry emerged pulling his caddy-car. From the bag he took out a driver, removing the chamois leather cap with dependent tassel in which the head was covered. Then he strode up to the tee and placed his ball to drive off. There was never any discussion as to precedence. Perry always took the honour and always won the match very easily. By the time they returned to the club-house the Captain's irritation had usually died down. It was only when he was entertaining wild hopes of reversing the inevitable order that he was vulnerable. When these were dashed, by fair means or foul, he resigned himself to his fate. Besides today he was looking forward to telling Perry all about his experience in Ralph's office. It was a chance to make himself important.

Perry always paid for the drinks—a beer for Loftus, Scotch and soda for himself.

The Captain was slightly cast down when Perry did not ask him to begin his recital and mortified when at last he got going to see Perry transfer his undivided attention to a young woman who had come into the bar. She never looked their way, and eventually Perry admitted defeat and turned dead eyes on to his 'cousin's' walnut countenance. But all the animation had gone out of the story by then, and in a desperate effort to recover lost ground he gave a highly distorted version of the encounter.

"Well—as I was saying—I gave it to young Ralph straight from the shoulder. I said 'Coppinger may be all you say; but he's not the kind we want on the Mile. For one thing, he's up to the neck in that arty crowd : we have never had that sort here; for another, the fellow is a traitor to his class. Because he has money he seems to think he can do what he likes. You can't pick up the newspaper without seeing his face or that wife of his—anything to attract attention. I'm speaking for everyone on the Mile when I say you have let us all down. The fellow shouldn't have been let into Cambridge; and if it isn't too late he should be kept out.' "

The Captain paused to get breath and because Perry's gaze had started to wander again.

"I hear he has the most awful taste. His present house looks like a souvenir shop in Bombay."

"Talking of souvenirs," Perry said. "I'd be obliged if you'd return my screw-driver when you've finished with it."

"I'll give it to you when we go back. I'd no idea you were in such a hurry for it."

"I didn't say I was in a hurry. I said I wanted it back. I wonder who that girl was. She has the finest fanny I've seen in years. I'd like to—"

Loftus, desperate, aimed below the belt. "I took a rise out of young Ralph before I had finished with him. He turned quite nasty. Had a dig at you."

"He had, had he? What did he say?"

"Oh, something to the effect that standards in the Mile had slipped so far lately that he didn't see how Bernard Coppinger could sink them further. The Coppingers were a very decent family."

"And?"

"And what?"

"I thought you said he had a dig at me."

"Well, I thought the implication was pretty clear."

"Did you? I don't. You and I both came within a year of one another; the Brownes had only just come and the Count came soon after that. Of course the Ormsbys look down on everyone—except that bloody Beddington bitch. To show you what I mean, I heard Ralph say that Wales used to be the stables of the old rectory. I meant to tell you."

"Did he? By God! I won't let him get away with that. I put him down properly yesterday. He thought I had come to make my will; but I let him know pretty plainly that I had my own man."

"Oh, come off it, Loftus. You don't mean to say that your business is such a bait."

"Why not? The young fellow is starting. My connection might mean something; and I pay on the nail."

Perry was suddenly very angry.

"I told you it was a damn fool thing to beard the boy in his office. What could he do? Miss Howard died. The place was put up for sale. The Lamber's solicitor can't order who is to own the lodge. A child would know that."

"Well, what would you have done?"

"If none of us takes any notice of Coppinger he will get the message from the start; but I would like to think the Canon and Miss Beddington will take a firm line. Look at the way they fraternise with that Nazi, the Count. I'm expecting to hear some news about him shortly, by the way. A very great friend of mine who used to be our Consul in Nice met him out there, and I have written to him to send me details in confidence. If we had all made a united front against the Count we could have frozen him out. Nobody will listen to me. By the way, did you notice an improvement in my tee shots today?"

"If you could learn to keep them out of the rough you'd be in line for the Open."

It slipped from the Captain without intentional malice; but he paid for it. "Yes, I will," said Perry, when he was invited to have 'the same again'. This was by custom a face-saving gesture, and the invariable rule was to have only the round Perry paid for. The offer and refusal of a second drink was the signal for the offer of the lift home which Loftus was always unable to take. Today the offer never came; but here Loftus showed unexpected resource. For once he had left his bicycle at home and walked to the links, and when he asked for a lift home, Perry had to agree to give it; but he made no effort to be civil on the journey, and Loftus had nothing to distract his attention from the view.

"What's that?" he said suddenly.

A horse-box was turning in the gate of Cumberland.

Perry slowed down, and both men strained their necks to see what was happening. The horse-box had halted outside the Canon's door and the Count with uncharacteristic haste had stepped out and was opening the door of the box. The proceedings were quite out of character; he had never been seen performing a menial task before. The grey rump and white tail of a horse now came into view. The watchers noted them, and by backing down the road, where the wall was low, were able to observe, without being observed, the grey being led round to the stable in the Canon's yard. Perry even noted the animal's sex.

"We had better be getting along," Loftus said. "We don't want him to catch us spying on him."

Neither spoke again. Each was baffled. Of course there was a perfectly innocent explanation. The Canon kept a horse; perhaps it had outgrown its usefulness, and the Count was supplying a replacement. But there was something furtive about the scene they had witnessed, suggestive of a sinister interpretation. They preferred it that way.

Each in his garden was to ponder over the scene during the afternoon; had either gone abroad he might have seen a strange horse-box arrive at the Count's, containing another grey filly to take the stall left empty by her predecessor, who was munching hay in the Canon's stable.

CHAPTER IV

"NOBODY IS FONDER of the Canon than I am," Mrs Browne had just said when she noticed that a corner of an unsavoury-looking garment which she had kicked under the sofa when Miss Beddington called was protruding. She tried to hypnotise her visitor with a smile while using a heel to push the offending woollen vest out of her range of vision. The ruse failed, not only because Miss Beddington had seen the object as soon as she came in, but because she resented the remark that preceded it; resented it because it was patronising and because it implied that criticism was to follow. She was not going to let anyone, much less Mrs Browne, criticise her oldest and dearest friend; but Barbara was not a fighter, and it always distressed her when she had to take a stand upon principle.

"You will meet competition if you say that on the Lambert Mile," Barbara said; then, changing the subject : "what a nice picture! It must be new. I don't remember seeing it before."

"Raymond picked it up at an auction. I'll tell him you liked it. He's at his hospital meeting this morning. These boards take up a great deal of his time; but he must be doing something. You know what men are."

"Yes, indeed."

Nobody had had less experience of men than Barbara, who had lived on narrow means with a widowed mother all her life; her father having been killed out hunting on a hired horse, but instinct may have told her that, except for her Raymond, Mrs Browne's own experience of the opposite sex must have been severely circumscribed by her manner and appearance.

"What I was going to say," Mrs Browne resumed, reading the glint of warning in Barbara's eyes correctly—"What I was going to say was that the dear Canon with his prodigious good-nature and utter innocence of the world may make a hames of the ball."

"A *hames*?"

"That's Sylvia's expression. 'A complete balls up' is what Raymond said. I am glad I know you well enough to repeat it."

Barbara's smile failed to confirm this. Her face became expressionless. "I don't know what his plans are. I only heard today from my woman who comes in to clean that Elizabeth was coming in August and the Canon was giving a ball for her."

Mrs Browne smiled, and seemed to swallow something large very rapidly.

"I heard more than that. I heard that the idea is to open up the house for the occasion and make it a coming-out for Elizabeth. And what I am afraid of is that the Canon in his own incorrigible way will invite every old fuddy-duddy he has ever met and give the party the air of a Harvest Festival."

"But I don't see how, if the Canon is kind enough to give a party, you or I or anyone else could possibly dictate his choice of guests."

"I couldn't agree with you more; but if I am to understand the position correctly the ball is for Elizabeth's benefit, and if it is to be given at Mount Lambert, I presume the parents will pay for it."

"Even so, it will then be a matter between them and the Canon. If fuddy-duddys, as you call them, are to be knocked off the list, that will wreck any chance I might have of being invited; so don't, please, expect me to support you if you are going to ask to supervise it."

"Now, Barbara! You are fishing. Raymond was only saying the other day that Lord Bray, whom he meets on some of his boards, was asking for you and described you as the handsomest girl in the county."

"I don't think Lord Bray has laid eyes on me for about twenty years; but, still, I am grateful for the compliment and I shall call on him as a referee if I hear that you are exercising a veto."

Barbara had arrived at that uncharted age which, in the case of unmarried women who are not frustrated by their lot, lasts indefinitely—a middle distance in the landscape of life through which the wife and mother is hustled by child-bearing and constant calls on her energy and patience. She would not change between forty and seventy to any greater extent than a tempera painting in which the fine feather of the *craqueille* is only perceived under the microscope : and nobody was going to be allowed an inspection of the minute order required. No one, that is to say, whom one could well imagine. For he would have to be enterprising as well as fastidious, and of the right age and with no impediments—a collector who determined to add her to his collection, as he might covet a fine piece of Worcester, in the shape of a jug, perhaps. But not devoid of spirit, not without an eye for the out-of-the-way, an ear for the incongruous, and a restrained but acute satirical sense.

"I am glad you came over," Mrs Browne continued. "There is so much I want to discuss, and you are the only person round here with whom I feel I can really let my hair down. I love a good heart-to-heart talk; but, you know, I very seldom get one. Raymond is a poppet; but you can't talk to men. They won't see the difficulties a woman sees in any given situation; he steam-rolls straight ahead. And, then, Sylvia is at the age when she just won't utter. She thinks we came out of the Ark, of course. I want to talk to you about Sylvia in a moment—don't let me forget—but first I must hear what you've heard about the Coppingers. Herbert Perry—not that I would set much store by anything he might say—gave Raymond a hair-raising account of what we are in for. He's stinking rich for one thing, and

39

surrounds himself with the long-haired fraternity. Modern art is the least of it. He plays up to everyone, and has the most extraordinary people in tow all the time. It's bad enough to have the Count—but, at least, he is discreet. This Coppinger man is said to have boasted that he is going to paint the Mile red. The silly little Captain went in to see Ralph Ormsby about it, so I've been told; but, apparently, there was nothing he could do. All we can do now is to agree to pull together and refuse to let anyone paint us red or green or any other colour. I hope the Canon will give a lead; but I'm just a weeshy, weeny bit afraid that he may be too charitable and sweet and let a hole be made in the dam, so to speak. That would be fatal. I mean, we would look silly holding out if the Canon gave in. Which brings me back to the ball: I rely on you to use your influence to keep the Canon from inviting the Coppingers. And one more thing—I hope I'm not talking too much, but I so rarely get a chance to *talk*—I want your opinion on another matter."

Mrs Browne leaned back so as to see her visitor from a new perspective, grasping a bulky knee as she did so in her large, brown hands and exposing a measure of suet-coloured thigh.

"We had planned to give Sylvia a season in London next year. Raymond's cousins would have fixed it up for us; but it costs a packet, and with things as they are and Willie's school fees, it is going to be rather a wrench...rather a wrench. When I heard of the ball for Elizabeth it occurred to me that it would be a perfect opportunity for Sylvia to come out. She is only sixteen, and it's far too young, of course; but nowadays—as Raymond says—they know more at twelve than we did when we married. I wouldn't like to say a word to Sylvia before I had your opinion."

"You are asking the wrong person. Sylvia would have a much better idea of what other girls of her age are doing. I know when I was sixteen I was just an awkward lump; and

I don't think I would have made a riotous debut. It's really up to you."

Mrs Browne leaned further and further back as Barbara was speaking. Then she let go her knee and shot forward as if released by a spring, letting Barbara see her uvula. She had returned to the barging way that she adopted whenever she was pushing through a family plan and scented opposition.

"I'd like you to discuss it with the Canon, Barbara: and then if he approves I'll ask him to write to Elizabeth to put her in the picture. It would make such a difference to Sylvia if Elizabeth were to take her under her wing."

The subject of the discussion appeared now in the doorway. She was wearing a white cotton vest and boy's trousers, rather stained in front. Cast-offs of Willie, Barbara surmised.

Sylvia had not grown into her full beauty. She was a martyr to acne; and tonsils or adenoids, or perhaps both, conspired to keep her mouth open except when she was speaking. She then shut it, and muttered in a surly and almost incoherent fashion through her teeth.

"The vet says the kitten's not old enough to be spayed," was what she was saying.

"Very well, dear. Barbara and I were having a little chat about you. Has Dormouse had her hay?"

Sylvia mumbled "Yep" as she planked herself on a stool in the corner and fixed Barbara with a stare. She had no idea of moving. Her presence had a gorgon quality guaranteed to kill any attempt at conversation. Mrs Browne gave a laugh of mock despair. Then she winked conspiratorially at Barbara, inviting her to share a mother's secret joy at such a display of madcap spirit.

"I don't think it would be fair to complicate the issue like that. If it's a ball for Elizabeth one wouldn't want her to carry responsibility for anyone else."

Barbara assumed correctly that Sylvia was well aware of her mother's project.

41

"Of course you're right. I never intended any such thing; I just thought it would make *such* a difference to Sylvia if Elizabeth realised the importance of the occasion for her. Sylvia is a shy thing under all that toughness. Come on, Syl, admit it?"

"Oh shut up."

Mrs Browne winked at Barbara again.

"Would you see if tea is ready, old woman. Annie was making hot-scones. And we would like some. What about you, Barbara?"

"I wasn't intending to stay to tea. I only dropped in as I was passing."

"Of course you are staying. Tell Annie we have a visitor, dear."

"She knows. She let her in."

Mrs Browne gave a furious wink at Barbara, suggesting that the performance was reaching its climax.

"Of course, silly! But she doesn't know Barbara is staying to tea. Tell her to put another cup on the tray."

"She doesn't bring in a tray when there's only you and me."

"All right, Miss Thunderbird, all right. But I think Barbara would be grateful if you'd just make sure Annie is bringing us all in tea."

Sylvia yawned heavily, rose, kicked the carpet, and lounged out of the room.

"She's shy," her mother explained when the noise of the door banging died down. It had rattled the chinoiserie standing on the mantelpiece and sent a current of air under the prints on the walls, causing them to flap.

"But she is a very sound kid and absolutely devoted to you. My dear! I can't tell you. I'd trust Sylvia anywhere; but still one doesn't want a girl at that age to come up against unpleasantness. That is why I think it's so important that we keep the Coppingers out; and may I say something else to you in the strictest confidence: I don't like the idea of Sylvia meeting the Count. I suppose he will be invited to the ball. I believe he is what my mother used to call a roué; and with an inexperienced girl like Sylvia, however sound she may be at bottom, a man like that could pull the wool over her eyes, if you know what I mean."

"You've expressed it very well; but I'm sure Major Paul would always behave like a gentleman; and anyhow, he would think her rather on the young side."

"Ah! But there's a special charm in the underdone for the jaded palate, dear. I hear the most frightful accounts of what happens in London even among our own sort of people. It's no fun to be a mother nowadays."

Sounds of an argument in the kitchen floated in under the door, followed by a short peal, like thunder, indicating the rough placing of a tray on a horizontal plane. Not long after, Annie, looking bustled, came in with the tea. There were four scones on a plate and some plain biscuits.

Mrs Browne smiled on the display as a good fairy might who planned to wreak a magical change. But the tray suffered no metamorphosis.

"Visitors! Visitors!"

Mrs Browne rescued the scones from Sylvia, and passed the plate to Barbara.

Conversation slowed down at this point. Mrs Browne had an agenda, and she had worked through the items. But when Barbara got up to go, she accompanied her to the door and reminded her that she was depending upon her to let the Canon know what she had in mind.

"I'll cadge an invitation for her. Don't worry."

Mrs Browne had hoped that she would go a little further than that; but she had wanted to ensure that essential preliminary. Now she could think about the frock. She waved to Barbara, and went in to bid her child rejoice.

"I don't know why you wanted to make me look a fool in front of Miss Beddington; and I've a good mind not to go to the silly old ball; and I wish you'd let me alone and not be always trying to push me around," Sylvia said.

Mrs Browne having nobody to wink at threatened her daughter with assault if she couldn't learn to speak respectfully. An impasse was avoided by Sylvia going up to her room where she had a copy of *Fanny Hill* which she had purloined during a routine inspection of her mother's chest of drawers.

CHAPTER V

"I SHALL CERTAINLY go to Mrs Molloy's funeral," the Canon announced at breakfast. Angela heard him say it and told the postman. Before lunch-time it was known along the Lambert Mile.

"The poor dear was so pleased with the marmalade. I'm glad I thought of it," he reminisced complacently. He was sitting at the study fire although out of doors the sun was sweeping the dew off the grass. His lips were moving slowly and his face was a shining mirror of beatitude, for his mind was occupied with an address that he imagined himself delivering at the humble graveside—a model of simple piety, within the comprehension of the most ill-informed, and at the same time strangely moving. Sincerity, simple faith, gratitude to God, resignation to His will—these would all be present; and in the most unaffected language. From the well of English undefiled, he would draw the words for a lesson from the example of this life, so useful, patient, meek and good. It would need to be done with considerable skill—the art that conceals art—because its very simplicity might encourage minds not attuned to meditation to seek for insinuations and allusions. Perry might detect a dig at him : the Brownes would be looking out for sly thrusts; and the Count was himself of so highly ironical a disposition that he would leap to the conclusion, if there was a shadow of encouragement, that the Canon was having a go at them all.

This labour of love, for that is what it was, occupied the Canon for the morning notwithstanding doubts and promptings that, perhaps, he was wasting his time; but the task was too congenial to be put aside for anything less than

45

the sternest summons to a higher duty; and the Canon had so arranged his life that none such was likely to disturb him.

He was preoccupied at lunch; and Mrs Ormsby, who was worried about the absence of a pudding—the Canon had a sweet tooth—was grateful for it and did nothing to break in on his meditation.

Michael had not forgotten to milk the cow, and Angela had ascertained that the funeral was to take place in the morning after ten o'clock Mass.

"Ralph will drive us," the Canon said at dinner.

"I'm afraid I won't be able to. There are some new clients arriving at eleven; and Mr Fox wants me to see them."

The Canon said nothing, but he put down his soup spoon as if deprived of appetite, and his forehead puckered in a way that was familiar to his family.

"I'm sorry. I'll explain to Michael; but I just can't help it. Besides he won't mind so long as you go."

"Penny, you will come with me. I shall have to drive you. Ralph's absence will make a very bad impression. These are the occasions when we show the spirit of the Mile."

"I just can't help it," Ralph repeated. "One must keep one's sense of proportion."

The Canon picked up his soup spoon again as if he, too, had decided that a hunger strike was disproportionate. He ate his soup, as did so many of his generation, with a certain boisterous noisiness. This got very much on Ralph's nerves as it was so inconsistent with his father's extreme fastidiousness.

Wiping his mouth with his napkin, the Canon proceeded to discuss his plan, and another cause for his disappointment at Ralph's desertion.

"I was thinking I might say a few words at the graveside, something informal, a mere expression of our regard for Mrs Molloy. I think it would give Michael pleasure. I am only thinking of him."

Mrs Ormsby recognised at once that the exaggerated

46

casualness of this suggestion gave no indication of the amount of thought that had preceded it.

"I think that is a very nice idea," she said at once.

Her husband beamed at her, and then turned to his son to see how he had taken it.

"Well, Ralph. What do you say, my son? Have you any objection to offer to our little plan?"

"I wonder how Father Flynn will like it. Suppose you were taking Miss Beddington's funeral, and he popped up at the graveside and gave an oration, wouldn't you feel that he was trying to steal your thunder?"

"I had no intention of moving without mentioning the matter to Father Flynn. We are on the best of terms. And, in his own way, he is a first-class fellow. It's not as though I were the rector of the parish. Then you might say the element of competition would be present. I am only a friend who happens to be a clerk in Holy Orders. I should be merely uttering what I feel are the sentiments of the whole neighbourhood, gentle and simple, about Mrs Molloy."

"The truth is that nobody ever knew her, Daddy. She was rather a mystery. One saw her going to Mass; and that was all. It would surely be an exaggeration to say that everyone shared the lovely sentiments which I'm sure you will express."

"Now, dear. Don't interfere with your father. I think everyone will be touched by his gesture. There is far too wide a gap between the people who live in the Lodges and the working class who depend on them. I am sure it is what breeds most of the current discontent."

The Canon nodded approval; what an angel among women he had married! Again and again he found good cause to tell himself this. She studied his every want.

"I think we depend on the working class much more than they depend on us," Ralph said.

"I don't quite follow that remark."

The Canon's irritation was chiefly due to the way in which Ralph had crossed the genial current. He was not

47

really much concerned with the argument. The older he grew the more he disliked arguments; the search for truth was carried out at excessive cost when it exacerbated friendly feelings. Comfortable truths, those were the ones to hold on to. The other kind were better left alone, like stray dogs which one petted at one's peril.

"It's quite simple. Nobody can get servants or labourers. The Count has to import them; and who could say Michael depends on us? What would have happened if he had asked for a day off? Who would have milked the cow?"

"I suppose I should," said Mrs Ormsby.

"I think our relations with Michael are a good example of what I mean." The Canon interposed. "Affection and respect on both sides. Reciprocal benefit. A long-standing relationship. A tie, if you like. When I called with the pot of marmalade the other day, Mrs Molloy poured down blessings on my head. Quite out of proportion to the presentation, really on account of what we have done for Michael. I shall always remember some of the things she said. I had no idea she was going to have to meet her Maker so soon."

"But what do we do for Michael? Because he is officially a part-time worker he gets less than a jobbing gardener. If he joined a trade union he'd be advised to go on strike at once."

"Ralph! Ralph!"

"Let him proceed," the Canon said. He looked like a man who was fully equipped to meet a developing situation.

"I don't want to say anything more. I know Michael is devoted to the family as he is to everything and everybody connected with the Lamberts; but I don't think he is sane on the point; and I think we have taken advantage of him. But as he seems to like it that way, it would be silly of us not to, I suppose."

"Ralph, you know your father is most just in his dealings always."

"I don't mean to criticise; but I think the pot of marmalade was rather symbolic."

"Symbolic of what, pray?"

"Of how little we pay for what we get."

"I see. I stand reproved. My son is too busy to attend this poor woman's funeral. His father is not to pay her a tribute, even though it would give immeasurable comfort to her son in his affliction. And all this high morality is to be found in the authorised version of the trade union bible. No wonder the world has come to such a sorry pass."

"Darling, don't get worked up. Ralph didn't mean it. We are all upset today. None of us is at his best."

"I'm sorry, Dad. This business in the office is rather on my mind. I'm sorry, really I am." Ralph loved, if he was exasperated by, his father.

"Ralph's sorry, dear. Let's talk about something else. Barbara Beddington called in on her way back from the Brownes. She was greatly tickled by Mrs Browne who wants her to make sure that Sylvia is asked to the ball. Who ever told her there was going to be a ball? That is the worst of the Mile, one thinks of something, and one's thoughts are read for one by everybody on the road at the same instant."

"What's the ball?"

"Your father heard from Elizabeth. She is coming over, and he thinks she should have a coming-of-age party. But I was trying to persuade him to let the Lamberts pay for it if they think it a good idea. We just can't make the money go round, and I think this would be quite an undertaking."

"When's she coming?"

"Who is *she*, pray?"

"I'm not in the nursery, now, Dad. I can do what the grown-ups do. I can put my elbows on the table."

"Ralph! Ralph!"

"Let him have his say. I stand corrected. Elizabeth leaves the date to us. I thought of August; but I'd like to know about your plans."

"Count me out."

"I will do no such thing. I shall depend on you to collect young people to entertain her. She won't find much society on the Mile, and I can't think of anyone more suitable than the Misses Tottenham."

"I'm not going to dance attention on Elizabeth. And I don't want her to be left under the impression that I am on the reception committee if she comes. If you've invited her, that's all right; but I haven't, and I don't want there to be any doubt about that. I was asked to go to Scotland in August, as a matter of fact; and I think I may accept."

"Your mother said you were planning to go to the Winter Sports at Christmas."

"That was an idea of the Coppingers. They make up a party, and they invited me to join them."

"And how can I explain your attitude to Elizabeth?"

"Don't explain it. I am only asking you not to count me in on your arrangements. Don't assume that I'll be there to help. I think you will find that Elizabeth is fully capable of paddling her own canoe. I shouldn't worry if I were you. Besides she knows the Count very well. I'd suggest that you consult him about your plans. He knows her form better than we do. And now, if you will excuse me, I have to go back to town; I said I'd be there at nine o'clock."

Silence followed his departure, the silence after an explosion when the last echo dies away.

Mrs Ormsby was the first to speak.

"I think he and Elizabeth had a tiff when she was on her last visit. He was mad about her; and then something happened. She probably made him jealous. She is rather flirtatious, and he is so intense, poor boy. He makes such heavy weather of everything. But I must say, I had forgotten all about it. One is inclined to underestimate the feelings of the young."

"I was staggered. Coming on top of that diatribe about the Molloys. What upsets me about it most is his lack of feeling. When you think what we owe to the Lamberts—the length of the connection; our position here. Why! Ralph wouldn't be in Mr Fox's office if it weren't for the Lamberts. I wrote to Julian at the time, and the suggestion came from him."

"Ralph doesn't seem to like the office very much; and, although he says very little, I think that he doesn't get on with Mr Fox. A most curious creature, I've always thought. I never could understand why he was held in such veneration. I don't think there's any use in appealing to Ralph on the score of gratitude. He is a profoundly discontented young man, if you ask me."

"I can see that he approves of nothing and of nobody. I can only hope it's a phase and that it will pass."

"Perhaps you should try to understand him better, dear. I don't mean to imply that you haven't always been an angel to him, as you have to everybody; but we are apt to forget the age barrier. It's hard on him to have been an only child, and that trouble with his back kept him apart from other children. I wonder sometimes if you try enough to enter into his problems. We expect him to be interested in what concerns us, and a lot of the time it must be just a bore for him."

The Canon laid his face between his hands. After a whole day spent on composition, he had come to the table to rehearse before his always sympathetic wife and intelligent son a little discourse which he hoped might be worth recording in his commonplace book, a collection of sayings and jottings, the compiling of which was one of the staple pleasures of his life. As a diarist he was too discreet to get the full pleasure that form of self-abuse offers its devotees. He preferred to give his genial spirit free play; and the extent to which the book was associated with the Mile, its people, and the Lamberts in particular, gave it almost the nature of a local history. Sometimes he played with the idea of publication. He had even thought once of approaching Jack Yeats, whose early drawings he admired, to ask him to design a cover—the dog-cart on its way down the Mile against the background of Mount Lambert and its satellite villas, perhaps. But the idea of a cover seemed somewhat premature at the time, and he abandoned it.

It was the artist soul in him that had been rebuffed by the wranglings at table when he had come almost bursting with his effort and his anxiety to give his speech a trial run. It was not until one heard oneself speak that one could really judge whether tone and emphasis were exactly right. He needed no practise for his sermons; but this was different; this had to be seen in its setting. To put it crudely, the Mount Lambert connection very seldom gave him the opportunity to indulge himself in this manner. He approached the self-imposed task as an artist; and at the very first mention of it his son unfeelingly tried to torpedo the scheme. Possibly not maliciously; but asking the Canon to visualise a ceremony which he was conducting and in which Father Flynn with his flat and nasal accent dared to attempt participation was as unkind as it was preposterous. Ralph had a habit in controversy of comparing small things with great and drawing inapt analogies; it was a fault of which his father—always happy in his choice of illustration—had tried to cure him; but in vain. In vain! And all Mrs Ormsby could do was to stroke that suffering head very gently with her hand, hardened by housework and chores of a description that matched ill with her husband's incorrigibly romantic temper.

CHAPTER VI

IF YOU WANTED to understand the inner workings of
that anachronistic phenomenon, the Mile, you could not
have done better than attend Mrs Molloy's funeral. Care-
fully observed and correctly interpreted it told you all; but
Captain Loftus, was not adequately equipped by nature to
be such an observer. He went to while away some of the
time that hung so heavily on his hands, from sheer curiosity,
without any feeling for the dead woman or her son; admir-
ably poised, therefore, for scientific investigation, but he
lacked imagination; there was nothing of the artist in him.
He went because he wanted to see who was there. He knew
the Canon was going; the news arrived in the kitchen with
the postman, but in itself that would not have tempted
Loftus out. It would not have been in the nature of a silent
command as it was, for instance, for Miss Beddington, who
went at once upstairs to inspect her black coat and make
sure the moths had not been having any fun and games in
the cloth or the fur. It was not a signal, as it was to the
Count, for the forces on the right to rally. Nothing could
have been more inconvenient for him at that moment than
a few hours' absence at a stranger's funeral; but his code
was rigid : one answered the call on these occasions and let
attorneys, bailiffs, actuaries, receivers and all their brood, do
their worst. The battle, in the long run, was decided in the
field.

Loftus was free from these feudal feelings. His whole
problem was to fill up his days with only a small pension to
spend. Sometimes he cycled all the way into the town to the
cinema. In the afternoon it was possible to buy a cheap seat,
even if it meant being surrounded by noisy, gum-chewing,
sweet-eating, orange-sucking, cigarette-smoking children.

53

Then there were the golf games with Perry when the latter had failed to pick up a more interesting opponent. In relation to the Perrys Loftus stood as a sort of first sub for all purposes; and if he had to sacrifice everything else, Loftus would have clung to his telephone : late in the afternoon Mrs Perry might ask him to make up a four of bridge that evening—after dinner. When Miss Beddington invited him to bridge it was always a decently long invitation, and not an S.O.S. He was only at the Perrys' when one of their regular four—Miss Beddington or Mrs Browne—had let them down at the last moment. Very occasionally the Browne's invited him when there was no emergency. But as a rule he went to York as a stand-in. The Count never invited him under any circumstances; the Ormsbys only to large gatherings. Hence the importance to him of such an occasion as a funeral. Nor was he lacking in shrewdness to realise that the Canon would approve; and it would enable him to have a word with Miss Beddington, still a fine woman, whom, when the moon was full and he had imbibed more than usually, he weaved amorous fantasies round. In practice these had gone no further than to clutch her shoulders when helping her on with her coat—a marginal approach which she was at liberty to ignore, and did.

The idea of the funeral itself was not wholly unpleasing either, in a case like this where it had nothing to do with him, he rather enjoyed the drama. That he and Mrs Molloy had shared anything in common never occurred to him any more than he felt an association with a dead cat on the road.

He decided not to attend the church. It would identify him too closely with the family. Moreover, the grave-yard was nearer than the church, a mile and a half away. He bicycled that far, hid his machine behind a hedge, and walked over to the church, arriving nicely, just when the hearse was beginning to pull out into the roadway. Behind it, Michael rode with the priest in a huge taxi. A rather battered car with a country registration mark containing,

54

presumably, relations came behind that. Then, seemingly, every poor child and tinker for miles around; and then a row of motor cars. Into these the Captain peered with unconcealed curiosity. It was for this he had come abroad.

Mr Fox, the solicitor, rode in the first car. He carried a wreath (purchase price £5.5.0), bought on behalf of Sir Julian, who depended on him to discharge his obligations on all these occasions. Mr Fox was very thin, very grey, and very reserved. Loftus was somewhat in awe of him. Behind Mr Fox came the steward, Bradshaw, in his small Ford. He seemed to fill the whole car up with his gross person; and his dark red face wore its habitual misleading expression of cheerfulness. Behind Bradshaw came the Canon and Mrs Ormsby. He had wrestled with the idea of ordering a taxi, but decided in the end, as the day was so beautiful, to come in the dog-cart. He wore a top-hat and, so far as appearances went, stole the show. Loftus, excited by the procession, very nearly clapped. Next came the Count in his Alfa Romeo. He had compromised in the matter of dress and wore a dark suit with a Locke bowler. It ruffled him, who was used to be the arbiter in every matter, to see that the Canon, whom he was present to support, had gone the whole hog in the matter of hats; but Miss Beddington, sitting beside him, was in a daze at his manly beauty. She had wondered whether to do what Loftus did on her own bicycle, and she had been quite overjoyed when a Ruritanian accent on the telephone invited her to drive. Miss Beddington was wont to blush when the Count's name was mentioned. He reminded her, she was known to say, of her father; he had fallen in the chase when she was an infant; one must suppose that the chest in uniform against which her little frock was pressed and the nutmeg of a razored cheek that scratched her baby-smooth plumpness—a half dream—was the total of her misty recollection of the first man in her life. The Count was a dream that had assumed living flesh. Moreover, and it may seem trivial in the context, Miss Beddington was extremely susceptible to smells;

and as the Count was liberally besprinkled with male perfumes and lotions, she got the pleasant sensation in his company that she associated with visits to the hair-dresser. Miss Beddington was enjoying the funeral; but her face expressed exactly the right degree of gentle seriousness.

Behind the Count's car came a few others: the doctor, the undertaker, the publican, farmers from the other side of the hill with their wives; and the rear was brought up by the workmen at Mount Lambert, two men and a boy, wheeling bicycles, and a few children who had arrived late and lacked the courage to push forward.

Captain Loftus was so interested in it all that he momentarily forgot himself; but when the drab tail of the procession hove into view he realised that he was in an invidious position. Wearing their funeral faces, none of the car occupants had pretended to see him. There was no question of anyone saying 'hop in'. Had he consulted with one of them beforehand he might not have found himself alone with the riff-raff of the countryside. Rather than trail along with them, bringing up the dusty rear, he decided to fall back and arrive at the cemetery when the internment had begun. As a solitary spectator he would cut a more decent figure than as one of the rabble.

Mrs Ormsby was preoccupied with her own thoughts. The Canon had been in a state of mild excitement all day after the deep melancholy into which he had fallen on the previous evening. And everything seemed to be conspiring to restore his usual complacency.

He had worn the tall hat and taken out the dog-cart against the advice of his family; but he knew with his deep histrionic sense, that he must not adopt half-tones. His support would be most effective if he was fully himself. To have come like everyone else in a closed car was to have denied the light. Then, his tall hat, which caught the sun with brilliant effect, was abundantly right. He was glad to see that the Count had a more modified form of headgear. It all built up to a crescendo: beginning with bare heads and cloth caps; dwelling on soft hats of different colours, shapes and textures; rising to the perfect correctness of the bowler; finally, the flourish, the organ note, of the topper—the high hat, on high, on the dog cart, crowning the scene.

Mrs Ormsby would have granted all that; but she wondered what surprises were in store. So far there had been no opportunity for a word with Father Flynn, who had said Mass and, after a painful delay, reappeared and stepped quickly, as by previous arrangement, into Michael's hired limousine.

It would arrive at the grave-yard before them; and how was the Canon to put his suggestion to the priest in the bustle towards the grave in such a manner as to let him consider and decide? From lack of diplomatic training, the priest might well, in the haste of the moment, express himself in a manner to give the Canon pain. On the other hand, he might acquiesce while resenting the imposition. Mrs Ormsby was struggling with herself whether to intervene in the public interest or to let Providence decide. Her husband's good spirits were her principal concern. These she would certainly dash if she suggested doubts. She decided, not without misgivings, to leave the matter in higher hands.

At the cemetery a boy had to be found and bribed with a shilling to hold the horse. This done the Canon and his wife made their appearance. The grave-yard was one of the horrible modern kind, a walled enclosure in a field with a crucifix at the entrance and rows of commercially designed memorials arranged in a regular pattern; some with artificial floral tributes on them, others more touchingly decorated with jam jars from which withered field flowers drooped.

The coffin, more gaudily decorated than the Canon's taste approved, was being let down by the grave-diggers into the pit they had dug. One or two children had crept forward to peep down, but officious hands thrust them back. The mourners were in a group round the grave; Michael, his head lowered, looking so dazed and ill that everyone stared at him apprehensively. Even the Canon, who had put so much thought into pleasing him, became instantly aware that Michael was oblivious to the surrounding scene. Instead of acting on this, however, he became more than ever determined to make a gesture which would give a pleasant turn to such a concentration of gloom. The grave-diggers, sweating and grunting, had struggled with the coffin's weight to fit it to the shape of the grave and moderate the pace of its descent. Now they stood back, rubbing their hands; and Father Flynn came forward and sprinkled holy water on the lid, murmuring as he did so invocations that the Canon could not follow. Then began the melancholy business of shovelling in the clay. Pebbles rattled on the coffin-lid; then the heavier, slushy sound of earth thrown in with practised spade-work went relentlessly on while those nearest the grave kept their eyes intently on the progress of the operation. At the outskirts there was more latitude. Some people conversed; the usual topic being a day by day account of the deceased's decline as it had been communicated to them. Was it Sunday fortnight or Sunday three weeks she had last been seen at Mass? Some said one, some said the other. Everybody noted how badly Michael seemed to be taking it.

The Canon had not been able to reach the inner circle, although there had been an instant stepping-back to let him through by those on the fringe. It was clearly impossible for him to converse with Father Flynn unless he raised his voice and held the discussion in public. Mrs Ormsby watched and wondered.

The filling-up was now complete, sods were thrown loosely on the clay. Father Flynn was saying the 'Hail Mary'. There was no time to lose.

The priest had done. Mr Fox now entered the picture. He had been content to stand well back hitherto. He walked up to the grave, and with the air of a man who does thoroughly whatever he has to do, he put the Lambert tribute on the grave. The Canon's heart overflowed. The Lamberts had, as always, done the right thing; and the presence of Mr Fox explained why Ralph had to attend the office. Clearly one or other had to; and it was right that the family solicitor of forty years' standing should be the one to deputise for them. Now others added their flowers. Mrs Ormsby had gathered a sheaf of roses, Miss Beddington an armful of azaleas. The Count's ten-guinea wreath—sent from the city, put everybody else's in the shade. Captain Loftus, from his point of vantage, noted it all. He had thought of bringing flowers; but he had brought himself. Neither the Perrys nor the Brownes had bothered to come. The Brownes had discussed it; but the idea never crossed the Perrys' minds. They would be upset when they heard that once again they had failed to sense local feeling. They had been warned; they knew just as soon as everyone else that the Canon was going; but not for the first time they put his behaviour down to some personal reason. They could not understand that the Molloys had a place in the community. Loftus rather looked forward to his visit this evening; he would drop in before dinner; they might invite him to stay. It would be fun to see them blench when he rolled out the names of those present and those absent. He sometimes got tired of the Perrys' patronage and resented their frequent snubs. He would get his own back.

Now the gathering was about to disperse. Father Flynn looked relaxed. People were coming forward to shake Michael's hand. The Canon took a step in the direction of Father Flynn, hesitated, stepped in Michael's direction, hesitated—these hesitations were fatal, for they allowed someone else to step in and begin a garrulous greeting while the lighter members of the crowd dispersed. If the Canon were to address anyone now, it would be the hard core of the assembly. Mrs Ormsby kept her eyes on him, noting the excitement in his eye. It lit on Miss Beddington. "I wonder if Michael would like me to say a few words."

She hesitated. Like everyone else she had noted Michael's broken-down appearance, and her understanding told her that the Canon's prescription was not what that stricken soul required.

"Blaze away, Canon. Blaze away," said the Count. He, too, perfectly, understood the situation, but he was only concerned for the Canon and looked forward to some diversion.

"Just a few words," the Canon murmured.

He stepped smartly forward, grasped Michael by the hand and raised the tall hat which he had resumed when the interment was completed. It was a call to attention. If everyone was not aware of it; once that rich voice, pitched to fill the furthest crevice of the dome of some Anglican cathedral, began the departing mourners would have been stopped in their tracks. But at that moment, as his lips pursed themselves and his fine head was thrown back, a donkey tethered in the adjoining field, prompted by who knows what desolation of spirit or pricking of the flesh, and desiring to communicate with its kind, gave forth a succession of melancholy brays.

The Canon was too much of an artist not to recognise that the scene had been stolen. He waited until the braying stopped, then turned towards the grave, and stood with his back to the crowd, head bent, communing in silent prayer with its pathetic occupant. A more affecting picture could hardly be imagined, and his timing was perfect. That done, he turned smartly about, clapped on his hat, seized his watching wife by the arm, and led the procession towards the cemetery gates.

"There's no one like him," Miss Beddington whispered to the Count. He pressed her arm affectionately.

Loftus saw it all. The funeral, all things considered, had been a resounding success. He hurried off to find his bicycle.

CHAPTER VII

THERE WAS A KNOCK at the door. Ralph settled his tie and arranged himself in his chair. This was the first important interview that he had had to conduct without Mr Fox at his elbow. He was regretting that he had not gone ahead with his plan of growing a moustache to age his face a little. It was too late now.

A young man dressed in city clothes, carrying a too-new leather brief-case, came in followed by a countryman in depressed tweeds.

"George Miller," the young man with the brief-case said. "From Grise & Grise," he added as if his own name had not made sufficient impact. "I sent a wire in case my letter didn't reach you in time. Mr Gallagher is advising us on the livestock end."

Mr Gallagher smiled sheepishly and slyly. His face was so thickly covered with freckles that it had the appearance of being camouflaged. Short sleeves made his wrists look abnormally long, and when he moved he cracked at the joints.

Ralph offered chairs. Miller took one at Ralph's desk on which he laid the brief-case, Mr Gallagher preferred to pick one out for himself a little removed from the lawyers. He sat down on it suspiciously, as if he expected it to buck him off.

Miller began to pull papers out of his brief-case with a self-conscious air of modern efficiency. His wrist-watch, clean linen, handkerchief in breast-pocket, and careful grooming, were all calculated to suggest an assurance that would have impressed Ralph more if he had not been to school in England. Familiarity with the type gave him a sudden accession of confidence. He even began to look forward to the interview. Now he was glad Mr Fox was at the funeral, giving him an opportunity to handle a case from the start.

"My firm act for Mr Tartan Young," Miller said. His tone conveyed that the conjunction was overwhelming.

Ralph nodded, and then wondered if it would not have been better to have looked blank.

"We have been writing to a Major Christian Paul of Kent Lodge, The Lambert Mile, Glenbray, Co. Wicklow, on Mr Young's behalf, but have not obtained any satisfaction. Certain information has come to Mr Young's ears which suggested that prompt action was required. I have come over to ask you to act for us. But we must first decide what is the best course to follow. Do you know anything about this Major Paul?"

Ralph nodded again. He hoped that his face did not betray the panic in his mind. Here he was looking after Mr Fox's business, listening to a proposal that he should take action against his father's friend. His immediate impulse was to warn the Count that he was in danger. He could only listen; but his composure was not increased when he glanced in Mr Gallagher's direction and saw that a small eye, somewhat larger than the surrounding freckles, and of much the same colour, was fixed on him. It was not a trustful eye.

"Major Paul owes Mr Young money, I take it."

"Eight thousand pounds."

Ralph was surprised but not amazed. His mother had made several homely observations on the Count's manner of life; and the campaign conducted by Perry against him was of course well known to Ralph; but he attributed it to pique because the Count ignored Perry and laughed at his pretensions.

"What do you know about Major Paul?" was Miller's next question. Ralph hesitated. Two pairs of eyes were now looking at his closely. This was the sort of situation that made his profession so hateful. Was he to deny that the Count was a neighbour and a friend of his father? Should he disclose his own difficulty? Why had Mr Fox to absent himself from the office on this of all days!

"He lives in considerable style and has a few horses. He is a friend of the Lamberts who are clients of ours; they let him take Kent Lodge on a repairing lease at a very moderate rent which is, I think, rather in arrear. He entertains lavishly. I believe one of his horses is very valuable. At the moment he is supposed to be negotiating a take-over of Mount Lambert as a stud-farm with himself as manager, but the Lamberts are not keen."

"I can understand that," said Miller.

From Mr Gallagher came a short, hideous laugh.

Miller searched among the papers on the desk and consulted a letter, then he began again :

"Mr Young met Major Paul at the house of a friend. He heard him talking about a grey filly with which he expected to win the Guineas and the Oaks at Epsom. Major Paul spoke of some difficulty with his bankers and Mr Young offered to meet this in order to keep the horse in training. Because of the circumstances under which he met Major Paul it did not occur to him that a formal business arrangement was necessary. He thought he was among friends, and very distinguished friends indeed. And he was impressed by Major Paul's insisting on giving him a formal I.O.U.

"It was only a few months ago, when a lady whom Mr Young met on a yachting trip happened to mention that Major Paul had borrowed ten thousand pounds from her, that he began to get anxious. He made enquiries in bloodstock circles and he got to learn that Major Paul had a very doubtful reputation."

Mr Gallagher gave another of his hoarse laughs and then fixed his eyes on the ceiling.

"We wrote to him and our letters were ignored. Then he wrote to our client and complained about the tone of our letters. Subsequently they had telephone conversations, and Major Paul offered to give Mr Tartan Young a partnership in the filly. But he never did any more about it. Mr Young is now very much annoyed, and he wants us first of all to check on the livestock in Major Paul's possession and get a charge of some kind as security for his money."

"If you want my advice," Mr Gallagher said, "you'se will get a few horse boxes and call at your Major's place and remove his stock."

"We couldn't do that without a court order," Miller said.

"If you call he will refuse to let you in," Ralph added. "He is not a man who is easily intimidated."

"How long would it take to get an order?"

Ralph hesitated. He wasn't sure. One was always meeting these elementary questions, and it was humiliating not to have the answer pat.

"Not long; but notice would have to be served on him."

"If you know him I'd suggest that you ring him up and say that you have friends who want to see him," Mr Gallagher suggested.

It was the very last thing Ralph wanted to do; but he might be able to slip out of the action if he could bring Miller and his friend into direct contact with the Count.

Benito, the Italian servant, answered the telephone. The Major was out, at a funeral.

"Will you tell him Ralph Ormsby was ringing up. Ask him to be good enough to ring me up when he comes in."

There was a short silence at the end of the line.

"I don't think the Major can do that."

"Why not?"

"It's the telephone. It takes the ring ups coming in; but it no answers the rings up going out. I am afraid I do not speak the English very well."

"When do you expect the Major?"

"The Major will be here at lunch time."

"I'll ring him up."

"There's some mystery about the telephone," Ralph explained. "He's out at the moment. I'll ring up at lunch time and if you call in this afternoon I'll let you know what I've arranged."

64

"We must go down today," Miller said. "Otherwise he will get rid of his stock."

"Leave it to me."

Ralph hoped he sounded authoritative; he felt miserable.

Miller and Gallagher went off arranging to communicate after lunch. By then Ralph would have seen Mr Fox. But Mr Fox was not back in the office and when Miller called again Ralph had to ring the Count up without having first had the benefit of his employer's advice.

"Who is that?"

The voice sounded sinister.

"This is Ralph."

There was a silence. The Count's fast-moving brain, prompted no doubt by the inflexion in the voice, told him that this was not a friendly call. Ralph was a solicitor. The Count was used to solicitors. Besides he had heard of the previous call.

"Ah, Ralph! What can I do for you?"

"A colleague of mine, a Mr Miller, wants to come down to see you today about the horses. He has a Mr Gallagher with him. They have been asked by Mr Tartan Young to look them over. Apparently he has some interest in them. May I bring them down?"

"I don't understand. Did you say Mr Tartan Young was there? I understood he was in Jamaica. He is a very good friend of mine. Who are these people? I'd be very careful, Ralph, if I were you. My horses are valuable. I can't let any Tom, Dick or Harry posing as Mr Tartan Young come down to do God knows what to them. Is Mr Fox there? No. I thought not. You tell him that I am very suspicious of these friends of yours. How many did you say there were?"

"Mr Miller is Mr Young's solicitor, and wants Mr Gallagher to take an inventory."

"Take an inventory! I am not letting my house to Mr Young. This is a very funny business. I'd have nothing to do with it if I were you. Tell them that you cannot help them. Let them find another solicitor. If you would like to come and have dinner with me tonight I will put you in the picture about Mr Tartan Young. You will then understand this little affair; but tell these people, whoever they are, to go to Hell, or some other suitable place. What time would it suit you to dine with me?"

"Mr Miller is Mr Young's solicitor. He has to go back to London this evening. That is my difficulty."

"No it is not. It is Mr Miller's difficulty. How do you know that he is Mr Young's solicitor?"

Ralph put his hand over the mouthpiece.

"He says how do I know you are Mr Young's solicitor?"

"Ask him if he got a letter from Grise & Grise this morning."

"Didn't you get a letter from Grise & Grise this morning?"

There was a short silence; then the Count spoke in a more confidential tone than hitherto.

"Bring him along with you to dinner tonight; but we don't want this Gallagher fellow. I know him; I would not have him in my house. Tell Mr Miller I will expect him here at eight o'clock. He can stay for one night."

There followed one of those pauses which can make a telephone conversation as nerve-wracking as a walk on a roof.

"Are you there?"

"Yes, Major. Thank you. See you at eight."

When Mr Fox arrived later, Ralph explained what he had done and was duly commended for his handling of the situation. "I think we had better get Counsel's opinion on the I.O.U.," Mr Fox added. "Major Paul is not to be underestimated."

"I wonder if Lady Lambert will approve if we take proceedings against him," Ralph said, remembering that the Count was her protégé.

"Lady Lambert is unlikely to hear about it from him and she certainly won't hear it from me."

What he knew, what he felt, Ralph could never fathom. It was like working with a sphinx.

Mr Fox never spoke to Ralph beyond telling him to do something and listening afterwards to his account; even then, his studied impatience of manner, as if arrested on the way to the lavatory, forbade anything resembling conversation. Mr Fox's favourite mode of communication was a type-written note slipped under Ralph's door. "Indicate suggested date of annual holiday. Leave address in case you are wanted. G.F." That sort of thing.

When, therefore, a note was pushed under Ralph's door asking him to call on Mr Fox at tea-time, he expected to stand uneasily at the door while his employer, without looking up, asked a question or gave an order.

As usual he knocked on the door, was kept waiting and wondering whether to knock again, risking an explosion of irritation, when a querulous "Come in" settled the question.

Today Mr Fox had a pot of tea on his desk, two very cracked cups in odd saucers, a bottle of milk and a plateful of plain dry biscuits. It was the first time that Ralph had ever seen him eat.

"Sit down."

His voice was high, with a slight undertone of hysteria. He sat in profile, looking out of a window at the ruin of a potting-shed. Ralph had never looked at him before. A mutual embarrassment had left only a general impression of leanness, dryness, petulance.

The forehead was high and narrow, suggesting an intellectual anchorite; the hair, a large tuft somewhere near the crown, left long and fanned out over as much of the skull as it could cover. The pale eyes were thoughtful, sad and disapproving; the lips mobile and thin, inclining to droop at the ends. To the hollow cheeks and delicate chin an indefinite growth of hair gave the appearance of a corpse. His suit, originally grey, and once rather pronouncedly in the fashion, had turned slightly green with age. He carried a selection of pens in the breast pocket. A semi-stiff white shirt

67

with long attached collar, of a shade that suggested about three days continuous wear, was set off by a piece of old black silk, loosely knotted. In detail the appearance was of dandyism gone to seed, an old-fashioned conjurer, perhaps; but the parts added up to something more distinguished and almost impossible to define.

"Have you time to take a cup of tea with me, Mr. Ormsby? I usually take some at this hour. Please take a biscuit. I always put some out for the birds. There's a robin out there. He comes back every year. I call him D'Oyly Carte for that reason; but they don't come any more alas! The name has rather lost its point. Perhaps I should call him Christmas or Easter; but somehow those names are too large for such a little joke. Is that chair quite comfortable? You may take the briefs out of it and put them with the others on the floor. I counted them yesterday. There are two hundred and twenty-three. I tell Mrs Hayes that she must never dare to move one of them—she complains that the room is impossible to clean. But any disorder in a system is fatal. I know where to put my hands on everything. Do you like my Diaz? I bought it years ago from an old Frenchman who said it used to belong to George Sand. Do you know whom I mean by George Sand? I used to read her novels once. I don't suppose you would care for them. That silver cup was given to me by old Sir Julian Lambert. I believe he stole it. The Lamberts are a curious family."

Ralph knew better than to attempt to answer the questions, but he was astonished by the transformation in Mr Fox's manner. This was a new person. What was the reason for the sudden change?

"The Lamberts have two characteristics that never alter. Every second generation is wild, and it always dies in time. You will have noticed that the estate invariably passes from grandfather to grandchild. There has always been a war to kill off the intermediate generation before they can ruin the estate. The present man is very like his old grandfather; but he doesn't want the place. He would sell it tomorrow if he

68

could. So long as Bradshaw is down there, he won't sell it. Bradshaw puts the purchasers off by telling them there is dry-rot under the roof, the lands are horse-sick, and the water-supply tainted."

"But why do you keep him on?"

Mr Fox continued to look out of the window as if he had not heard the question.

"Sir Julian appointed Bradshaw. I suggested that an accountant should look into his returns, but the idea was unacceptable. Elizabeth is coming over this year; and, no doubt, she will find out the position for herself. This is the first time there has not been a male heir; and the question arises : will she change the pattern? or will she go early and leave a child to inherit? I am determined to live long enough to find out."

At the mention of Elizabeth's name Ralph, as always, was plummeted into the past. The high voice with its note of insistent complaint receded, the weird figure against the light became a shadow; and he was walking with Elizabeth in the wood near the cottage which they had discovered and were furnishing with tea boxes and chintzes stolen from his mother's trunkful of oddments. One day he had picked the roses in the garden and put the petals in a sack to make a bed for Elizabeth. He had waited for her to come as she had promised, waited until his heart was sick and heavy and the excitement that had attended the spreading of the roses had died down to a foreboding that he had been made a fool of. At twelve o'clock he had gone, stumbling through the wood along their special pathway, into the field behind his father's house. The lights were still on in the drawing-room, and he stood staring in through the open window where he had left Elizabeth two hours before. The room was empty. There was a light peeping through the curtains in his parents' room. His father always read himself to sleep. He went round to the front of the house. The doctor's Austin 10 was still there. It had been borrowed for the evening by his flashy son, three years older than Ralph.

This morning she had complained about the party; it would be much better if they were alone in their little house. It was then that he had collected the roses; and during the evening he had said, "This is awful, let's slip away. I'll go ahead and wait for you there."

It was possible that she had not been able to get away while there were guests. He knew this, and comforted himself with the thought when he was approaching despair in the cottage; but that the only guest to remain should be the smooth young man had been a knife through his heart. He raged with jealousy.

Were they outside in the garden? The car had the appearance of a sentry. The horrible thought had struck him that they might be in the back of it, a degradation that it made him sick to imagine, but he had looked to make sure.

He stood in the hall, listening to the night. Upstairs the old Ormsbys guaranteed safety. No sound came from there.

Suddenly a laugh, clear, mocking, hideously familiar, rang out. It was followed by the muffled sound of voices. The sounds came from the sanctuary, the Canon's study, a place in which Ralph did not think for a moment to look. He stood outside the door, ready at first to burst in and vent all his feelings of disappointment, misery and rage on the couple; but now the moment had come, he couldn't do it. But the torture of waiting while God knows what was going on inside was more than he could bear. He went into the drawing-room and put the *Emperor Concerto* on the gramophone, full blast. It burst upon the night with an effect that was truly dramatic. He poured himself out a glass of wine-cup (the Canon put his foot down on the suggestion of anything more potent) and threw himself on the sofa.

A knock on the ceiling proclaimed his parents' distress at the sudden irruption of sound; but he ignored the protest until Elizabeth and the young man appeared together in the door-way.

She gave him a look he had begun to get used to, of imperfect repentance.

The young man, whose hair had come down over his face, seemed to have been taking violent exercise.

"Where've you been all evening?" he said. "We've missed you."

"Where have you been is more to the point?"

Elizabeth turned off the gramophone.

"Don't do that," Ralph said.

"You'll wake up your parents."

"That's my business. Put that record on again."

"Don't be a baby," Elizabeth said. Ralph got up, and pushing her aside, put on the record.

"Mind what you are doing," the young man said.

Ralph took a glass of wine that lay on the table beside the gramophone and threw it in the young man's face.

The next minute his head seemed to split open, and he felt darkness descend on him down a path of stars.

When he came to he was lying on the sofa with his collar open and Elizabeth was mopping his forehead with a wet handkerchief. At a great height above her in a mist stood the young man.

"Are you sure he's all right?" the young man was saying.

Ralph kept his eyes closed.

"Yes. His colour has come back and his pulse is steady. You'd better go home. If he doesn't come round I'll ring up, and you had better tell your father to come."

"I'm sorry. Really I am," the young man said.

"You'd better go."

"I'm sorry."

"It can't be helped."

"He shouldn't have thrown the wine at me."

"It's my fault really."

"But you do think he's all right—I didn't mean to knock the little fellow out."

"You won't do him any good staying here. And your father may want the car. Can you let yourself out?"

71

"Well—Good-night. Will I see you again?"

"I'm off tomorrow. Don't bang the hall-door. Good-night."

Elizabeth had taken Ralph's head on her lap and was spraying it from water in a finger-bowl. His head was aching terribly. His jaw felt as if it was cracked. His teeth pained. He felt young and foolish and inadequate. He kept his eyes closed and let her bathe away until she bent down and said:

"Look, are you awake? There's going to be hell to pay if we are found here."

This had put the situation into perspective. After a short interval he had opened his eyes, and sat up very gingerly. He said nothing; there was nothing to say. He walked out of the room with Elizabeth at his elbow as if he were a baby taking its first steps. At the foot of the stairs, he grasped the banisters.

"I'll clean up down here," she said. She sounded every-dayish, reassuring, sensible.

He stayed in bed next day and did not see her again. The Canon asked no questions.

Ralph came back to earth; while his mind had been wandering his ear had been receiving a ceaseless flow of family history which would float up from the back of his mind in due course. He had not been told anything that bore on the problems of the moment; that he felt sure of. A man looking out of a window is inevitably looking backwards. What had recalled Ralph's attention was a change in tone. Reminiscence was at an end.

"I am telling you this," Mr Fox was saying, "because you might as well know the history of the family if you are going to become involved in their business affairs."

A habit of speaking as if he was alone in the possession of facts, however widely known, contributed not a little to Mr Fox's reputation for universal wisdom. He was evidently not interested in other people's minds; apart from this, his method precluded interruption. You just listened all the time, irritated or impressed according to your opinion of your own capacity.

He put down the cat, and proceeded to walk up and down the room, winding his central tuft of hair round and round his first finger as if to symbolise the complexity of the situation.

"Major Paul will try to inveigle you into some scheme of his own. I met him at the time of the lease and he did his best to put his spell on me. Enquiries had already produced sufficient evidence to put me on my guard. He has borrowed over a hundred thousand pounds in the last ten years, and he has been declared a bankrupt on two occasions; but he has some influential friends.

"Lady Lambert—this, of course, is not to go beyond these four walls—has been under his influence for some time. I am not aware of the nature of the services he may have rendered her; but she persuaded Sir Julian to give him Kent, the best of the villas, free of rent, on the pretext that he will improve it. In fact, I believe he has done a great deal of work on the house and the stables. I fancy he wants to get his hands on Mount Lambert. Bradshaw told me as much. It wouldn't suit Bradshaw at all, as I should think the Major would get rid of him at once. A poacher turned gamekeeper. You must let this Mr Miller take full responsibility for anything that is proposed. You must not let us become answerable to Miller's client for the Major's future conduct. I shall be very interested to hear what happens."

Like many other men who are normally inaccessible, Mr Fox was impossible to get away from when once he had made an exception to his rule. Perhaps it was another manifestation of the urge to dominate : not letting people in, and when invited in, not letting them out.

The falling sun was playing strange tricks with the long dark room in which it seemed all the waste paper in the world had come to rest. Mr Fox had ceased to perambulate and was now reading some document in the worst possible light with the aid of a magnifying glass. He had apparently forgotten about Ralph's presence; and he was tempted to creep out of the room: to excuse himself required an effort of which he was incapable. However, when Mr Fox put down the paper, seized the telephone and emitted a loud wail, Ralph felt it was safe to go. He murmured something for civility's sake; his employer replied with another wail; but this was addressed to the telephone.

CHAPTER VIII

As soon as they arrived at the Count's door Ralph realised that he had made a tactical mistake in agreeing to interview him on his own home ground. Such smoothness of gravel, such sleek lawns, such neat edges; the perfection of the roses, the shine on the door knocker, the newness of the paint, the general air of prosperity, order and good taste—all combined to inspire a feeling of inferiority in a caller. Ralph found himself glancing at his shoes, settled his tie, feeling his flies, pulling down his shirt cuffs—exhibiting in innumerable little ways that there was an ordeal ahead. Miller cultivated an air of not being impressed by anything; but his prominent adam's apple might have been seen to move more than was its wont. For all his pin-stripe ostentation, he was still rather junior in his firm.

The knock was not answered at once; then the Italian servant whom Ralph had seen before on the two occasions he had come to the Count's for cocktails, opened the door. He led them through the small hall into the drawing-room where, as was the fashion on the Mile, a fire was burning in the grate, although the windows were wide open and the evening sun lit a path of gold across the Aubusson carpet.

"The Major asks you to excuse him, he went late to dress; but you are to have whatever you want while you are waiting—sherry, whiskey, gin, vodka, Dubonnet . . ."

"We should have dressed," Ralph said.

"He couldn't expect me to bring over a dinner-jacket for the occasion." Miller looked defensively hostile.

"I'll have some gin and tonic water, if you have any," Ralph said, trying to sound confident, conscious of having lost ground.

"If the sherry is dry, I'll have some," Miller said.

Ralph resented his tone. One didn't gradate civility on the Mile.

"What wonderful roses," Ralph said, hoping to cancel his companion's arrogance. A corner of the room was filled with roses, banked up in artful profusion.

"The Major arranged them himself," Benito answered with admiration in his tone.

Miller glanced at the flowers, and looked away. He was not going to be impressed by anything. His faculties were harnessed to the tasks of exposure and bringing to book.

The Italian reeled off the names of six brands of sherry with perfect good humour. Miller, as if making a concession, settled for one.

"Help yourselves to anything you like the Major says." With an indulgent smile Benito left them.

Miller's bearing antagonised Ralph at once. He somehow shrank in stature the more *blasé* he tried to appear. An air of cynicism did not become him, and he looked far from impressive as he stood in the centre of the room, sniffing and, at the same time, taking a mental inventory. Ralph turned away and pretended to be absorbed in a picture.

The Count came in wearing a velvet smoking jacket over evening trousers.

"My dear boys. I am so sorry for having kept you. I asked my man to tell you to make yourselves at home. What are you drinking, Ralph? And your friend?"

"Oh, this is Mr Miller from Grise & Grise, Major."

"Mr Miller, I don't think we have met before and I have not heard of your firm, although I know many of the leading firms in London. Do you pronounce it Grease & Grease or Grice & Grice? Lawyers' firms have so often such funny names; and this is curious because there is nothing funny about a lawyer's office. We will compromise, we will pronounce it Grease & Grice. But your name is Miller; how is that? You are not related to Grease or Grice are you? Just in their employment? A clerk? Someday you will be a partner. I can see it written on your noble brow. You are—

you will permit me to say—too distinguished-looking for the junior branch of the legal profession. Your forehead would look well under a wig. What are you drinking?"

Miller's face underwent many changes during this soliloquy, but whenever he saw an opportunity to jump in, he found that it had flown past; he was experiencing the chagrin of one who reaches the platform in time to see the rear lights of the train disappearing into the tunnel. And, as if the simile had occurred to him, the Count turned round abruptly and moved with surprising swiftness for a heavy man towards the array of bottles on a side table.

"I was drinking Tio Pepe," Miller said sourly.

"I am sorry we are not dressed, but Mr Miller didn't expect to go out to dinner," Ralph again tried to set off his colleague's manner.

"It was very good of you, Mr Miller, to come all this way. I do appreciate it very much. Could you take a few days off? I'd like to show you the country. Do you ride?"

"Yes and no."

"There goes the lawyer—Yes *and* No."

"I used to ride, I mean, but I don't get the opportunity nowadays."

"What I suggest, then, is that you come over for a few weeks in the winter. I can mount you; and you will find the hunting round here very mild indeed. Ralph's father keeps a horse for his trap. He goes very well. Ralph took him out a few times last season. How is the Canon, Ralph? Please give him my kindest regards."

"He was at Mrs Molloy's funeral today."

"So he was. So was I. How time flies. Let me give you some more, Ralph. Is that gin? The tasteless death. I meant to mix you champagne cocktails but I was so busy. Miss Beddington came back with me to lunch and helped to pick the roses."

"We were admiring them."

"Thank you, Ralph. I have the best roses in the county. Miss Beddington was amazed. She played in the garden as a

77

child. I can imagine it! I see her in a spotted muslin dress, her hair in plaits, and long black stockings. Perhaps she enjoyed her first kiss there under the rose—a lady of the utmost discretion. I was going to ask her to join us at dinner and then I remembered you said something about business. You have some business to discuss, haven't you? It won't take us very long; but, even so, I thought that it was better to keep our party intimate. Miss Beddington, though delightful, is a little old for you Mr Miller. We must collect some *jeunes filles* when you come over for the hunting."

Benito came in and announced dinner. The Count propelled his guests towards the dining-room with slightly exaggerated gestures. Miller gulped down his sherry in the manner of one who proceeded systematically, keeping his feet on the ground, holding tenaciously to what he had. Ralph, unable and unwilling to pretend that he was in the enemy's camp, remembered Mr Fox. What had been the purpose of today's interview but to warn him not to get involved? He could play the rôle of amused spectator and leave the Count and Miller (who grew less attractive with every passing minute) to fight their battle out. Already it was apparent that Grise & Grise had underrated their opponent and would regret having sent over a member of their second eleven.

The dining-room had an enormous table in the centre of it, unlaid, but with three chairs arrayed around it at the greatest distance geometry allowed. In the window a round table was laid with three places. The Count caught Ralph's eye as he looked at the large table and winked. The wink was the first concession. It told Ralph that the original plan had been to put Miller at one end of the table, so far away from his host, that he would have had to shout at him. This would have been the technique of cold war. It had been abandoned in favour of the friendly arrangement at the small table where the Count could employ his weapons of diplomacy. Perhaps if Ralph had not been there he might have shown an unfamiliar self; but on the Mile the Count had taken pains to appear in one character only, and that a very urbane one.

Having decided that the young English lawyer was of poor conversible material, his host made no effort to draw him out; instead he resorted to his Othello technique, and as he plied his guests with wine and dishes of such variety that it was obvious most of the ingredients were imported, he soliloquised about the time he was faced by a lion on safari, aimed coolly between the eyes as the beast sprang and the trigger stuck. A keeper's cross shot brought down the lion at the Count's feet.

"I held my ground but I felt its hot breath on my face. I was reminded of the incident when I was sprung at by a contralto in her dressing-room. I bear the scars of that last attack still."

Miller did his best. "May I ask in what army you were a major?" he said, his daring being a sad effort to emulate the Count's manner.

"You may. I wouldn't if the circumstances were reversed; but these are questions of taste. I was a major in the Foreign Legion. How do you employ your time, Mr Miller, when you are not collecting debts? Do you take part in charitable work? organising bazaars and concerts? Are you musically inclined? Do you go to the Opera? I have some good records if you would like to hear them after dinner? You are married? Perhaps Mrs Miller would like to come with you when you are with us for the hunting."

"I'm not married."

"No doubt you have made satisfactory arrangements. I never married; but that is because I am something of a perfectionist. I am only satisfied with the best; and if I were a husband I would wish to be a perfect husband. There are therefore two risks involved, and one of them would not be under my control. You are not drinking, Mr Miller. Finish this claret and we will have a little champagne. What a power of strength you must be to Grease & Grice. Tell me

79

about them. What does Mr Grease look like? Has he side-whiskers? Does he come to his office in a hansom cab? And Mr Grice, what about him? Does he pull well with his partner? I smell a conspiracy. Mr Grease is old-fashioned and easy-going? Mr Grice is keen and ambitious. One day Mr Grease will wake up and find that Mr Grice has bought him out or sold him up. When that day falls, Mr Miller, on which side will you be found? With Mr Grease, your back to the wall? Or with Mr Grice who will command the big battalions? I attach a lot of importance to the answer because it will tell me whether you are a romantic *au fond,* in spite of appearances, or the realist that you present yourself."

Miller made no effort to suppress his sulkiness.

"There is no Grise in the firm."

"No Grease in the firm! No Grice! Where are they? What have you done with them? You are a dangerous man, Mr Miller, a Turk among attorneys."

"Our firm is eighty years old," Mr Miller solemnly said; but his speech was a little thicker than it had been. "There is no member of the original firm alive. But the senior partner is a great nephew of the founder, Sir Plowman Grise."

"Ah! You don't say! Let us drink his health. Sir Plowman Grease! Eighty years! What a little has gone a long way! Have you a portrait of Sir Plowman? Has he not got mutton-chop whiskers?"

"He had, as a matter of fact; we have a painting of him by Sir William Richmond in the board-room."

"There! What did I tell you!"

Refusing a cigar, Miller tried to take over the conversation.

"I wonder if we could have a word now about Mr Tartan Young's business. He is anxious about the money you owe him. You see he thought that it was only for a matter of weeks, and he took no security."

"Anxious! That absurd little man anxious! Security! What impertinence! I met him at the house of a friend of mine where he happened to be filling the place of someone who had called off at the last moment. Incautiously— thinking myself among friends—I spoke about a filly that I had which I was going to sell, because I couldn't afford to keep her in training, when this Tartan Young gentleman insisted on pressing me to take a few thousand pounds—I'm not quite sure how many—five, I think—hoping to get in on a good thing."

"Eight."

"Eight or five, the principle is the same : he thought apparently that by doing that he would have some sort of stake in her. The silly fellow didn't realise that one doesn't syndicate mares. That's the mistake these business tycoons make. They think just because they have money they can become connoisseurs of pictures and authorities on blood-stock breeding. One grows up with that sort of knowledge. It's partly in the blood. I wouldn't like Mr Young—what is the significance of 'Tartan' by the way?—I wouldn't like him to be anxious. His money is perfectly safe. He shall get back every penny, and interest if his tastes run to usury."

Were it not that nobody could be quite so opulent as the Count looked, it did seem somehow foolish to be worrying about money in his presence. It seemed worse than foolish, it seemed petty and second-rate.

"Ralph, I'm afraid your friend is not a romantic after all. You brought him to see me on false pretences."

But Miller was not going to be deflected now in his own area of operations and in full control of himself and the situation.

"I'm sorry; but I'm afraid Mr Tartan Young is a business man, and he doesn't employ me to be romantic on his behalf."

The Count smiled as if the picture gave him secret plea-sure. Benito had returned and at a nod from his master let a champagne cork off so close to Miller's ear that he jumped in his chair.

"A little more wine, Mr Miller? Mr Tartan Young has

almost gained my approval. I wish that I had you working for me. What admirable persistence! I will do nothing for your Mr Young. I have a code, and it lays down a very definite rule about conduct of his sort. My father used to say: never do business with friends, never borrow except from bankers, and confine your *affaires* to women of your own class. I have never departed from that advice without regretting it. And Mr Tartan Young was very definitely not up to snuff. I did not want to snub him. I did not want to say 'Keep your five thousand pounds and invest it in Bearer Bonds'. I did not want to humiliate him by pointing out the obvious, that one does not offer money across the table to a friend's guests. My good heart has been the cause of this very tiresome business; but it has also been the cause of my meeting you, Mr Miller. For that I thank Mr Turban Young."

"*Tartan* Young, and I must remind you that it is not five thousand pounds, but eight thousand pounds."

The Count bowed ironically, and then signalled Benito who let off another cork behind Miller's ear.

Miller made a gesture as if warding off the assault of champagne until agreement was reached about the business.

"I can't subscribe to an attack on my firm's clients. Mr Tartan Young is very well thought of in the City, and extremely lavish in his contributions to good causes. I don't expect he detected your reluctance to take the eight thousand pounds he offered without security or interest. He has not given me the impression that he thought you resented it; nor does the file of correspondence give this impression, I must say. You are profuse in your thanks even if you continually evade the matter of repayment."

Ralph glanced uneasily at the Count to see how he was taking it now that all pretence of friendliness had been dropped. The change was interesting. The look of mockery had gone, and in its place a pair of very dark eyes were staring at Miller, but apparently not taking him in, a dark film made the irises look as if they were covered with an inky fluid. The impression was of intense concentration; but not on what was being said.

"Do you not think your friend's money is safe?"

"Mr Tartan Young is not a friend; I represent him. His money, you will forgive me for saying so, seems to me to be about as safe as if it were loose on a raft in mid-Atlantic."

"Mr Miller, I will not forget that phrase. And now will you please say what you want to do to secure this gentleman who is suddenly in such pressing need."

"What security have you to offer?"

"My word."

"That is not legal security, unfortunately."

"I daresay. I have a project, a stud farm, into which that very friend in whose house it was my ill fortune to encounter your client, is prepared to invest a quarter of a million pounds. I had intended to suggest that Mr Young's five or eight thousand pounds should be regarded as entitling him to a share—he was extremely anxious to associate himself in any projects of this kind that I had in mind—but now I'm afraid that's off. I shall have no more dealings with Mr Young. I should not employ him as a groom were he to offer his services. His appearance would produce contagious abortion among my mares."

"I must ask you not to attack my client to my face. I don't imagine that he wants to involve himself in any fresh enterprise before he sees his money. The question is where is it to come from? Is this house mortgaged."

"I beg your pardon."

"It occurred to me that this house would be fairly adequate security for the amount you owe."

"In the east, Mr Miller, a remark of that kind at a man's table would endanger your life. There are sacred laws, Mr Miller, laws that are older than those which you seem to be very superficially versed in—if you will pardon the observation of one who is descended from a family in which there were eminent judges."

"It was you who suggested that we should talk business at

dinner. I thought we might meet in a law office. If you prefer, we can postpone our talk until the morning and have it in Ralph's office."

The Count had lapsed into his tranced state and did not seem to listen to what Miller was saying. At length he put up his hand, and as if nothing had been said before, he turned in perfectly business-like manner to Miller.

"You can take any horses of mine that you want. I only ask for a return of that note and a clear receipt from you to end my liability to your client."

"I don't think—"

"Mr Miller, you can't have it both ways. Mr Young pressed his money on me to stop me from selling my horses. Very well; now he employs you to harass me when I have plans of the greatest importance on foot. I can't be bothered with Mr Young, tartan or no tartan; my life is not geared for annoyances of that kind. I shall in future work in partnership with people of standing. I don't own this house. It belongs to the Lamberts, as Ralph will tell you. I live here at their request while I am going into the matters I mentioned, in which I've promised them they will get a share. At the moment I have only the horses in my stable as Mr Young knows very well. Why would I have been pressed to sell them if I had other resources? Let him take the horses. I will sell them to him. But I insist that you take them away at once and I insist that you give me a clear receipt."

"I will have to take instructions."

"By all means," the Count said, then his jaw fell. He had it back in place within a fraction of a second; but Ralph noticed the phenomenon.

"Something has gone wrong with my telephone. I can't make outgoing calls," he said.

"Come over to my house, George, after dinner and put through your call from there. It will only take us a few minutes in the car."

"George! Is that your name, Mr Miller? Perhaps you can tell me why in every English play to which a footman is

84

introduced he is invariably called George. Is it because of all those fat Kings? The idea of service and at the same time liberal pickings from the pantry, raids on the cellar?"

Miller, unable to cope with the speed of the onslaught, decided to ignore it, nor did he look particularly grateful for the association of ideas.

"I think we had better go at once. Mr Tartan Young may not be easy to find. I'll ring him up at home."

The Count made no protest; but he was obviously perturbed. In the hall, he turned dramatically and raised an hieratic hand.

"No. I cannot allow it. I cannot have my business bruited over the local telephone service. If Mr Miller's client does not give him plenipotentiary powers, I can't help it; but I am not going to have it common gossip on the Mile that the bailiff is in my stables."

"Then we must wait until tomorrow. George can ring up from my office."

"What about Gallagher?"

"What about him? Oh...Yes...I suppose you ought to ring him up and tell him to hold on for the present."

"And who is Gallagher?" A certain sharpness in the tone of the question showed that the Count saw an opening for a counter-attack.

"He's my adviser. I'd arranged for him to come down in the morning."

"Without my permission. He may be the sort of man whom I would not allow in my stables. I regard this as an outrage. You came tonight to discuss the position—what right had you to anticipate the result? I might have preferred to write you a cheque."

"That's always on. I'd much prefer it."

The Count raised his hand, then moved it very gently as if to fan away some unspeakable unpleasantness.

"I think George could easily warn Mr Young on the telephone not to mention any names, and then he could say he had arrived at a solution, and would Mr Young authorise him to act on his own discretion."

Ralph's intervention had an astonishing effect on the Count.

"I want to make one thing quite clear, Ralph. Your father is my friend. Friendship is sacred to me. I absolutely insist that he is not brought into this sordid business. It does not concern our relations. I ask you to give me your word that you will not bring Mr Miller across your threshold or mention this matter to the Canon. If not, I will leave the Mile tomorrow. I will not stay anywhere after a friendship is dishonoured."

Miller grasped the door-handle.

"I'm tired of all this play-acting."

"Mr Miller, will you please leave my house. Your client can do his worst. I will not allow his understrappers to insult me in my own house. Please go at once."

Bizarre though his behaviour had been, Ralph had no doubt that the Count meant what he said. He had done as he pleased since he came to the Mile, picking his friends, snubbing the rest, running, by all reports, a discreetly disorderly house, and getting away with it. His panache was all-conquering. A few minutes before it seemed that the Young debt had been solved, and now they were fighting again, because, if the truth were known, the Count had not paid his last telephone account. It was not too late to make an effort at a compromise.

"Perhaps we ought to sit down again and sort this out. I'm sure George didn't mean to be rude. Did you, George?"

"He called me a clerk as soon as I entered his house, then a footman, then an understrapper. I wouldn't stand that sort of thing from anyone. All I'm concerned with is trying to get security for £8,000 which Major Paul borrowed and hasn't repaid. It's as simple as that."

"You touched my honour, Mr George. No man can do that. In Legion days, we would now be facing one another with revolvers. That is the clean way to live. If you agree to keep my friendship with the Canon out of this, I am quite prepared to come to a compromise."

"I don't really understand how your friendship with father comes into it," Ralph intervened.

"Quite simply. I want you both to promise he hears nothing of tonight's entertainment and that Mr George does not cross his threshold. I want you Ralph to promise that in no circumstances, *in no circumstances whatever,* will you disclose to the Canon that there is a dispute in which my horses are involved."

"By all means," said Ralph. "I quite agree it has nothing to do with him."

"Well, where are we now?"

Miller looked from one to another. He was lost.

As if perfectly at ease now that the Romantic element was in order, the Count put his hand on Miller's shoulder.

"Come with me. We will visit the Guards—the police. From there you can ring up London. I trust them. They will not talk, They are all friends of mine."

Miller jumped at this suggestion. All three huddled into Ralph's car and drove to the barracks in better humour than they had been all evening. Miller had been very pleased with his work, and the last minute hitch had been a disappointment. The Count's only concern was to make sure that Miller did not discover the grey filly in the Canon's stables. Ralph was glad to have made the peace. It did occur to him that a call from the barracks would go through the same exchange as a call from a private house; but if the Count had overlooked this, he was not going to queer the pitch. He, too, had the private satisfaction of thinking that in this detail he was more astute than the Count.

The Count's standing with the police force was high. He had taken trouble to endear himself, and tales of his sexual prowess gave them opportunities to exchange anecdotes of a pleasing character. Their lives were dull and they were full-blooded men.

There was no trouble in putting through a cross-Channel call.

Mr Young was at dinner : and he expressed delight at the way things had gone.

"It's not the money, old boy. It's being taken for a fool that stuck in my throat. Nobody has ever done that to T. Young with impunity. Don't let him palm off a dud on you. I heard him say the grey filly was the valuable one. Get me that."

In this manner the business of Mr Tartan Young and Major Paul was made known to the Mile. But as no discredit attached to suggestions of fraud in connection with horse-dealing, the Major's credit suffered no hurt. The excitement was all in character.

After some joking with the Guards, and a rabelaisian tale, the party returned to Kent Lodge, where the Count insisted on opening another bottle. He then became very insistent that Ralph should stay the night and not return to Cumberland a little under the weather. And Ralph, with the prospect of more champagne, allowed himself to be persuaded.

CHAPTER IX

"WELL, THIS IS very nice. Very nice as it always is with you, Barbara, dear."

The Canon referred to the pretty drawing-room, decorated with Bartolozzi prints and Victorian water-colours; the faded chintz; the prevalence of *petit-point* on cushions and chair-backs; the stuffed birds; the souvenirs of Eastern service; the oval pastel portraits of Barbara's father and mother, made at the time of their marriage; the card-table furnished with sweets in a silver dish and a whole packet of cigarettes; the sofa-table on which a tray stood, prepared for coffee and biscuits later on; the pomeranian asleep on the tiger skin at the fire-place; the neat sewing basket between the sofa end and one side of the Bossi mantelpiece; the photographs of the two young princesses in a silver frame; the budgerigars in their cage at the window; the china-cabinet with its Dresden and Meissen figures and a Worcester tea-set; the general air of gentleness and established modest comfort; and Barbara, herself, an ungathered rose, blooming serenely, oblivious to the onset of autumn.

"As it always is with you and Pen, Canon," Barbara replied. In a silk dress which made Mrs Ormsby look somewhat homely in her blouse and skirt, she looked as if she had stepped out of a Gainsborough group. "You will marry Barbara when I go aloft." Mrs Ormsby used to tell her husband frequently. He found his errant fancy playing with the thought now. Barbara had an aromatic delicacy which appealed very much to him, and of which he was pleasantly aware. Penelope always smelled of soap. It was bracing, but not seductive.

"Mabel Browne will be a little late, George had to attend an emergency meeting at the hospital, and they weren't able to dine before eight. However, it's cosy to be able to have a little chat between ourselves before she comes," Miss Beddington said.

The Canon leaned towards his hostess. "I missed you after the funeral, Barbara. I wanted to have a word with you."

"Poor Michael. He looked quite terrible. He must have been very devoted to his mother. She was such a complete recluse. I wish we could find him a wife; but I suppose he will never marry now."

"He has been working for me for twenty years, and I have never known him to say anything except in answer to a question. I have no idea what's going on in his mind. I think he might kill himself if Mount Lambert were sold. He has constituted himself a sort of watch dog."

"He will be more excited than anybody at Elizabeth's visit. If only she would marry your Ralph and settle down there, Michael would become their guardian angel. I'm sure he is longing for that to happen."

"Elizabeth will look further than our Ralph," the Canon said, trying to distract attention from his self-consciousness, by brushing crumbs off his broad front. Barbara had a way of reading his mind. Perhaps it was because they saw eye to eye on so many matters.

"Did you hear about Elizabeth's coming?" Mrs Ormsby enquired. "Did she write to you too?"

"The grape-vine brought me the news this morning. And that reminds me before we get any further—when I dropped in at the Brownes' this afternoon to ask Mabel to make up our four this evening, she was most anxious, poor dear, that her Sylvia should be included in the invitation to the ball. I promised I'd put in a word; Mabel is so ambitious for that child, and really I think all she wants is to be left alone. She looks at the moment far more suitable for a rugby scrum than a dance; but if her mother wants to bring her out, I'm sure you'll have no objection."

"Well, isn't that the limit? Who said there was going to

be a ball? And who is supposed to be giving it?" Mrs Ormsby looked genuinely upset.

"You, my dears, in honour of Elizabeth's coming of age; and you are going to take Mount Lambert for the occasion, and it's going to be the greatest occasion since Lord Bray came of age, and that wasn't yesterday."

The Canon threw up his hands in mock despair.

"It's no use, Canon. The Mile has read your thoughts. It will feel cheated if you don't persevere. If I'm going to be on the list, I must start to get a dress ready."

"We can talk to you, Barbara, as one of ourselves. It's perfectly true that the idea did come into Oliver's head. Can't you imagine it! But I think it's quite absurd. The Lamberts can well afford to give a dance for Elizabeth. Why should we act as if we were mayors of the palace? It's ridiculous."

"But you are. Without the Canon there would be no Mile. I got the impression you were going to address the mourners today. I was quite disappointed when you didn't. You looked so impressive at the grave-side; and you had the look of someone with an oration prepared."

"I don't know what gave you that impression, Barbara. I think any intrusion by me on today's proceedings would have been sadly out of place. But I was glad I went. I think it gave some pleasure to Michael. As you know he is very reserved. I called on his poor mother with a pot of Pen's marmalade the day she died. I'm afraid she never got an opportunity to taste it. I suppose it will go to waste now."

"Michael will preserve it as a burnt offering, I'm sure." Then she betrayed her own preoccupations. "Major Paul was very good to go. He always does the right thing. He invited me back to lunch. It was very kind of him."

"I hope you had a chaperone. Oliver refuses to listen to gossip; but I must say the stories about the parties at Kent Lodge are hair-raising. I wonder if royal ghosts attend them. It must seem quite like the good old days if one can believe one's ears."

"Now Pen! You know I have forbidden you to take away Major Paul's character. He happens to know people in the horsey set, and he doesn't think they would mix in very well with the Milers."

"I couldn't go; but I was longing to. I've only been there in the evening, and he always has the same party for me. It's just like being at home, only the food's so much better."

"Angela had a story that at his last dinner one of the guests, a horse-trainer, had a bet with a girl as to what she wore underneath and turned her upside down to see during the fish course."

"Pen! I'm amazed at you. Why the fish course, I wonder?" The Canon was surprised to see how calmly Barbara took the news.

"That was going rather far. No wonder he doesn't let us meet his sporting friends. We mustn't let the Perrys hear that story. They are so anxious to hear the worst about the Major," was all she had to say.

Mrs Browne's arrival brought about a change in the conversation. Everyone concentrated very hard on bridge because there was a certain self-consciousness in the air. Mrs Browne was wondering whether Barbara had already spoken to the Canon, and if so what was the result. The Canon was aware that gossip had anticipated any announcement on his part, and he was determined not to be rushed. Mrs Ormsby was worrying about the jam she had been making all day. Miss Beddington couldn't get her mind off the picture that had formed in it of the Count's rowdy dinner. Supposing that she was there, and that had happened—not to her. Good God no!—but in her presence ... She had wanted to say 'yes' when invited to lunch. The Count was fascinating in a way that the Canon was not. They were both the finest-looking men she had ever met; and to have married the Canon would have been a perfect development in her life on the Mile. It could only have happened if God's inscrutable will had decided it was best to remove Mrs Ormsby from the earthly scene. It had not so decided, and if appearances were any guide, was not likely so to decide in the ascertainable future. The idea of a marriage with the Count was too bizarre to be mentioned except in scandalous jest. He belonged to another world, of whose existence she got occasional glimpses, a world full of mysterious attraction, of mystery—and it had to be faced— evil, a world of which she had sometimes received frightened and fascinated intimations in her dreams—especially after wine at dinner.

The rubber proceeded. Threepence a hundred. The Canon looked detached; Mrs. Ormsby worried; Mrs. Browne alert; Miss Beddington *distraite*.

At ten o'clock there was a halt for coffee; and the state of the game was seized upon as a neutral and engrossing topic. Mrs Browne was a scold, and she had a great deal to say about some of Barbara's leads and answers to her signals.

"How astonishingly unattractive she is," the Canon mused, keeping out of the discussion. Mrs Ormsby was sticking up for the hostess, a united front against a lesser Miler. Barbara looked sweetly penitent. Mrs Browne wanted a frank acknowledgement from all present that her interpretation was the only correct one when, like doom, a loud knocking was heard at the door.

"Whoever could that be?"

Barbara, maidenwise, became nervous at once. Mrs Browne looked peeved that dialectical victory was being snatched from her grasp. Everyone else welcomed the interruption.

The maid opened the door to let in Captain Loftus. He looked as if he had been running.

"I rang you up, Canon, but your maid said you were out for the evening."

Loftus seemed to have a grievance over this if he had only time to pursue it. He had a way of opening conversations with remarks which were made in a tone of interrogation but took the form of incontrovertible statements of fact.

It led, as now, to pauses. Everyone waited for him to carry on.

"I couldn't think of anything else to do; so I rang my cousin. But he was out. They dine at the Yacht Club on Thursdays. I didn't want to ring him there; so I came round here."

"I'm glad you did. Would you like a cup of coffee?"

"No, thank you, Miss Beddington."

The Captain rather pointedly turned away from the women and addressed the Canon exclusively, as if he were the presiding officer at a Court Martial.

"I was at the funeral today; and it so happened that I left my bicycle near the wall of the grave-yard. I couldn't find it when I came out, and I reported the matter to the Guards. They found it afterwards; apparently some young ruffian had looted it—I'd have flayed him alive if I'd caught him. But that's not the point. The young Guard who called this evening—quite a decent, well-spoken young fellow—let drop a remark which I thought was too serious to let lie there. He was going out, and in that familiar way these people have nowadays, he said : 'Nice place you have here.' I said nothing, of course. But he didn't spot the reproof—thick-skinned—and, as if I had encouraged him, he said : 'I hear Mr Coppinger has great plans for Cambridge. My uncle is in the contracting line and he says that his firm expect to get thousands out of it. He's adding a new storey and throwing out a garden wing and a bridge across the river.'

"'Is he?' I said very firmly. 'Well I think Mr Coppinger will learn before he's much older that there is still some law left in the country.' He gave me a look. I think he realised by this that he had said too much. And he took himself off without trying to prolong the conversation. I thought I'd better act on the information at once. We may not have much time. If Coppinger gets away with this the Mile is finished. The next thing will be a pub at the corner and 'bed and breakfast' notices on the villa windows."

The Canon gave the utmost attention to the Captain's outburst, realising that all present would rely on his final judgment. He could sense that Mrs Browne was at once on the Captain's side, prepared to respond, if necessary, to a call to arms; but Miss Beddington, who was so much more of the true Mileage, was not so much impressed. Like the Canon she ever so little resented this passionate concern for tradition from one who was only a Miler by sheer accident—the Perrys would be in full cry tomorrow also. One had to be wise and calm and judicious. But all these were qualities with which the Canon—in Barbara's sight—was pre-eminently endowed.

Mrs Ormsby, as a rule, barely concealed her distaste for Loftus whom, in the privacy of their bedroom, she had more than once discussed with the Canon, and he had not contradicted her assertion that he was an 'officious little bounder'. It was she who was the first to speak when Loftus, exhausted after his efforts, let his eye roam in search of a decanter. But he had to solace himself with coffee. Miss Beddington did not offer drink to bridge guests, although she always 'did whatever was the right thing' at her little dinner parties.

"I believe the Coppingers have a crowd of small children. I never could see how they were going to fit into that house."

The Captain made a gesture of impatience with his foot, exposing long underwear in the process.

"If Mr Coppinger employs a good architect, he may be able to keep the character of the house. It can be done," Miss Beddington said to the Canon.

He was thinking to himself, and as always his imagination had been stirred by any suggestion of enlargement. He saw a building like Blenheim arising on the site of that neat Regency villa; and in its grounds, made enchanting by statuary of the Rococo period (to which his taste inclined), girls in vague draperies, which enhanced their elegant figures, moved rather aimlessly about while he gazed out of the

95

window of the library (in which as the Dr Johnson of the Mile he had the right to browse), and feasted his eyes on the peaceful magnificence of the prospect. Peacocks spread their prismatic feathers on the lawns, doves in the elms...

"I think Canon that you should go and see this Coppinger person yourself. I gather from Ralph that Mr Fox is not prepared to take a stand." The Captain's voice crackled through the reverie.

"But who says Mr Coppinger can't do whatever he likes to the house," Mrs Ormsby interjected. "It's a pity if he changes the look of it; but Oliver can't be expected to invite a snub by trying to interfere. How would you have liked it, Captain, if the Canon had called on you when you moved into Wales and found fault with the way you were looking after the house? He's not the Lamberts' agent. Mr Fox is."

His wife's voice, as always so redolent of common-sense and practical considerations, broke up the Canon's dream. Never did he look so sagacious as when he hadn't heard the question. Experience had taught him that it was fatal to try to answer on those occasions. By looking wise and keeping silent one conveyed the impression of not approving of whatever had been proposed. At worst, the question would be repeated. The great thing was not to rush in.

"Fox only thinks of the legal end," the Captain continued. "He doesn't live here. Besides, though I hope I'm not a snob, I don't think an attorney is qualified to understand our concern for the social atmosphere of the place."

"Mr Fox is a friend of mine," the Canon said.

If the Captain had been a real Miler he would have known that he had been reproved, that his reflection on Mr Fox was resented; but he was not; he was 'an officious bounder' as Mrs Ormsby had recognised from the start.

Miss Beddington knew; and when Loftus began, "Oh, that's all very well——" she interjected with as much acerbity as she was capable of assuming.

"We never discuss our friends on the Mile, Captain. I'm sure the Canon is right. I am as sorry as anyone to see any

96

changes; but let us face the fact there have been several, and I daresay there will be more. I only hope Mr Coppinger employs a good architect."

"I hear his house is full of modern art and all that sort of God-forsaken rubbish. Mark my words, he will put up something that will look like a glorified glass-house. I'll bet my life on it."

Brave as his words were, the Captain's spirit was punctured. His zeal had been killed. Once again he had tried to recommend himself by giving a lead, and once again his enterprise had fallen flat. If neither the Canon nor Miss Beddington were impressed, who was left? Mrs Browne had held her tongue—an effort in her case—to see which way the cat jumped. For herself she welcomed the idea of the Coppingers. They had children. They gave parties. The opportunities of entertainment this offered were dazzling. What an absurd figure this monkey of a man cut protesting against the arrival of added life. What had *he* to offer? But she did not want to commit herself until she heard what the Canon and Barbara had to say. *Noblesse Oblige.* Now she had a licence, and she used it.

"I don't suppose you know the Coppingers, Captain."

"I meet him in the Club."

"Then you can tell us all about him. I'm longing to hear."

Loftus was trapped. He had asked the porter once who Coppinger was, struck by his rather mannered good looks; but he had never had a word with him, and what he had heard were grumbles from one or two of his own kind who were not in touch with anybody and even resorted to telling one another what was in the morning's paper. Mrs Browne, a name-dropper of many years, understood the Captain's predicament. She had been in it often on her own account, and as she was less than an angel she looked forward to a little sport. But her hostess had no illusions about her, and at once suggested a resumption of the game. She even insisted on dropping out in favour of the Captain, to the disappointment of the others. He jumped at the chance, threw off his bad humour, ignored Mrs Browne's strictures, and had the satisfaction of ending the evening by taking seven shillings off her.

He even ventured to put his arm round Miss Beddington's waist in the hall. And as the Ormsbys went past, tactfully averting their eyes, he called out after them, "I hope you got a vet's opinion on your new horse, Canon."

The Ormsbys drove home in silence. She knew that her husband was never happy when she laid down the law; and she concealed her curiosity about the Captain's remark, waiting for an explanation to be volunteered. She was astounded to hear her husband was buying horses without consulting her. Robinson was perfectly satisfactory. What new folly was this?

"Was Loftus referring to the grey mare in the stable?" she said from her brass-headed bed after each had bade the other 'Good-night'.

"I don't know what he was talking about. He is a very consequential little fellow."

"But who owns the animal in the yard?"

"The animal in the yard?"

"Yes, the animal in the yard."

"Oh, that's the Major's; he asked me to keep it for him. I'm not quite sure why. But I don't want to be unfriendly. I hope Michael gave it some hay."

"I see. Are we now keeping the Count's horses?" Mrs Ormsby asked the desert air. She had never been more keenly aware of the discrepancy between the world as it was and the world that occupied her husband's picturesque and disordered imagination.

CHAPTER X

RALPH WOKE UP and wondered where he was. His own room had changed very little since he first occupied it on leaving the nursery; but through half-awakened eyes this was a scene of oriental splendour in comparison. The deep comfort of the mattress, the delicate splendour of the silk sheets, the feather touch of the blankets—these were unaccustomed luxuries; and their soothing properties gave his back and legs a delightful sensation of embracement which contrasted with the ache in his head as it turned in confusion on the plump pillow. A Chinese carpet covered the floor; Chinese prints, many depicting tortures, made a pattern on the Chinese wallpaper. The pieces of furniture in the room were oriental, and there was a Chinese Chippendale cabinet and chair.

He had drawn the curtains before going to bed, and the room was gay with sunlight, summer sounds came through the window. What time was it? He looked at his watch; the hands said two o'clock precisely : it had stopped. He threw back the coverings, and painfully and slowly got out of his bed. His head was certainly very sore. He moved with great care.

He always felt shy in other people's houses, and this accounted for the rather furtive manner in which he opened his door and peeped out to see what was happening in this one. Facing him an open door revealed a bed that had been slept in. Further along the passage another door was open. Ralph had a picture in his mind of Miller, rather talkative and not quite coherent, going in there while his host stood at the door looking like Gulliver in Lilliput.

The Count had a faculty for conveying contempt without using word or gesture. It must have been endemic, an attitude

99

towards the world which he concealed behind his elaborate and dated manner, modelled one might think on those central European film stars, recruits from the Vienna and Berlin theatres, who had a potent and guttural attraction for the more sophisticated film-viewers between the wars. They looked so experienced and dangerous to know; contrasted with the brash American heroes, they were like survivors of the Medici in competition with garage hands and horse boys.

Ralph had assumed that the Count was merely a picturesque fraud with a talent for raising money and a genius for spending it; the legendary background—Foreign Legion, lion hunting—the Hemingway details—he had accepted as part of the act, the conjuror's apparatus. Last night, for the first time, because, perhaps, the Count was unaware that he was under scrutiny, Ralph detected a formidable, a sinister quality which filled him with a vague apprehension about the outcome of this unreal episode. He had regarded it as fun, a break in routine; now, inexplicably, he was sorry he had accepted the Count's invitation.

He went into Miller's room; his clothes lay in a heap on a chair where he had tossed them the night before. He was not in the bathroom, because a pair of borrowed pyjamas had been dropped on the unmade bed. From downstairs came the voices of the Italian servants, a welcome evidence of cheerful life. Why—the question crossed his mind—did Italians have to converse either in shrieks or whispers? Feeling like Fatima he looked into the other rooms upstairs. All were furnished luxuriantly, and all were empty. From the window of one he got a view of the whole extent of the Count's grounds.

This window looked across the roofs of the stables into the fields. Kent had more land than the other lodges, and the fields stretched down to the river at the foot of the valley. A figure on horseback came into view on the track which ran down towards the river and then came back through a little wood, making with the fields, into which it ran, a gallop of about a mile. The rider was now hidden by the trees, but when he emerged, Ralph saw he was riding a splendid black mare which the Count had produced at the end of the hunting season, but only when hounds met. He had not taken part in the hunt. This, someone explained, was a token participation to qualify it to run in point-to-point races; by this manoeuvre a racehorse could, without being subjected to the risks of a hunt, be certified as a hunter.

The Count, like many men whose legs do not live up to the promise of their torso, looked at his best on a horse. Stern, upright, elegant; he formed with the tall horse, whose coat blazed like a shield of black metal in the sunlight, an heraldic figure. Each was the perfect complement to the other. The Count's ascendency was never lost for long; at such a moment as this his superiority was incontestable. And by force of contrast this was emphasised when the figure of Mr Miller emerged, in a pair of borrowed jeans—they were too large for him—and approached the horse and rider.

The Count, capitalising on his advantage, as if aware of an audience, talked down to the skinny figure at his horse's shoulder. At that distance it was not possible to make out their facial expressions, but the Count seemed to be mocking his companion.

Then the scene changed suddenly. In a moment the Count was on the ground, the solicitor had taken the reins and was facing the saddle, with one foot in a stirrup. The Count took the other leg and seemed to heave him into the sky. Now he was in the saddle and the Count on the ground. The moral positions were less unequal, but not reversed. On the ground, though his appearance had a military correctness, the Count's rather short legs diminished the impression he should have made; but not to anything like the same degree as Mr Miller fell short of the glory he might have attained in the saddle. Crouched, and with elbows akimbo, he looked comic and craven at once. The Count held up a whip, the rider hesitated and then grabbed it with a gesture indicative of nervousness and a precarious balance.

The mare walked at first; then the rider gave her a half-hearted kick with his heels. That seemed to ruffle her, as if the animal were in a reverie, but she broke into a trot for a while, and then relapsed into a walk, which slowed down gradually to a standstill. In this manner the ill-assorted pair made slow progress along the edge of the field. As they disappeared over the breast of the hill, the horse had passed from a stand into a sluggish trot. Ralph watched with an awful fascination. The scene exactly accorded with the sense of ill omen with which he left Miller last night.

Now the rider had come into view again. The mare was trotting and had come to the place where, a few minutes ago, Ralph had seen the Count. Here she halted, and the rider flapped his legs, indicating that he was using his heels. This time the mare did not make a reluctant response, instead she seemed to gather herself together, as if an experienced rider had 'collected' his mount, drawing in the head, and matching the movement with a sustained pressure of the knees. Coiled like a spring, the mare began to execute a sort of Indian war dance, as if the ground was too hot for her hooves. Then the coil released itself; with black mane flying and black tail waving ominously the huge animal came at full gallop across the field. Reduced to insignificance the man on her back swayed from side to side. Only the tip of his head showed : his face was buried in the mane. The reins hung loose, an iron swung like a hanged man at one side of the animal, the rider's foot still retained the other.

The Count would, no doubt, come to the rescue. But there was at least a quarter of a mile to go, and if the mare left the path and decided to jump a fence Miller was in serious danger. As it was, if the mare bucked, he was likely to be badly hurt. He could even be killed, because the ground was hard and to be bucked off, going at that speed, was tantamount to being shot out of a cannon. Now they had entered the fields. The gate was at the top corner; if the mare elected to charge through it she would probably knock her rider against the post.

Ralph leaned out further. He could just see the gate. The Count, he expected, would stand in it to head them off. Miller's best chance was if his mount made for the corner. She would then have to stop, and he might be able to slide off.

The Count was not in the gate. Ralph looked round despairingly. Then he saw him, legs crossed, propped on his arms against the fence, watching the show. No sign of perturbation: no effort to help; his posture was relaxed and exuded philosophic detachment from the spectacle of horse power and human incapacity.

That glimpse of the Count frightened Ralph more than the mad charge of the mare, now approaching the gate.

"Pull the right rein," Ralph shouted.

Miller acted as if he had heard; the slack on the horse's neck was suddenly gathered in, and the sharp pressure on the mouth made her wheel to the right facing a twenty foot haycock which, even in her savage excitement, she could not attempt to leap. As she slid into a halt Miller shot over her head and disappeared, all but his legs, into the hay.

Ralph, still in his pyjamas, ran downstairs. The hall door was open. The gravel was agony to run on. He skirted the yard and saw ahead the open gate through which the mare was now trotting quietly, having dislodged her rider. The Count emerged on the right and caught the hanging reins.

"Whoah, my beauty! Whoah, girl!" he said.

Anyone could see that he had a wonderful way with horses.

"Why did you let him up? You could have killed him."

The Count turned to meet Ralph. His eyes had their opaque look, when the irises were inked over.

"Your friend cannot ride."

"That horse is dangerous. It meant to kill him."

"Not this time, Marlene wouldn't. Next time. She would say 'I recognise this chap. He can't ride. I'll soon get rid of him.' But I don't suppose Mr Miller will give her the opportunity."

"Is he all right?"

"He's very comfortable in the sweet hay. Have you had your breakfast? It's in the dining-room. Ring the bell and Benito will bring you fresh coffee. I must put Marlene back in her stall. It would never do if Mr Expert found that she was not there." He walked off, the mare rubbing her nose affectionately on his sleeve.

Miller met Ralph in the gateway. Covered in hay, his face was a grey white. He looked as if he were going to faint.

"I've been having a ride," he said. "Nice animal. Rather hard in the mouth. I let the reins go when I was dismounting. She must have gone back to the stable on her own."

Ralph said nothing. What was there to say? Here was courage. Mr Miller, for the moment, had assumed a Don Quixote appeal; a surprising metamorphosis.

Each had his own reason for not mentioning the ride at breakfast, and the Count made no attempt at conversation; but the silence was so pregnant that it provided a sort of communal wealth from which each was able to draw as much as he pleased. Miller's colour gradually returned. When Benito came in with the post, the Count said: "I shall be in my study when the horse-dealer comes."

Ralph found that he could not talk to Miller. It would be like this if there are reunions beyond the grave, he thought. Miller, wondering how much Ralph knew, and feeling limp after his experience, was glad not to be questioned. They spun out breakfast, and then Miller pretended that he had papers to look at. Ralph took a stroll in the fields, digesting the morning's experience and his new vision of the Count.

Not more than half an hour late for his appointment, Mr Gallagher and his double horse-box drove up to the gate. Ralph saw the roof of the box from the fields and hurried in. When he reached the gate, Gallagher was walking up the drive—it was too narrow for his trailer. He had the slightly aggressive air of the ill at ease, and as Ralph watched him approach, he became aware of someone else at his elbow.

"Behold, Esau my brother is a hairy man," the Count intoned as he, too, observed the horse expert's self-conscious gait.

Gallagher recognised Ralph, and greeted him with a sharp side-way motion of the head accompanied by a violent contortion of the mouth. Ralph introduced him to Major Paul, who got the benefit of a head jerk and grimace all to himself. Miller, appearing in the door-way, was similarly honoured.

Miller fussed over his friend; but the Count refused to be impressed.

"If you want to see my horses, you may follow me to the stables."

He wheeled around and marched off, leaving the others to follow.

All morning he had maintained this attitude as of a great general compelled to sign an armistice with an opposite number of inferior social position. There was an air of magnificent grievance about him, and Ralph was left in no doubt that he was included among the enemy, in the character of a deserter. Last night's revelry was forgotten. Truth had come with the dawn.

Mr Gallagher, as his method of greeting showed, was a man of few words; but the nearer they got to the horses the more knowing he looked. He also nodded in the direction of the Count's proud back and winked at Miller, implying that he had taken the measure of his man.

There were two loose boxes in the yard : over the door of one a grey face looked out, a black out of the other.

"Is this the lot?" Gallagher asked derisively.

"You may inspect the garage if you care to," the Count replied.

"May I see that one?" Gallagher indicated the grey.

"Certainly."

The Count went to fetch a bridle. Miller and Ralph

looked at the black face, but neither said anything. The mare seemed to be taking an intelligent interest in all that was going on, but the grey had the expression of a village idiot in her pale eyes, as with amazing persistence she continued to chew the saliva-soaked residue of a wisp of hay.

"Both mares?" Gallagher said.

The Count who had returned made no reply. The matter could be ascertained by superficial inspection. Did he sense—Ralph wondered—the other's attitude, of which the overt evidence had been shown behind his back?

The grey filly was not impressive. Even to Ralph's untutored eye there was no suggestion of latent power in those straight shoulders or drive in the inclined plane of her hindquarters.

"How did you say she was bred?"

"I didn't say. Her pedigree is here."

"Grey filly by Grocer out of Nasturtium by Fumble out of Careless Hands. That's not a very impressive strain. I seem to remember a yearling out of the same mare withdrawn at Ballsbridge without a bid."

"I am not trying to sell you anything, Mr Gallagher. Your visit was not made at my invitation. You asked to see the grey filly. I have shown her to you."

Mr Gallagher with a head-jerk indicated that he wanted to speak to Miller alone.

"Why don't you follow your friends, Ralph?" the Count said.

As he did so Ralph experienced the sensation of having lived through that second before.

"They are not friends of mine."

"You led the invasion."

"That's not fair, Major. I had never seen Miller until he called at the office. It's not my office, it's Mr Fox's. He was at the funeral yesterday. What was I to do?"

"If you will be an attorney, Ralph, you will find yourself in these ignoble situations, in unworthy company. Remember your promise, Ralph. Not a word to the Canon. That is between ourselves, outside the Fox's lair. If you fail me, I shall never forgive you."

Jack Hawkins and Long John Silver in the stockade on Treasure Island. That was it. Ralph suddenly remembered why he got such a vivid impression of having lived through this scene on another occasion.

Meanwhile Gallagher was assuring Miller that in his opinion the filly was worth only a few hundred pounds.

"I can't help it. I was told to collect her."

"There's one born every minute. I prefer the black. Let's have a look at her."

"What about the other," he said to the Count.

"I am training her as a show jumper. She is not a racer."

"Half-bred?"

"I do not have half-bred horses in my yard, Mr Gallagher. You have heard of thoroughbreds as hunters I presume."

"Don't fancy them myself. Too skittish."

"I know how to ride."

"Did you ever hunt her?"

The Count was aware that Ralph knew the extent to which he could be said to have hunted on the animal—a brief appearance outside the gates of Mount Lambert, a hat raised to the master, and then home again to Kent Lodge.

"Never seriously. I am going to concentrate on the Show Ring; but I thought you wanted my grey."

"We can discuss that," Miller said. "Perhaps you'd show Mr Gallagher this one."

The mare's affectionate manner as the Count bridled her was surprising. The noble impression she made when she came out evoked an unspoken admiration that had been noticeably absent when the grey filly appeared.

"Would you like to throw a leg across her," the Count said to Gallagher. "I can get you a saddle."

"Don't," Ralph called out with such emphasis that Gallagher turned to him.

"Do you think I couldn't sit on her?"

107

The idea seemed to tickle him, and he gave one of his head jerks in Miller's direction, inviting him to join in the fun.

"George was nearly killed riding it this morning," Ralph said, not looking at Mr Miller who blushed a deep red. He thought he would bring the story of his humiliation a secret with him to the grave, acknowledging it to himself as the end of a duel with the Count who had sought his revenge for the humiliation of having to acknowledge defeat in their diplomatic encounter. As he had maintained an ascendency over Ralph from their meeting, it was galling to think that he knew about that dive into the hay.

"If you call my mare 'it', Ralph, she will certainly buck you off if you ever try to ride her," the Count said, as he tightened the girths.

As always in the situations that he engineered, he was standing impassively waiting for lesser mortals to play the rôles he had assigned them.

"Do you want to see if I can ride?" Gallagher enquired of Fate, and Fate not answering, he vaulted up on the mare with the agility of a monkey.

Then, with winks all round, and a tremendous head-jerk at Ralph, he coaxed his mount into a walk across the yard.

"I don't like this. You shouldn't allow it," Ralph said to the Count who was following the procession this time.

Miller, from motives of national prestige, perhaps, walked beside the Irish victim. If the worst happened his injured vanity would be smoothed.

"Don't mix yourself up with these little people, Ralph. They came down here to hunt me. I am smoking them out," the Count murmured.

Ralph ran forward. "For God's sake be careful, Mr Gallagher. I don't believe that animal is fit to ride."

"Will you listen to your man," the rider said to Miller, but the jerk that ordinarily accompanied his mockery was cut short by his mount who had seen something in the hedge and had not liked what she had seen. A violent swerve to the left threw Mr Gallagher over to that side; before he could recover, the mare reared, bucked and then set off across the field making antelope jumps of incredible agility and beauty. Rejoicing in her freedom, because Mr Gallagher lay on the ground.

He was very little the worse, no bones broken; but he had lost his jesting habit.

"That animal should be shot. If she were mine I'd shoot her. It's bloody well murder to put anyone up on her."

Ralph and Miller had run to pick up what they feared was a corpse; when they had him on his feet, they saw the Count talking to his mare in the field. She was walking hesitantly towards him, her mane and tail drooping now—a beautiful penitent. She nuzzled him and he patted her, not with the effeminate gestures of the sentimental pet-keeper, but with the gentle vigour of a satisfied lover. Then he vaulted into the saddle and performed a series of equitation exercises, followed by a leap over barrels. As he rode into the yard, patting the mare's neck and shouting endearments, he ignored the group for whose benefit he had performed.

The three on foot resembled prisoners of war in a Victorian picture of military disaster as they followed the victorious figure on horseback. Mr Gallagher muttered a great deal and spoke of revenge. Miller wished that he had never left his predictable surroundings in the Strand. Ralph had a feeling, which he knew was immoral, that he was ashamed of his association with the losing side.

Mr Gallagher halted in the yard.

"Do what you like about the grey filly, but I wouldn't touch the mad mare if I was you. It will kill someone, and there will be law. Nobody would buy her after a trial, and she will eat you out of house and home."

Ignoring their parley, the Count was handing over the mare to a man who had appeared in the yard, to whom he was giving instructions with a certain military emphasis.

"You'd better go and talk to him, Ralph," Miller said.

"Tell him we will take the grey. I was told to do that, but you might let him know Paddy Gallagher says she is a very ordinary animal. I don't want him to go on as if he was conferring a benefit by parting with her."

Ralph, not enjoying his rôle, did as he was told. Once again he had an absurdly juvenile feeling that he was Jack Hawkins running between the loyal crew and the pirates.

"I want a clear receipt. If my filly goes, he is to write down that it completely discharges any debts due by me to Mr Whatever-his-name-is."

Miller hedged. The diplomatic success of the night before looked pale and wan under the light of day and the discouraging report of the red-haired horse expert. Why had he been so cock-a-hoop? Was it the Count's champagne? It was unwise, very unwise, to have negotiated under conditions chosen by him. One lost the initiative. He would have to try to make an eleventh hour effort to justify his expedition.

"Tell him that we had better fix the matter inside," Miller said. But, again, he was making a mistake in keeping the Count at arm's length now. It was at the early stage of the negotiations that he should have refused to be talked at. Now the initiative had slipped away.

Ralph and Gallagher stayed outside when Miller went in with the Count. Ralph watched their faces when they came out five minutes later. The Count had won. He looked like a much-tried monarch who has been petitioned once too often to exercise clemency in a clear case of high treason. Miller looked downcast.

"Take the grey animal, Paddy," he said. "That's the toughest rogue I've ever had to deal with in my life," he said to Ralph.

At parting the Count bowed to them all and insisted on accompanying them to the gate. The ink blots in his eyes, where the irises should have been, told Ralph that the punishment for his part in the affair was under consideration. As it was he had to retreat with the beaten army.

CHAPTER XI

"WHAT IS IT, dear?"

The Canon, disturbed in his study by his wife's voice outside the door, put down cat and newspaper, and assumed an expression of long suffering. Mrs Ormsby put her head round the door.

"Angela says that a man in the yard is taking the grey horse away."

"What man?"

"The Count—the Major—Ritzy... Is it all right?"

"We had better pretend not to know he is there. Tell Angela not to go near him. She is an incorrigible gossip. I don't know why we keep her."

"At three pounds a week, dear..."

Late that night, having turned the matter over in her mind many times, she said : "Are you awake?"

"Yes, my dear."

"I believe the Count gave Angela five pounds."

"That was very generous of him."

"In fact, I know he did. She was clutching it in her apron."

Having said so much Mrs Ormsby lay back and waited to see what her lord would make of this. She waited and she waited.

"Have you fallen asleep?"

"No, my dear."

"Well, why don't you say something about the Count giving Angela five pounds?"

"I said it was very handsome of him."

"Now, dear, you know it was most odd. And you have never told me why he stabled his horse here. Hasn't he plenty of accommodation in Kent?"

"I can't remember the reason he gave. He asked my permission, and as a good neighbour I was only too glad to oblige him. I will admit there was something in his manner—not exactly furtive, conspiratorial, perhaps—which disturbed me. I had the uneasy feeling that he might be avoiding his creditors."

"Expecting the bailiff, you mean?"

"I suppose that is what I do mean."

"But that doesn't happen to people on the Mile."

"The Major has been in serious money difficulties before. Perry dug out that information and broadcast it. Very remiss of him. Quite nasty in fact. There is some vendetta between them apparently. I refused to listen, of course; but I heard. One can't help hearing that sort of thing. It went out of my mind until the Major asked me to put up the horse."

"Doesn't that make it all the more extraordinary that he should give Angela five pounds?"

"It certainly gives the lie to my theory."

"But she had done nothing whatever for him. Michael gave the horse hay, and cleaned out the stable what's more."

The Canon, if he was thinking, did not communicate his thoughts.

"You don't suppose—"

"Don't suppose what, my dear?"

"Oh, no! It's absurd and too unpleasant to think of."

"What is?"

"She is far too old in any case."

The Canon remained silent.

"Perhaps it was hush money."

"Hush money?"

"Dear, don't parrot everything I say. He may have asked Angela not to mention to the postman that the horse was here. Everyone knows that he is the source of all the gossip in the Mile."

The Canon remained silent.

"I didn't mean to offend you, dear; but it is disconcerting to say things and have them echoed every time."

The Canon after a suitable delay decided to capitulate.

"I think we would all be well advised to talk as little as possible about this matter. It is none of our business. And if there were—I am not saying there is—but if there were any irregularity we had better not know about it. It could be awkward for Ralph, being in the law. I don't know whether he saw the horse, by the way. He was out last night."

"I don't think he did. And what about Michael?"

"Michael only talks to himself."

"I think you are very wise, dear. But may I say that it all bears out what I told you about Major Paul. I cannot understand the attraction he seems to have for you. From all accounts he is not a very suitable friend for you."

There was such a long silence that Mrs Ormsby ventured.

"Are you asleep?"

"No, my dear; but I think I shall turn over and try to drop off."

"Good night, dear."

"Good night, my love."

The Canon dreamed of a ball in a palace. From the ceiling, rich with rococo plasterwork, five chandeliers depended, lighting a scene of unparalleled splendour and picturesque frivolity. Miss Beddington appeared at the top of the stairs, dressed in a splendid gown of peacock blue which showed off to perfection her diamond necklace, while her white powdered wig, and the intriguing patch on her cheek, gave a new lustre to the sea blue of her splendid eyes. The dancers halted as the orchestra stopped in the middle of a bar. All eyes were on her when he, dressed in plum-coloured velvet, with a waistcoat of blue, covered with silver stars, stepped forward to claim her for the dance.

She came forward, her hands stretched out to meet his and, at the very moment their fingers touched, the band, leaping a hundred years, broke into a Strauss waltz. Grasping her gently but firmly round the waist, he spun off in a heady succession of whirls, with the vast assembly looking on, with admiring eyes, some were even clapping. Lord Palmerston waved his partner's fan. Byron was in the crowd; so, too, were Marie Antoinette, Jenny Lind, Coleridge, Florence Nightingale, Talleyrand and Mrs Humphry Ward. After a time they, too, began to dance; but the dream fragmented and became confused just at the moment when the Count swirled by, clasping Diana of the Crossways very close to his cherry-coloured waistcoat. From then the dream seemed to concern a horse race on the Mile, and that in turn melted into a congregation, to which Michael was preaching, holding up in his hand a pot of Mrs Ormsby's marmalade.

Mrs Ormsby's dream, which she did not afterwards recall, was about cleaning a mountain of silver.

PART II

CHAPTER I

Loftus usually went on foot when he paid a
local call; but there was something so urgent in his 'cousin'
Perry's voice on the telephone that he took his bicycle out of
the garage and pedalled, regardless of his heart, up hill to
Sussex. Perry met him at the door. His eyes were bulging
more than usual, and he was snapping his thumbs against
his second fingers in a manner that suggested savage impatience.

"You've seen this?" he said when he bustled his cousin
into the drawing-room, taking down an invitation from the
corner of the looking-glass over the chimneypiece.

Loftus seized the card and read,

> "Mr and Mrs Bernard Coppinger request
> your presence
> on Friday, August 26th. Dancing 9 o'c.
> EVENING DRESS. R.S.V.P.
> Cambridge Lodge."

In the corner was written "To meet Elizabeth Lambert".

His 'cousin's' astonishment and unconcealed indignation
were all that Herbert Perry had hoped for. His habitual
expression, as of a man watching his wife being boiled to
death on his own instructions, left his face for a moment.
He looked appreciative. Loftus noticed this and determined
to keep it up. Perry might produce whiskey if the favour-
able atmosphere was retained for long enough.

"What do you make of it?"

The Captain's feeling of outrage had not been simulated:
but now that he was asked to express it in words he realised
that it was the absence of a similar invitation which had
upset him most of all.

"I call it cheek, especially that bit in the corner about meeting Elizabeth Lambert. Who does the fellow think he is?"

"You appreciate that we are going to be asked to dance in the modern excrescence that he is adding to Cambridge!"

"I suppose so. The builders are working like beavers. It will break Sir Julian's heart. I suppose somebody will tell him. He loves every inch of the Mile, and this will hurt as much as if his own place were to be devastated by vandals."

"I always understood that the reason why we never see him is because he hates the place. It's been on the books for ages you know. We had better think of ourselves and not worry too much about the absent baronet."

Loftus might have sulked at being put down like this; but he knew that his 'cousin' would retaliate by not producing the whiskey, so, instead, he continued to play.

"What's the worst element in it—the invitation I mean—what do you see to object to most in it?"

"I should think it sticks out a mile."

"Putting the note in about Elizabeth Lambert, you mean?"

"The whole thing, old boy—the vulgarity of it, the brazenness of it—after all he must know we resent his extensions. He has ruined the character of the Mile. Secondly, it was surely time enough to offer to entertain us after we had entertained him. The note about Elizabeth, I wouldn't mind. That's just bravado."

"You don't think he will invite her?"

"Of course, he will invite her. Has done so already apparently, and she has accepted. It's the most barefaced piece of push I've seen in a lifetime."

"Bounder!"

"I wouldn't say that. He's all right. Why do you say he's a bounder?"

"I mean, he acts like a bounder."

"Do you know him? Have you ever met him?"

"Not exactly."

"What exactly do you mean by 'not exactly'?"

"Damn it all, Herbert. I don't want to be cross-examined. I'm entitled to my views about the man. I've seen what he has done here. Now this invitation confirms what we all expected."

"They haven't invited you, I take it."

"Certainly not."

"Why 'certainly not'?"

"They knew I wouldn't accept."

"How could they know that, old boy, if they don't know you?"

"I assumed that they made enquiries before they issued their invitations and left out anyone who was likely to resent their overtures."

"I think you are letting your imagination run away with you. They've only left out the people they don't know."

Having endured so much it would be a pity to break down now; Loftus had never realised before what a common drop there was in Perry. No wonder he had been at such pains to establish his cousinship with the Loftuses, remote as it was.

"How did he get Elizabeth to come, do you suppose?"

"Just invited her. He would have heard she would be over in August."

"I'm surprised that Julian didn't put out a feeler before he let her accept. He usually writes to the Canon."

"I'm sure his reverence was delighted to have this entertainment provided. He has been making such heavy weather about the girl's visit. You'd think she was the Queen of Siam or somewhere."

"What about the Canon's ball? I thought we would never hear the end of that; but he hasn't given tongue about it lately, and Elizabeth is due in a few weeks' time."

"What I heard was—and this you will keep in confidence—I wouldn't tell anyone else—they got an estimate for a caterer and the Canoness put her big foot down—it's she who has the money, of course you know—and refused to cough up. Then they wrote to Julian to suggest that he should give a ball at Mount Lambert. He was very definite in his refusal, I believe. Apparently the young lady has been costing him quite a lot, and he regards the trip to Ireland as a temporary passing of the buck."

"I heard something about this. Mrs Browne was nearly fit to be tied. She has bought a dress for that fat trollop of hers to come out in, if you please."

"So I heard."

"There's no news in the Mile. Everyone knows everything. I often wonder how the grape-vine works."

"I can't tell you. I mind my own business and I expect others to do the same."

"I wonder who else got invitations. We won't be long waiting to know if the Brownes did. I see her coming along the road. The missus won't be pleased. She has a bloody awful stomach ache. Poisoned."

"Good God!"

"Only food poison. What an alarmist you are. That's the Browne knock all right. You'd want to have the courage of a lion to keep the door shut when that tattoo sounds on it. What a woman!"

"Such a pusher."

"Everyone's a pusher with you, today. Did you get out of bed on the wrong side?"

Loftus was accustomed to the contrary trait in his 'cousin'. Whenever he invited Loftus over urgently, apparently expecting him to share his indignation, he promptly took the other side once Loftus had committed himself. Conversation became a sort of table tennis with Perry always serving. However, the arrival of Mrs Browne as it increased the possibility of liquid refreshment was a welcome break. He might even venture to say, 'The good woman looks as if she might do with a drink, Herbert.' That would be fun.

Mrs Browne came in to the room waving a card.

"We know about it. We know," Perry said, pointing to the looking-glass.

"Oh, that! It's this," she said cryptically.

Mr and Mrs Browne
Major Christian Paul
invites your presence
on Saturday, August 27th at 10 o'c at Mount Lambert.
Dancing.
R.S.V.P. Kent Lodge, The Mile, Glenbay,
Co. Wicklow.

Loftus took the card, but Perry snapped it from him.

"When did you say it came?"

"By post this morning. I think it's very, very mean of him, and spiteful of the Canon and that repressed female, Barbara Beddington, whom I've never liked or trusted. Too sweet for my fancy. But I'm downright. I must say what I think if it chokes me."

She was certainly red enough in the face to suggest that this was no idle threat.

"I think the poor lady could do with a drink," Loftus said.

Perry waited to see if she rose to it; and, as she made no demur, made a fine show of enthusiasm as he went off to fetch the glasses.

"What is upsetting you, my dear?" Loftus said as soon as his 'cousin's' back was turned. He wanted to recruit an ally and to be first with the news.

"Leaving Sylvia out of the invitation. It's cruel. Imagine the feelings of a girl of that age whom the Canon swore he would ask to his mythical ball when she hears she has been left out of this, and at Mount Lambert, too!"

The Captain, so seldom consulted by anyone, tried to look preternaturally wise. He shut his eyes to gather interior inspiration undisturbed.

"I wonder if a ball under the Count's auspices would be a suitable place for Sylvia," he began rather ponderously. "I

121

don't know the gentleman. I made it perfectly clear to him that I wanted to keep myself to myself when he took Kent. But I can't help hearing what's being said, and I gather there are pretty rum goings on at his weekend parties, ladies tumbled in the hay, and elsewhere no doubt. Herbert"— Perry had appeared with tray and decanter—"I've been saying to our little friend here that I don't think the Count's ball is exactly the setting for a nice girl like Sylvia."

"Balls!"

"Hear. Hear," Perry said.

Having poured a careful glass of sherry for Mrs Browne, barely reaching the plimsoll line at which hospitality sinks, he had the excellent idea of starting to fill his 'cousin's' glass and then breaking off to brandish the decanter, its normal task unaccomplished. He waved it with a slightly circulatory motion while he expressed the view that the news confirmed the impression he had formed of the Count long since. It was not merely mean, the omission of Sylvia conclusively proved the man had no idea how decent people behaved. How right he had been to refuse to know him, to put up a barrier from the start.

Mrs Browne did not look so cheered as Perry might have expected. She would have preferred counsel that offered some promise of getting her daughter to the ball. Rhetoric was no good to her; moreover, she suspected rightly that it was the Count not inviting him that gave Perry his cue.

While Loftus peered sadly at the drop in the end of his glass, Mrs Browne afforded him some melancholy consolation by turning the attack on Perry.

"I'm tired of all this rot about the Count. If he decides to ask you, Herbert, will you and Molly refuse? Give me a straight answer."

"Yes, tell us what you'd do, and may I remind you that you were interrupted when you were kindly filling my glass," his 'cousin' chimed in.

Perry's eyes bulged and his neck grew so red that it

looked as if he might have a stroke. Hardly knowing what he was doing he filled up the Captain's tumbler.

"That undischarged bankrupt. I would be afraid he might pick my pocket."

Mrs Browne who had called for counsel and a plan to outwit the Count now felt impelled to come to his rescue. After all he had asked Raymond and herself and she was throwing away her advantage by consulting with these rejects. She bitterly regretted having shown her hand.

"Talk about gossip—men are much worse than women. Major Paul may not realise that Sylvia is out. I am sure it is a mistake. He is a very good friend of ours and I should no more think of discussing his affairs behind his back than I would yours, Herbert, behind your back. And that goes for any friend of mine. I thought it was the rule on the Mile, I must say. Neither the Canon nor Miss Beddington will allow it in their houses; I admire them for it."

"I declare to God, I am sick and tired of the Canon and Miss Beddington, sick and tired of them. So far as I am concerned you may b——"

But the extent of Perry's permissiveness was never known because the fist that descended with extraordinary emphasis on the chimneypiece sent a Dresden shepherdess to ruin in the grate.

"Broken, smashed to bits," the Captain said, bending down to pick up the pieces.

CHAPTER II

"Barbara, my dear, you will forgive me for blowing in on you like this, but I want to ask you to do me a great favour."

There is always an appeal to vanity in applications of this kind when they carry no undertone to suggest that the favour has anything to do with even a small loan.

Miss Beddington, who always looked benevolent, leaned forward to diminish the distance between her soft face and Mrs Browne's, which had the texture of crocodile leather.

"Tell me what it is and I'll do it if I can."

"It's awkward for me; I don't feel we are on sufficiently intimate terms—he isn't my type—Major Paul, I mean—otherwise I'd just pick up the telephone and settle the matter in a jiffy."

"Come on now; own up; what's the trouble?"

Miss Beddington was all smiles, encouraging.

"It's about the Count's ball. We've been invited, of course, but he forgot Sylvia. He may not know she is to come out this year, or it may be a mere slip, but you can see how I would hesitate to put him right. I wondered if you . . ."

Mrs Browne was a shrewd dealer in ponies and dogs and as the shopkeepers knew, a keen bargainer and a sharp appraiser of values. Someone less dedicated to the attainment of her ends might not have noticed that Miss Beddington, albeit faintly, blushed.

"I don't think that I really know him well enough for that. I'd be uncertain how he might take it. He's unpredictable. He might think that it was unfriendly of you to use an intermediary."

"I see that, but I thought that you were such close friends... a word from you..."

"I couldn't possibly say that Major Paul and I were close friends. Whatever gave you that impression?"

"I just thought."

"Then you thought very wrong, dear."

If her vehemence was a surprise to Mrs Browne, it was a revelation to herself. Why did she feel so upset?

"Perhaps the Canon..."

"I really think you ought to manage this for yourself. I'm sure if you drop the Major a line and say Sylvia is coming out and if numbers permit may you bring her—I'm sure he will be only too delighted. I find him always most sympathetic."

Again for no reason, Miss Beddington blushed.

Mrs Browne noted this. One was never without some new topic for conversation on the Mile, and this was a very intriguing development.

"I'm sure you are right. I'll drop him a line, as you say. Elizabeth's visit has been a wonderful promoter of parties. We must do something. What do you suggest—a gymkhana?"

"I'm not sure whether she is interested in riding now. She will have grown up a great deal in the last three years, don't you suppose?"

"I saw very little of her. Syl was only twelve, and rather young to make a pal of. Between these four walls and our two selves—I suspect that the Ormsbys had their eye on her for Ralph. They monopolised her. But Ralph had his nose put out of joint, I hear, by the Fagan boy. He's off the map now."

Miss Beddington was not averse to filling up gaps in her own information on this absorbing topic; but she felt that the addition, however intrinsically sweet, was polluted from this source. The uninvited intimacy, the confidence about the Ormsbys—all this was immensely distasteful, and added to the embarrassment of the Major Paul topic, gave her a

125

guilty feeling. It was as if Mrs Browne had suggested they should both undress and compare themselves. It verged on nastiness. She was glad, therefore, as she would not have been on another occasion, when a loud knock at the door heralded the entry of Captain Loftus.

He had come in for a glass of sherry and a chat—in that order. Mrs Browne found herself in a quandary. If she stayed he might disclose that she had been at the Perry's on a similar errand; if she left, her retreat would leave her exposed to God knows what. If Miss Beddington had pressed her to stay it would decide the issue; but she didn't —she let her say that she "would have to push on if anyone is to get any lunch in my funny little house" without demur.

Loftus buttoned himself in as if to imply that he would not open up until the evacuation had taken place; so there was nothing to do but go and trust to Miss Beddington's good breeding to restrain any gossip at her expense. Meanwhile she was looking forward to enlivening her own lunch table by asking Raymond to guess what the latest romance was. It would be—although she hated to admit it—a relief from the inevitable recital of what had happened at the board meeting of the Children's Hospital, the Soldiers' and Sailors' Benevolent, the Institute for the Blind, the Georgian Society, or the Bespoke Tailoring Co., which actually paid him to act as a director.

CHAPTER III

A N E X C H A N G E O F letters passed between York Lodge and Kent Lodge.

26th July, 19—

My dear Major,

I am writing informally to say how delighted Raymond and I will be to accept your very kind invitation for the 27th of August. It will be like old times dancing at Mount Lambert.

When we met at the Ormsbys' pleasant party in the spring, I think I told you that we had decided to let Sylvia come out this year. You can't keep them back nowadays! I am only mentioning this because I think Elizabeth may be a weeny bit disappointed if Syl is not at the ball, though not quite the same age, they were always tremendous chums. You will forgive me for mentioning this, but I thought it must have slipped your memory.

Yours gratefully,
Mabel Browne

26th July, 19—

Dear Mrs Browne,

I am so glad that you and your husband will be able to come to the little party I am giving to celebrate Elizabeth's 21st birthday and her return to Mount Lambert. It seemed to be appropriate that every family on the Mile should be represented on this occasion.

You are very kind to recall the conversation at the Ormsbys'. I must confess it had slipped my mind; but memory plays us tricks as we get older. My own recollection is that you asked me the time and I was crestfallen to find that my watch had stopped. Fortunately the room was furnished with a clock. I'm glad to hear that Elizabeth and your daughter are 'chums', as you so charmingly put it. They will have many opportunities to renew their friendship, I am sure.

Remember me to your husband.

With my regards and esteem, I remain

Yours very sincerely,

Christian Paul

CHAPTER IV

E VERY MORNING AND every evening since his mother died Michael Molloy came to Cumberland and did the chores for which he received two pounds and ten shillings on Saturday. He made only one change in his routine. Instead of fetching the Canon's newspaper in the morning, he arranged with the postman to have it delivered with the mail.

This fitted in with what was not so much a change in his personality as a new emphasis. He had always been a solitary, but now he refrained from even the most superficial intercourse, averting his head when he passed people on the Mile, leaving the milk in the kitchen for Angela without as much as bidding her the time of day. He no longer looked for the odd jobs that supplemented his weekly wage; but when sent for he did whatever he was asked to do quickly and silently.

Angela was the first to notice the strangeness of his behaviour and she mentioned it to her mistress. She also spoke of it to the postman, and it became at once a leading topic on the Mile. This was not conducive to a cure, because Michael found himself the mark for searching looks and expressions of concern for his welfare, all of which obviously embarrassed him and drove him deeper into his shell.

The Count, who did not have conversations with servants, seemed to know by telepathy whatever was in the wind. Michael's condition intrigued him, and he was not satisfied with the local explanation.

"A man of his age does not grieve like that for a parent." he said, "unless there is something incestuous in their relationship."

Barbara, to whom he made this observation, contrived to

look as if she was accustomed to Freudian topics. The Count had taken to calling on her, and it had given her life a new dimension. She never knew what he was going to say next; but he was such a gentleman, as well as a man of the world, that she did not resent even his most shocking revelations, while she felt contemptuous of Herbert Perry's stockbroker smut, which he was always prone to fall into after his second glass.

Perry's jokes like Loftus's feeble attempts to hug her at the end of long parties were an insult, the sort of thing a woman on the Mile should not have to endure; but the Count's esoteric depravity was an exciting extension, a Brighton Pavilion, in the classical severity of the landscape, a bizarre and amusing contrast, a daring innovation—but whatever it was, it was in the family, as it were; the characteristic contribution of its most uncharacteristic member.

It is hardly necessary to say that the Count's visits and Miss Beddington's not so frequent visits were the talk of the neighbourhood. Perry said things to Browne about it which he, in the privacy of their rather chilly bedroom, repeated to Mrs Browne (who said "Hush, Ray. Syl hears every word."). Angela knew all about it and managed to convey the news by contriving to put it in the form of a respectful questionnaire to her mistress.

Mrs Ormsby told the Canon in the watches of the night. He got quite cross about it and in doing so contrived to make his wife jealous.

"I daresay the poor thing would like a cuddle from somebody," she said.

Her lord made no reply but his wife—even at a distance—felt the radiation of hostility and knew his plump body had stiffened under the sheets.

When she said 'Good night' he echoed her too rapidly, and turned right over as if to shut her out for the night.

The extent of the Mile's interest in her would have astonished Barbara—as well as alarming her—because it would have told her something that she had never admitted to herself.

The Count always rang up before he called, not like the Captain who dropped in invariably when least welcome. And this little warning, exciting in itself, gave her time to titivate herself a bit. Not that she was ever 'not fit to be seen'; but what would have been satisfactory for many another woman was below her own fastidious standard. Sometimes she even changed her underclothes after she had answered the telephone : and a suspicion of a ladder in her stocking was enough to make her whisk them off and substitute the very best pair in her wardrobe.

When the Count's knock came at the door, it found her in the drawing-room ready, but not so satisfied with herself that she didn't take a last long look in the Louis Quinze glass to make sure a hair was not out of place, lipstick marks on the teeth, or powder in request on nose or forehead. When he came in he always kissed her hand—he got the best of both worlds by a judicious blend of continental tricks with the severest officer and gentleman standards, characteristic of a foreign nobleman who had been through Sandhurst. In fact his English ways were the result of intense observation and an unequalled gift of mimicry.

Today she was particularly pleased to see him. She had come running down the stairs when she saw his head over the wall as he came down the road. Her eyes were sparkling when she greeted him. She almost said, "Now try the other" when he pressed his lips on the back of her soft hand. He made her feel so pleased with life. After the salute, they both stepped—by habit now, like two dancers who had the choreography by heart—back to the regency sofa. Barbara fitted her comely back into the high end, the Count sat at the foot. They were arranged at such an angle that he could have put his hand on her knee without moving. If she could be imagined to have had a reciprocal impulse, she would have had to bend forward. Her principal gesture was a rhythmical shaking of the shapely foot on her crossed-over leg. The movement put the shoe into some jeopardy, and it was fascinating to watch. She had also a way of stretching out her right arm and holding away her cigarette while she leaned her head back and blew out smoke rings, whose gradual ascent she watched as if they contained messages from a sibyl.

The Count leaned forward because he pulled his stomach in. His cigarette smoke went ceiling-wards past his eyes which he kept half shut. His stubs he put in an ashtray laid on the ground at his feet. Barbara had her own on a table at her head. Although these telephone calls were given a casual air and took her by pleased surprise, they came every other day lately and always at a quarter to twelve. This meant an hour's talk until lunchtime. Barbara had lunched once with the Count, but he always refused to stay with her although he must have guessed she was well prepared. His refusal and her invitation were as much part of their routine as the positions they adopted on the sofa. If there were to be any change in that routine now, it would amount to a crisis. Had he, for instance, said today 'Yes' instead of 'They're expecting me at home' when she said 'Won't you stay to lunch?' it would have amounted to a declaration of a kind, a first move towards...

Barbara never entertained such thoughts. She had the reserve of perfect breeding. But she did know that these visits were what she lived for. Her friendship with the Canon and their mutual esteem were very tame in comparison with these talks in which the Count spoke to her with a daring that she would hardly have believed if she met it in a book. She was quite amused to think how coolly she passed her shockedness off—the complete woman of the world. She found herself using words like 'lesbian' and 'queer' or 'fairy'; and even if four letter words were not the Count's style, he talked of love-making in a racy way that was quite new to her. Until he came the Mile confined its references to such matters to the misfortunes of servant girls. That is to say, in talk between herself and the Ormsbys—the others didn't count.

What astonished Barbara in retrospect was the way in which she unconsciously led the Count on to dangerous ground. She found herself doing this with a mixture of self-contempt and curiosity, with a quite unholy if anxious thrill, as if she had come upon the Count bathing and had watched from behind a bush. It was all the more strange because no one could have been more adept than she in anticipating looming indecencies and disrailing them with a sudden turn of the conversation on to another track. She acted as a sort of pointsman of propriety when Perry was present, never failing to detect his drift when he leered at his plate as he waited for an opening to tickle the company with a retailed risqueness or an improvised bawdry. Many a time Perry had sworn to 'take a rise out of that old prude', but he had never succeeded.

And here she was reclining—almost—at her ease, like one of those Greek hetairai—she told herself afterwards—encouraging this charming man with quite obviously an unspeakable past to let her glimpse through the interstices of his rather stilted sentences such bits and pieces of it as she could assimilate without positive embarrassment in a male presence. As she led him on she felt as if she was very gradually pulling up the end of her skirt under his scrutiny. It was only when he laid his hand on her thigh, having twice emphasised a point with his palm on her knee, that she actually as well as metaphorically drew her skirt down and changed the subject.

His talk was always of far away places and times past, so that it was possible to give him a certain amount of licence on that score; his confidences had all the differences between a description in a book and an experience in real life. That fairly describes Miss Beddington's sensations when she encouraged the Count to reminisce; she felt as if she were reading the *Memoirs of the Count de Gramont* or some of the other books on her shelves which she had sometimes

133

wondered why her father collected them. It seemed so out of character, according to his character as her mother described it.

She rescued the Count from life in the French colonies just before he went down for the third time, and dragged him on to the safe shore of the Mile, where he was quite happy to land because it was a suitable opening for a subject that he had intended to introduce at the right moment.

The ball was on his mind. He described Mrs Browne's letter and repeated, word for word, his own reply, laughing very loudly. Miss Beddington told herself that she had never heard him laugh before. Laughing gave his face the look a tiger has when it appears to be laughing; it was highly expressive but lacked mirth. It also showed off the inside of his mouth and reassured her that his teeth, though revealing expert dentistry, were all his own. This pleased her, she hardly knew why. She was perplexed, conscientious person that she was, whether she should tell him about Mrs Browne's request to her to put in a word for the uncouth Sylvia; but the Count's attitude did not suggest the least likelihood of his obliging the Brownes on any score. They were not 'up to snuff'. Moreover she was rather disgusted at the further evidence of Mrs Browne's brazenness. On the whole, she decided, justice would be done to all parties by remaining silent on the subject.

"I am a romantic fool," the Count suddenly declared, jumping up from the Récamier couch and striding towards the fireplace, head down, hands behind his back, like Napoleon on board the *Bellerophon*.

If Napoleon had been a gentleman and had not grown a paunch he would have looked like the Count, Miss Beddington thought. Perhaps the Count was a bigger man; but he could have done with another few inches. She was tall.

"What's the matter. What's worrying you?" she enquired. He did seem perplexed in the extreme, and it had all come about so unexpectedly in the middle of laughing at the silly Brownes.

134

"Miss Beddington—Barbara—I am going to call you 'Barbara' whether you allow me to or not—and I am Rex to you. That is the name those who know me well have always used. 'Christian', I abominate. I am not a Christian."

"Oh! Now! Come!"

"You must take me as I am, a lion in a cage—Hell and Death! how I wish to break through the bars sometimes and...Enough! What I am telling you is a secret between two campaigners, good comrades, blood brothers—am I right?"

She could only nod. She felt as if she wanted to loosen her stays, although she had never worn any. She was carried away on the rising tide of his emotion. This extraordinary man.

"I know Elizabeth's mother very well. You understand. I will say nothing more; but if you don't know this it is impossible to follow the rest. She wrote to me to say that Elizabeth was coming to stay with the Canon; she hinted that I was to keep an eye on her. She knew that I could be trusted to see that whatever was appropriate was done. Naturally I expected to hear that Mount Lambert would be opened for a celebration. Elizabeth is twenty-one. She is a beautiful girl. What a condition of things to think that she can come to the place she will inherit, the last link with the past, and spend it at the Canon's with that spineless young man as an escort and Sylvia Browne as her chum! My sense of what is appropriate—when I heard that the Canon was backing out—was to throw a ball. To be candid, when I wrote to Julian for permission to use Mount Lambert I thought the dear boy would at once assume responsibility. I was wrong. Julian lacks—what shall I call it? Flair? Certainly; but that is rare enough." The Count paused for a fraction of a second. "We don't demand that. We might expect some sense of loyalty to his order, some sense of history, some sense of the fitness of things. But so long as he can get his golf and his bridge and his occasional mild flutter at the tables, he wants only to be left in peace. *Après moi le déluge.*

"You might say it was no business of mine; but I felt it was. I have been Ritzy to Elizabeth since she was eleven. Ritzy has panache in Elizabeth's eyes. Ritzy has a feeling for the right thing done in the right way. So Ritzy gives the ball, Ritzy orders the champagne and caviare. And why not? You will ask if Ritzy can afford it? My bank manager says he can not. A cursed mortgage to whom I was kind in a soft moment is pressing now. Ritzy has given his word, and in his code, his word is his bond. There will be a ball if Ritzy goes bankrupt. There will be a ball if Ritzy has to sell his lovely filly. Why am I telling you all this? Because you are a woman, I suppose; and a lovely woman. I have never told you how much your beauty disturbs me. Keep away. I am not to be trusted. In this mood I am capable of enormities which nobody would regret more than I."

To lessen the temptation presented by Miss Beddington who had come towards him with hands of comfort outstretched, the Count turned away; holding the chimneypiece he stared into the empty grate and kicked the toe of a well-polished shoe on the ground.

She, her eyes brimming with tears, looked on.

He turned to face the world again. "There. That's over. I am sorry. I lack friends. I have no one here that I can open up to. The Canon is an old dear, but a child. I cannot show the weak points in my armour, only to a woman who is a sympathetic woman and a friend. May I call you a friend?"

"Major—Rex, I mean. How well the name suits you—I want you to do me a favour."

She paused : he seized a hand and kissed it.

"Anything in my power."

"I have a few hundred pounds on deposit receipt. I don't need it. I put the money there so as to have an emergency fund. Now, this is an emergency, a much pleasanter one than I could ever have imagined. I want you to prove you are a friend by taking a loan of this. Afterwards you will pay me back. I can quite understand how you must be situated with all the expense you were put to, moving in here."

The Count shook his head firmly. His face was very stern, like marble. He could have been a Caesar refusing a widow's plea for clemency.

"I insist. I will post it to you, and I want nothing more said about it. You are putting me under a compliment in accepting my help. You know how much the whole idea of entertaining Elizabeth appeals to me. I even played with the notion of giving a party; but it seemed rather pretentious for anyone in my situation. Now I feel that I am sharing in yours. It will be such fun. And as for friendship—you have no idea what your coming has meant to me and to the Ormsbys. They often say so. Until you came we felt we were alone, the last outpost with a miserably ineffective force to man it. But you from the very first have been a tower of strength. You are like Colleoni, whom Venice called on in her hour of need. Do you know his statue on horseback? I'm sure you do. You know you do remind me so much of him. Especially when you are riding that black mare—the one you let us get a glimpse of at the last meet. I have a picture of him here, in this guide book."

She went to the book-case and ran her eyes along the shelves.

"Here! Look! It's you to the life, looking so stern and so—" She blushed a little because it was the virile horse that had caught her eye. Instead of finishing the sentence, she bent over the book, spread out on the sofa table, and pretended to be absorbed in it. But for all her appearance of concentration even her back radiated the emotion within. Her back seemed to be listening when the Count, from behind her, exclaimed:

"What a coincidence! Do you know as a child of ten I stood with my mother under that statue in Venice, and she pointed up at it and said 'Frederick, some day you will be a hero and will ride a horse like that and go to the war. Remember your mother prophesied it.' "

"She called you 'Frederick'," said Miss Beddington in a tiny voice.

The Count did not answer. He was surveying Miss Beddington as an experienced athlete might a jump to decide the best place to take off, the required distance for a preparatory run, and the amount of spring the height occasioned. On the Wagnerian level their duet had arrived at, she might have been surprised at the coolness of his appraisal.

"Rex," she said, turning round suddenly, eyes sparkling with joy, through the undispersed mist of tears.

"Rex, let us shake hands on it. Some day I may call you Frederick, too. I feel that I should have loved your mother."

The Count changed his plans. She had turned round too soon. He was not prepared for a frontal assault, and if the town was going to disgorge its treasure before it fell, no further effort was required. That was his immediate reaction. Had she been a widow he would have engaged; but long experience had taught him that a single shot would not end a campaign in this quarter.

If Miss Beddington were to surrender, he would be involved in endless attentions, reassurances, misgivings, conferences, post mortems—it would become a confounded bore. If only she could be satisfied with a sample of his prowess, for he was loth to take and not to give what would mean so much to her and cost him so little : and he had often done more to oblige someone to whom he owed only a civility. But Miss Beddington deserved and would expect to be treated as a great occasion. Hers would be the equivalent of the capitulation of a reverend mother. He knew Miss Beddington—rather, he knew what he would know if he knew her; and he knew what an unholy fuss he would be expected to make over the treasure he could so well do without.

He guessed that she had expected to meet a glance no less
emotional than her own when she turned round. It was not
unreasonable when his emotion had been the cause of hers.
To turn aside and look in the book-case was easier than
working up his face to the required pitch of noble feeling.
And it gave him time. Besides he wanted to bask a little
longer in the glow he had induced.

"Ah! Keats!"

He took down a volume and opened it at a venture.

"What are you reading? I shouldn't have thought you
would care for Keats."

"Barbara! You don't know me. I lay a sheaf of roses on
his grave whenever I am in Rome. Listen :

"Thou still unravish'd bride of quietness,
Thou foster-child of silence and slow time,
     Sylvan historian, who canst thus express
A flowery tale more sweetly than our rhyme :
What leaf-fring'd legend haunts about thy shape

"Of deities or mortals or of both,
In Tempe or the dale of Arcady?
What men or gods are these. What maiden loth?
What mad pursuit? What struggle to escape?
What pipes and timbrels? What wild ecstasy?"

The Count dropped the book at every line to fix Barbara
with what she would have called in another 'a knowing
look'. It was ill-bred to make a woman feel so self-
conscious; she would have thought so once. He had an
extraordinary way of making the poem seem to refer to her,
and the emphasis he gave with his deep voice and foreign
intonation to the words 'unravish'd' and 'shape', not to
mention the way he seemed to give her the first line for
perusal with a slight gesture of the hand; and the *excitement* in his voice at the last two lines. She could hear the
cymbals clash and saw herself legging it down a forest glade,

with the Count, his lower half metamorphosed into a goat's, pursuing her.

She hardly heard the lines, but she was anaesthetised by the voice: and he kept on emphasising what he chose to consider appropriate.

"Bold lover, never, never, canst thou kiss,
Though winning near the goal—yet, do not grieve;
   She cannot fade, though thou hast not thy bliss.
For ever wilt thou love, and she be fair!"

The Count could hardly believe that he was not dreaming. He had never heard of this poem before, had chanced upon it; and it was as suitable to his purpose as if he had specially commissioned it at ruinous cost.

"More happy love! More happy, happy love!
For ever warm and still to be enjoyed,
For ever panting and for every young;
All breathing human passion . . ."

It was certainly exceeding its promise; but how would it end? Would it go too far? If it were to be more explicit he might as well have embraced her and got it over. She believed that he knew what was coming, and she would take the word for the deed. He tried to take a quick glance at the last verse as he read on—

"Who are these coming to the sacrifice?
To what green altar, O mysterious priest
Lead'st thou that heifer lowing at the skies."

Not so good. "And all her silken flanks with garlands drest," which followed, went for nothing after that reference to the heifer. He took it very fast. The end he had ascertained by now was most suitably equivocal. And if

"O Attic shape! Fair attitude! with brede
Of marble men and maidens overwrought"

gave him more or less what he wanted, "a friend to man",

when it came, was an unexpected bonus. He paused to stare into her glowing and startled eyes—a reassuring stare. After the whirlwinds and the quicksands they were back on the rock of friendship.

It was the appropriate moment to go. Once again he seized her hand. This time he kissed it twice; and on the second occasion she felt the pressure of his large teeth through his warm lips.

Then he walked swiftly out, unmanned by so much feeling packed into an hour before lunch.

Barbara made no attempt to accompany him to the door. As if in a trance, after sitting quite still for five minutes, she got up and went round the room, standing in the places he had been, touching things, seeking to rediscover her identity.

CHAPTER V

Passing through the general office, Ralph was surprised to see Michael Molloy sitting on the horsehair sofa provided by Mr Fox for his clients.

"Hello, Michael."

"Master Ralph."

Michael's acknowledgement was accompanied by the faintest expression of recognition. He had the air of a man on a mission, and he clutched a large box as if he would not trust it to anyone else's care. Clearly he did not want Ralph's advice; and that young man, a little piqued, went on about his business. Michael presumably was in about his mother's affairs and the tenancy of the lodge now that she was dead. He had never discussed business with Ralph, whom he saw every weekend.

Mr Fox never hurried one client to make room for another. Consulting him on the smallest point meant often a morning or afternoon gone west. As he had no other hobby outside his work, which he brought home in the evening as well as attending to in the office over weekends and on holidays, he had naturally come to suppose that life centred round his desk. Here he fought his battles and enjoyed his conquests; here he levied tribute and paid ransom. His reputation was enormous for one who operated on such a modest scale; but he could not bear to delegate or to allow others to take credit. Ralph's chief complaint was that he was so rarely allowed to take on the full responsibility of any case. Mr Fox either began it and then passed the work on, or presided at the kill.

He had a dominating personality; speaking he commanded silence; his own silences were daunting. Even after a client had stated his business, Mr Fox in measured terms repeated it again as if to demonstrate that until then it was a mystery. He had enormous curiosity and a splendid memory, being tenacious of everything, especially facts. And as he had no temptation to share anything, he was a perfect confidant. Even if his office was not equipped to take on large cases, many sought his advice on points when they wanted an expert opinion. It was believed that in government departments his appearance sent a tremor down the corridors and clerks consulted their files in fear and trembling. He had found holes in hasty legislation and tied Ministers of State into knots on more occasions than one. So the story went; and it was part of Mr Fox's mystique that nobody was able to say whether the story was true or not. In legal circles he combined the reputation of Machiavelli with the mystery of the Loch Ness monster.

Michael thought of him as a god. For so long as he could remember Mr Fox had been visiting Mount Lambert, and on those occasions nobody except Bradshaw the steward, had ever spoken a word to him.

After a two-hour wait he was told to go into Mr Fox's room. The outside of the door had for him the semblance of a bomb-pin or safety-catch; he hesitated before knocking, and hesitated when a voice invited him in. This led to a scream from inside, and his entry was consequently hurried and confused.

Mr Fox was staring at him from the shadows, behind a table, in a corner, at a great distance from the door.

Michael saw a chair with its back turned which he concluded he would be invited to sit on, meanwhile he was much concerned for a place to put his hat. His movements, in any case, were somewhat impeded by the box he clutched against his chest.

"What can I do for you, Michael?"

He sounded less angry, and it was reassuring that he knew whom he was talking to.

"There's a chair there," Mr Fox indicated where with his

spectacles. These he used for every purpose except as an aid to vision. While Michael was arranging himself, his hat, and his box, Mr Fox, to save time, continued to read a letter; before doing so, he replaced his spectacles and pushed them up on his forehead.

Then, seizing a dictating apparatus, he recorded a short letter. That done, he turned all his attention on Michael, not thinking of what his business might be, assuming that he was merely concerned about his future in the lodge; but he was glad of the opportunity to study the face of one who had cropped up so often in estate correspondence and whom the steward had designated an eccentric and habitual thief.

Michael would not look him in the eyes; but his expression was not shifty, he looked down as if lacking self-confidence. His expression was excessively humble.

"What have you there?" the solicitor said at length.

Michael jumped to his feet at this and put the box on the table.

"I found this and I thought I should give it to you. It must belong to the Lamberts. I can't make it out at all."

The box upon which the Lambert crest was engraved was not locked, and Mr Fox displayed an unexpected lightness of finger in getting it open and laying out the contents on his desk.

There was a chamois bag full of gold sovereigns, two letters in a schoolboyish hand, tied in a piece of faded ribbon, several newspapers of the first war and two gold lockets. In one there was a lock of brown hair, in the other a miniature photograph of a man in uniform.

"Where did you find this?"

"In a trunk in my mother's room. I was tidying up after she died (R.I.P.) and I came across them."

Another and more impulsive man would have assured Michael at once that these were his. But Mr Fox had not earned his reputation by good-natured impulsiveness.

"I shouldn't be keeping you," Michael said, looking

round at all the papers. Mr Fox made him feel very insignificant indeed; but, in his own way, he was pleased to see that he had made an impression. It was also exciting to be in the great man's own room.

"I must see what all this is about," Mr Fox said. It would have seemed in keeping with his cautious character to have put the contents away for perusal later, but he was inordinately curious to see what was the explanation of the mystery, and he had never seen so much gold in his life outside the vaults of a bank.

"Help me to count these," he said to Michael. His tone was conciliatory; this innocent was the man who had been accused of systematic pilfering.

Michael stood beside his chair, and when he had poured out the coins on the desk they made a sand castle. They were all sovereigns. Mr Fox suggested making piles of ten. And there were soon ten little gold pillars on his table.

Mr Fox now opened the letters. One said "My poor little darling, We arrived here yesterday. The journey was not so bad. I expect we will go into action very soon. But don't worry. I will be back. I am thinking of you. I send you 1,000 hugs and kisses. J."

The other

"My poor little darling. I am worrying on your account if anything should happen to me. I wish I knew about you. It worries me dreadfully. I have written to my mother and if anything should happen to me I know she will be kind to you for my sake. I wish we were in the cottage now. I have the little curl you gave me in a locket. I wear it next my heart. Did you get the one I sent you with my photograph? Not a very flattering likeness. I do not need a picture of you. Your face is in front of my eyes day and night. It will be tomorrow when we go into battle. A thousand kisses from your loving J."

Mr Fox darted a glance at Michael who, as always, had his head down. Then he opened the newspapers. They were all for the early months of the first fighting in France. One

145

had a sombre casualty list. He was not surprised to read : *Lambert, Julian Charles Andrew: second lieutenant Connaught Rangers; missing.*

There were other bits and pieces in the box, crumpled handkerchiefs, pieces of lace, rings and brooches of no intrinsic value.

"Tell me, Michael," said Mr Fox at length, "when were you born?"

"First of April, 1915, sir. It's a queer class of a day to have for a birthday."

"Did your mother make a will?"

"Not that I ever heard of. But what had she to leave? The few pieces of furniture in the lodge wouldn't be worth what it would cost to carry them away. She had a few things she took a pride in—some linen and suchlike which old Lady Lambert gave her when she married my father."

"He was the coachman at Mount Lambert, wasn't he?"

"He was, for fifty years and more. It nearly broke his heart when the old lady took to a motor-car. But he learned how to drive it."

"He was older than your mother?"

"That he was, old enough to be her father."

"You were the only child?"

"Yes. I was the first, and there were no more after me."

Mr Fox as his way was when he was thinking got up and walked up and down behind Michael's back. He changed the subject from the box to the lodge and told Michael that there had been provision made at the time of his parents' marriage in 1914 that they and their children should occupy the house free of rent.

"My mother (R.I.P.) told me that. It was very generous of old Sir Julian."

"The family were under a great obligation to your father, I am sure they were glad to be able to assist him. It all happened before my time, you understand. My uncle was the family solicitor in those days; but he told me all he knew about their history."

146

Michael became increasingly ill at ease having to converse with a voice, and constantly turning round was giving him a crick in the neck; so he was relieved when Mr Fox seemed suddenly to forget all about him and taking up the telephone began a long conversation with someone in London.

He got up then and waited to be dismissed.

"I will look into everything and let you know," Mr Fox said.

Michael was satisfied. He knew that Mr Fox was the trusted agent of the Lamberts and that once he had given him what was obviously belonging to the Lamberts, he had done his duty by the family. He did wonder why his mother had never told him that she had that box. She had been old Lady Lambert's personal maid, and it could be that the box came to her in that capacity and she had forgotten all about it. He had done what his father would have done in the circumstances. Of that he was quite certain, and it left his mind at peace. The responsibility of the box had been killing him.

CHAPTER VI

THE SUN HAD banished the silver mist which had lain over the Mile since soon after dawn; swallows and martins swooped in circles round the villas before sailing in under the eaves. In the fields cattle grazed on the close grass and chewed the thistles to which the cuckoo spit clung. Sometimes a cow would look up and give a deep low which a calf out of view would answer with its baby moo. A lark in the clear air went on as if suffering from St Vitus's dance; bees guzzled in the clover. From the stables of Kent a high whinny sounded every now and then along the valley, and it was answered every time by the stout cob feeding on the Canon's grass. He hardly lifted his muzzle off the ground to neigh reassurance.

All nature was profitably occupied and Perry was coasting along the Mile in his Jaguar. He saw from the top of the hill the flurried figure of the Captain rushing towards the gate, waving a piece of paper. Perry was not in any particular hurry—if the truth were known he had come out from sheer boredom—but he felt an immediate resentment at his 'cousin's' assumption that he was available whenever he wanted to discus his insignificant concerns. In fact he played with the idea of accelerating and leaving Loftus standing there; but this would possibly spark off a quarrel and was hardly worth it.

He pulled up, looking peeved, and said.

"What is it? I am in rather a hurry."

"A letter from the Major. Look at it for yourself. He says that his secretary made a mistake over the invitations, and he wants me to support him at the dance. That's a very nice way of putting it. I think we have been too harsh in our criticism of the Major. You may say what you like, but a man who serves in the Foreign Legion voluntarily has guts—he is a hundred per cent he-man. I am going to drop him a line this morning and leave it round by hand to show I appreciate his gesture. What do you think?"

"You must either refuse or accept the invitation: surely to God you are old enough to know that without asking advice from every passing motorist."

"I resent that, Herbert. I would discuss this with nobody but my most intimate friends, yourself, the Canon and Barbara. What I was going to suggest—but I will do nothing without first getting your marching orders—I was going to see if I could get a chance to drop out to the Major that you never got a card. I don't see why he should not have included you and your missus."

"I will tell you why; because I made it clear from the start that I could see through him. He may be a match for the fossils round here, but he will need to sharpen up if he wants to take in a man of the world."

"I think you are being unfair. We never heard his side of the story. And, I ask you, why should we take sides with a fellow like Bernard Coppinger, who looks like a pansy, against a red-blooded fellow like the Major?"

"I notice you are giving him his military rank now. Yesterday it was 'the Count'."

"The Canon and Barbara always call him 'Major'. I think they are right. I have taken myself rather to task about my attitude, and I don't mind telling you I think I've behaved badly. I'm not ashamed to admit it."

"Well, this is not getting me anywhere. I was late as it is." Perry put his foot down on the accelerator and shot away at a quite reckless speed.

The Captain watched him with glee. Only one thing could have taken the patina off his pleasure, and that would have been to have heard an invitation had also gone to the Perrys. Herbert was 'fit to be tied'. He could see that. It would be some time now before there would be an invitation to the golf links, and when it did come Loftus resolved that he would decline unless a lift both ways was made part and parcel of the invitation.

Perry was in a filthy humour. He saw the invitation to his cousin as a calculated slap at himself, not to mention his wife, who was longing to go to the dance and had unsuccessfully tried to wangle an invitation through the Brownes. Mrs Browne could talk about nothing except her spotty daughter, whom, very naturally, the Count had excluded.

As the Jaguar passed Kent at the end of the Mile, Herbert increased speed. It was a reckless move because the road narrowed there as it approached a blind corner. As the car came round the hedge on the corner it faced a van. Perry swung violently into the hedge, and to the accompaniment of cracks and scrapes as the briars flogged his paintwork he felt his rear bumper meeting some projection on the van. It wobbled and then pulled up. Perry, whether in the right or the wrong, always lost his temper after an accident. He jumped out at once and marched purposefully towards the van, from which nobody had emerged.

MOUNT LAMBERT was stencilled across the door. This was the estate van, appropriated by Bradshaw for his private use. Shook by the collision, he was not too much upset to make quick calculations. He had recognised both the car and the driver; he should not have been in the middle of the road, but the other car should not have come round the corner so fast. Unfortunately its place in the ditch on the left hand side of the road gave its driver an appearance of being in the right. His own car's tracks were there to show that he had not hugged his proper side. Moreover, he was well aware of the fact that he had not been using the van on estate business, and a query about the amount of petrol consumed had been made on a few occasions.

Perry found himself confronted by a leer.

"It's in Brooklands you ought to be with that machine," Bradshaw said.

"What the devil do you mean by taking up the middle of the road at a blind corner? I've a good mind to write to Sir

Julian about this. Nobody is safe to drive on the Mile if this sort of thing is tolerated."

Perry had been thinking too, and it had occurred to him that as there was no witness of his speed, he stood a good chance of putting all the blame on Bradshaw. "That car will never be the same again, and there wasn't a scratch on her until you came along racing in the centre of the road round the worst corner in the county in your enormous van."

Bradshaw avoided fights, and the dialogue might have gone on indefinitely if the Count had not appeared at that moment.

He had reason to believe that Bradshaw had been making mischief and was a serious encumbrance to his plans for Mount Lambert. Some day or other they would have to clash. Why not now?

"I saw the accident. It's a pity that you didn't keep on your own side, Bradshaw. Mr Perry was well over on his. I had better ring up the Guards. Meanwhile leave the cars where they are. You can stand at the corner, Bradshaw, and warn approaching vehicles. Mr Perry, come along with me and have a tot of brandy. You had a very nasty fright."

"Nobody wants the Guards," Bradshaw said.

"It's the law," Perry said.

"Get your car mended and send me the bill," Bradshaw wheedled. "I'll get it off my own insurance company."

Perry pretended to consider this, and only reluctantly agreed.

Bradshaw then drove away. His left rear mud-guard in a state of pulp. The Jaguar was without any serious damage. Its rear bumper had done execution without suffering in the process.

It was a very happy ending to what might have been a very tedious business; and Perry was magnanimous enough to accept the offer of the brandy in the circumstances.

"Where did you see from?" he said. The hedge was thick and about twenty feet high.

151

"I saw nothing until I came out on the road and looked at the cars. I heard the collision. I put two and two together, and I don't believe in giving a hesitant opinion. I like to decide matters and have done with them—drumhead court-martials, I have taken part in many a one. I know a guilty face. Bradshaw is a blackguard. In the desert he'd have had a bullet in his brains long ago. Besides I have a code, Mr Perry, and Bradshaw offends against it."

"Call me Herbert, Major. I think it is silly of neighbours to stand aloof, especially here with people like Coppinger, pulling the houses to bits, and sending out invitations to strangers. I think we should take a stand. And after what I saw this morning I think you demonstrated your own loyalty. Noblesse Oblige."

The Count watched Perry, and considered. Perhaps he had insulted him long enough, and he had an uneasy feeling that Perry had seen him the day he hid the filly in the Canon's stable.

"By all means, Herbert. And I am known locally as 'the Count'. You may call me that. By the way I was giving a little party for Miss Lambert when she comes over next month, a most unpretentious affair—nothing, I am sure, like the Coppingers' splendid entertainment—would you and Mrs Perry—what is *her* Christian name by the way?— would it bore you to drop in and support me that evening? I didn't like to send you a card before I had an opportunity to sound you."

"Molly and I will be delighted to come. She is always saying that we don't see nearly enough of you. I think you are quite right to restrict invitations. There's no compliment to anyone in being invited to a jamboree."

"Splendid. Splendid. I will send you a card."

"There's no need to. I'll pass the message on."

"No. No. Protocol must be observed."

"We are the last of the Mohicans."

"I must think about that."

With the servile look which he invariably assumed when

his company matched his pretensions, Perry departed in a flutter of waving hands; but he saw in his driving mirror that as soon as he took the wheel the Count cut off the salutes and stared after the retreating Jaguar with stolid indifference, with no indication of good-will in his stance or his stare.

"Funny chap."

As he passed Wales, Perry wondered what he was going to say to Loftus. But, really, it didn't matter a damn. The thing to do was to lie doggo at the moment and let Loftus become aware by degrees of an intimacy between Kent and Sussex, something from which he was implicitly excluded. The little matter of the invitation would then fall into its place. Meanwhile the poor little fellow could nourish his illusion that the Major wanted his support. What a sense of humour the man must have to think of that one!

CHAPTER VII

BRADSHAW   HAD   ATTRIBUTED some of the losses
at Mount Lambert to Michael's maraudings, this convinced
Ralph of Bradshaw's infamy; and he recalled strange stories
that had been going about that Bradshaw had businesses
scattered over the country. He determined to go into the
matter himself and felt not a little impatient with his
employer who seemed to be incapable of moral indignation.
Bradshaw had also reported the Count's frequent prowlings
round the place.

Now, in fact, Bradshaw was not the sort of man who
made wild assertions. Truth was a slippery pole where he
was concerned; and he contrived to grease it in such a
fashion that anyone who tried to hang on dropped off at
length from the exertion. He had perfected a system of hints
in preference to the crude policy of plain statements. His
victims usually gave him credit for knowing more than he
knew. Until their encounter on the road Bradshaw had
thought of the Count as a remote source of danger to his
livelihood because he plainly coveted Mount Lambert; after
the road accident he saw him in a more formidable guise as
someone who knew too much about him. For it had not
occurred to Bradshaw that the Count's arbitration—plainly
dishonest—was inspired by frivolous motives. He saw it as a
show of strength. For this he bore the Count no ill will : he
had always assumed that life was entirely competitive and,
if anything, admired a ruthless opponent; but it put him on
his mettle. He had been slacking : there were chinks in the
Count's armour by all accounts; he must find out at once
what they were. In the end they might reach a compromise.

One moonlit evening, the Count before going to bed
decided to take a stroll through the woods of Mount Lam-

bert. He wanted to perfect his knowledge of the place, and the scope and value of the timber was an item of which account would have to be taken.

On that same evening Bradshaw also decided to take a look at the woods; he had heard what sounded like sawing the night before and it had aroused his curiosity. Bradshaw left home at least half an hour before the Count made his more leisurely way; and he walked like one who is stalking game. He heard more sawing tonight and he made for the direction whence it came.

Peering through the undergrowth he was not at all surprised to see Michael Molloy beside a fallen tree which he had cut into neat sections. One of these he was now lifting up, and Bradshaw hastily moved back to further shelter because he was standing on the path to Michael's lodge. But Michael did not appear and the snapping of twigs in the distance indicated that he had walked the other way. Bradshaw emerged cautiously and tip-toed back to his former spying-place. There was nobody there, but sounds in the distance indicated that Michael was coming back. He appeared in the clearing, picked up another of the planks and took it in the same direction as the first. This time Bradshaw followed him.

Less than fifty yards away was the cottage which had never been re-let and in which Elizabeth as a child used to play house. The door was open and a lamp standing on a table showed that a scheme of repair was in progress: the planks in the clearing were being used for a form of rustic panelling; the ceiling joists had all been renewed. It was quite an extensive job. Bradshaw watched with intense interest. This accounted for missing timber; but what was Michael's purpose? Did he propose to try to use the cottage surreptitiously? Had he some crazed idea that by repairing it he was acquiring some proprietary rights in it? Bradshaw was fascinated. A lesser man would have reported the matter at once to his principals. He had no such intention: hints delivered at intervals in the near future would let

Michael know that the game was up; it would be time enough to report the matter when it was examined from the point of view of Bradshaw's interest first of all.

The Count had often passed the dilapidated cottage on his walks, and had even noted it as worth putting in repair to house some of the stud farm staff; but tonight was the first time he had seen it open. He did not hesitate to look in. An oil lamp on a rough wooden table lit up a room like a hunter's lodge.

The Count took careful note of everything; and was so busy that he did not hear Michael coming into the cottage, hauling one of the planks with which the wall was being decorated. As neither had any right to be there it was appropriate that each should look taken aback and then relieved when he saw who the other was.

"Nice little hide-out you have here," the Count said. His brain had entertained and as quickly rejected the idea of saying he had called to condole with Michael on his recent loss.

"It's Miss Elizabeth's. I am trying to get it ready for her by the time she comes over."

"Ah! I see. A summer house."

"No. She used it whenever she was here as a place of her own. It was a secret. She didn't let on to anyone. But I used to see her come and go. She never knew I did; and when I heard she was coming back I thought I'd do it up like, to give her a surprise."

"And is the worthy Bradshaw in the secret?"

"That man! I don't have any truck with him. Of course I wouldn't mind for my own sake if he found out—I'm only doing it for Miss Elizabeth; but I'd be afraid he might be wanting to put the place to some use if he thought it was in repair. That's why I'm leaving the outside just as it was with the ivy grown up over the window. You won't let on to anyone, Major—will you? Miss Elizabeth would have my life I'm certain sure if she thought I'd given away her hiding-place."

156

The Count gave all the necessary reassurance. He went even further. He had rugs and curtains and cushions, fans and peacock feathers—all sorts of decorative material—which he said he would be more than ready to contribute to make a 'bower' as he called it for 'Miss Elizabeth'.

"Look what I have for her," Michael said. He warmed to the Count tonight, remembering gratefully his appearance at the funeral. Although he was suspicious of his interest in Mount Lambert, fearful of anyone who might try to filch it from the Lamberts he had heard that he was their friend; and as he was someone of whom the Canon approved he must be on the right side.

"Look-at."

He took out a miniature and hung it on a nail over the fireplace.

"Very nice. Very nice. Where did you get this?"

The Count had taken down the picture and was subjecting it to inspection through a magnifying glass. A worthless miniature, the sort that the toucher-up in photographic studios used to produce at about five guineas a time. Michael could have bought it at a local auction for a few shillings, and the Count's appearance of interest was only to flatter. At the same time the face had a certain familiarity.

"Oh, it's mine all right. It's mine to give away; for what would the likes of me be wanting with the likes of that? Mr Fox sent it back to me and said I could keep it."

"And where did Mr Fox get it?"

"I found it in a box under my poor mother's bed (R.I.P.) and I took it in to him."

"Have you no idea who it is?"

The Count looked from the miniature to Michael and back again.

"Unless it was one of the Lamberts; but if so, I don't know why Mr Fox says it is mine."

"There's a remarkable likeness," said the Count.

"To Sir Julian?"

157

"I was going to say...Yes, yes, of course! To Sir Julian."

"Well then, Miss Elizabeth ought to have it, seeing it's her father."

"Not her father, Michael, her grandfather."

"Now, I never thought of that. He was killed in the War, did you ever hear of it? Poor man. I never saw him, and how could I? He died the year I was born."

The Count took up the miniature again and appeared to be studying it; when he turned back to Michael the latter noticed with some alarm a look in his eyes as if they had filled with dark fluid— quite a wicked look.

"You won't tell Bradshaw," he pleaded.

The Count stretched out his hand. "Michael, if Bradshaw ever gives you any cause for worry, come and tell me. I will break every bone in his body."

Michael accepted the outstretched hand. He had had an uncanny feeling that Bradshaw was hovering near, and knew every secret of his soul.

In this he was clairvoyant; but Bradshaw, making his way back to his house with enough to think about to keep him awake all night, found that the Count's threat took all the pleasure out of what seemed, until the very last moment, to be one of the most rewarding half hours he had spent for many a year.

CHAPTER VIII

"I MUST SAY I am sorry Ralph was not able to take time off to meet her."

The Canon was pacing up and down the morning-room; from the bow window he would get the first glimpse of the Count's Alfa Romeo when it started up the Mile.

"Perhaps it's all for the best. Ralph is unpredictable these days; he might have quarrelled with her in the car and ruined her visit from the start. The Count is an old friend and will have a lot to talk to her about."

"I wish you wouldn't call him 'the Count', dear. It's a local vulgarism, and I am always afraid you will come out with it some day in his hearing."

"But I think he enjoys it. I've heard him use it himself. No doubt he sees it as a patent of nobility and will adapt it to formal use in due course."

"You don't like him, dear. You never will. Your prejudice keeps on breaking through."

"Well, you know as well as I do that he is a ruffian. I am still curious to know what that business of the grey horse was all about. I have a suspicion we took part in a fraud on creditors. It will be very interesting to see where the money for the ball is to come from. According to Angela, he has thrown discretion to the winds—the most expensive band, champagne, and I hear that the invitation list has been extended. We are to have the President, no less; Ministers of State; Ambassadors and a cabaret show from Paris to do God knows what during supper."

"I wish you wouldn't listen to Angela's stories, dear. It's unworthy of you. We were brought up to avoid kitchen gossip; and a very good rule it was. It is so easy to become second-rate. Up to this we have avoided it on the Mile, and I think we should struggle to maintain the standard."

"That's all very well, but you know Angela gets the news a day before we do. Mrs Bartholomew called yesterday with a present of honey from Barbara. Angela got all the gossip from her."

"Kitchen gossip."

"Mrs Bartholomew got it from Barbara."

"Key-hole gossip."

"You *are* being pompous, today."

"Pompous? Nobody has ever called me that. Pompous? If there is one thing I despise it is pomposity. Surely there is a distinction between the ordinary decencies of society and—"

"Here they are!"

The Canon forgot himself sufficiently to run to the window. He was just in time to catch the gleam of the sun on the roof of a blue car. It would be visible again when it came to the wall of Cumberland's grounds.

With one accord the Ormsbys left the bow window at the back of the house and moved towards the hall. They were out on the steps when the car drove up and a girl jumped out: long legs, auburn hair—that was what the Canon saw: his wife noticed with approval white, un-Irish teeth.

They made an arresting tableau: Elizabeth with her arms stretched out; the Count behind her, smiling—the producer with his star; the Canon on the steps, swaying like a giraffe on the qui vive. In the background, Mrs Ormsby, gentle, welcoming, restrained, against a porch pillar; props of the house, rounding off the composition in its setting of summer sky, lambswool clouds and a violet hill-top smoked in mist.

"Uncle Silverpenny! Aunt Penny! How lovely to see you both. And Napoleon. What a tum he's grown. These are my best stockings, Nap. Lay off them. Nothing has changed! How well everyone is looking. The parents send all their love to both of you. Aren't they awful never to come? Dump my bags there, Ritzy. I'll bring them in afterwards."

"You will do nothing of the kind. Look who is here," the Canon said. This was the signal for Michael to step forward, blushing, hanging his head, pulling furiously at hair concealed under his cap.

"Michael! Well this is nice of everyone to turn out. How is the old house, Michael? I know you are keeping an eye on it."

"Fine, miss. It's fine," said Michael.

Dazzled, he was glad of the excuse to pick up the bags and bring them in. Angela now came forward to greet and be greeted. Reuter had been caught napping for once. News of the arrival would fly forth now in every detail.

Mrs Ormsby had made her best cake for the occasion. They all sat down in the drawing-room; but Elizabeth kept on jumping up to look out of the window or examine familiar objects in the rooms.

"And how is Ralph?" she said.

The matrimonial telegraph operated for a fraction of a second between the Canon and his wife; the lightning exchange of messages ended when Mrs Ormsby said, "He was awfully sad not being able to get off to meet you. He is really working very hard, too hard we think at times. But I believe Mr Fox is very pleased with him. You will see him at dinner."

"I hope," the Canon took up the task, "that you will be able to make him frivolous. He has become far too serious. I am depending on you to shake him up."

"Now, Elizabeth, you know what you have to do," the Count said. "If Ralph fails you, you will have to turn to me. I am always frivolous."

"Not frivolous, Ritzy, gay, gay—the most precious thing anyone can be. Ma is like a corpse when you are not there. At the moment she is trying to revive herself with a one-eyed Armenian, and it just won't work. And as for Pa; he lives in terror of the newspapers and television, and won't keep away from either. He is expecting an attack from South America at any moment. He wants everyone to dig air-raid shelters. Ritzy you must come back and make Majorca gay. It's stifling."

"Anywhere Lizzy is won't be stifling for long," the Count said. "But what we want you to do, Liz, is to come here and stay with us. If we can entice your aged parents over here— the one-eyed Armenian as well—well and good. But you must stay. I have plans for Mount Lambert—"

At this moment Angela came in with the tea on a tray, and a contest took place. She arranged every detail of the feast with meticulous care, the Count assisting, but not going on with his conversation. It was a siege. When it was clear that nothing was to be gained by waiting, Angela withdrew.

But Elizabeth did not allow the Count to disclose his plans for Mount Lambert. Instead she went to the chimney-piece and started to discuss the invitations on display.

"Ritzy, dear, have you taken leave of your senses giving a ball for me? I tried to get Pa to do it, but he just groaned and said the floor would fall in."

"He seems to have communicated his fears. Mr Fox has asked me to go into his office to discuss fire insurance, possible collapse of floors, injuries to third parties, and other matters which I never dreamed about."

"And, tell me, who are the Coppingers? Mrs Coppinger wrote to Ma and asked if I might go to their ball. She said they wanted to celebrate their arrival on the Mile. They had rather a nerve to ask for Mount Lambert. If they were to have it, why not everyone? It would become the local *palais de danse*. Pa didn't rise to that one."

"We are all rather worried about the Coppingers, my dear. They are like what used to be known as The Yellow Peril, a distant threat which might at any moment assume calamitous proportions," said Mrs Ormsby.

"Besides it was mean of them to try to steal Ritzy's thunder. At the time, I must confess I thought that it was a good lark to have two dances instead of one; but I have aged and matured considerably since then."

"A month is a long time at your time of life," the Count agreed.

"You see the dance idea was put up when I was reacting rather violently after the breaking of my engagement. But I've sobered down. I see life steadily now and see it whole."

"We were very sorry to hear about the breaking of your engagement," the Canon said, looking suitably grave.

"Well it was one of those cases where everybody is praying secretly for a swift release but pretends they want the patient to keep alive, for decency's sake. You know what I mean."

"I'd have to know more about your engagement, dear," said Mrs Ormsby, to whom the question was put.

"He was a catch, far too good for me, stinking rich, rather handsome, like a *New Yorker* ad. for English tweed; not too old; healthy; unmarried; vaguely Christian; perseveringly cultured—and bloody awful really. Now do you know what I mean?"

"If you felt like that about him you were certainly right not to marry him," Mrs Ormsby agreed.

"But it wasn't me who broke the thing up. I was all for it. He got qualms when he found that I was still seeing Jock. Finally he said that if I didn't promise to give Jock up it was all off. Of course I wasn't going to take that from him or anyone, so I told him to——. I won't say it. But Uncle Silverpenny knows what I mean."

"And who," the Canon enquired, "is Jock?"

"Elizabeth's former fiancé, Captain Jock Redman Pulbrick, wing-forward for Harlequins, 15 stone 10 lb of unreflecting beef."

"Ritzy's jealous. Jock may not be a highbrow—in fact, he is definitely not. God knows I am not educated; but whenever I'm with Jock I feel like a mixture of Mary McCarthy and the French woman who's mixed up with Sartre and

163

flies all over the place telling people how miserable they are. I've forgotten what she's called."

Nobody answered this, and Elizabeth put back the invitations.

A light chill had descended on the evening. The sun that had been so much in evidence when Elizabeth arrived had gone down. Shadows in the garden were beginning to lengthen and, as if in sympathy with them, so did the shadows in the house.

CHAPTER IX

"WHAT WE WOULD have done without the Major, I am at a loss to imagine," the Canon said.

He was standing, suitably framed in the Corinthian porch, waving to Elizabeth as the Alfa Romeo disappeared down the drive. They were off to an evening race-meeting, to be followed by a supper with some friends of the Count who lived luxuriously by a lakeside. And this had been the pattern of many days. Mrs Browne was heard complaining all along the Mile that Syl had no chance at all to play with her old chum. But she had sent out invitations to a tennis party; and the Perrys were doing one better with a buffet supper. Captain Loftus, anxious not to fall behind in paying a tribute to so decorative a representative of the Lamberts, his sponsors, consulted Perry on the question. He, as usual, seemed to find it hard to apply his mind to his 'cousin's' problem, it being engaged with matters of greater moment.

"Oh, they won't expect you to do anything," he said at last, but hardly in a tone to soothe the Captain's anxieties.

"I know I can't put up much of a show, especially for a gay young thing, but I thought a little gathering of the inner circle might be a pleasant contrast to all the rather garish entertainment that's on hand, something intimate I had in mind that she would remember afterwards as if it were part of home."

"I don't know what exactly you mean by 'garish'. Certainly the sort of evening we have arranged would hardly come under that heading, unless having enough to eat and drink is garish. But I have never heard it so described."

"I wasn't thinking about your party, Herbert. I heard Miss Beddington say that Elizabeth had refused two other engagements so as to be able to accept your invitation. Have no worry on that score."

"I wasn't worrying. By this time I have a fair idea what Molly and I can do in the way of entertaining. It was you who seemed to be casting doubts on it. I don't know why; you used to seem to enjoy yourself at our parties."

"Be reasonable, Herbert. I'm damn sorry now I ever mentioned the subject of my little party. I can see that it would be a bore to everyone."

"There you go, Loftus. Why should it be a bore? I admit that the prospect of meeting only the faces I see every day of the week doesn't exactly make my heart miss a beat—you might stretch yourself a bit and ask one or two off the Mile. We are none of us the sort of company a girl of that age is likely to write up in her diary."

"She seems to be going everywhere with the Count. If I were master Ralph, I'd have had a go myself; but that young man seems to be so fully occupied making gaffes in Fox's office, he has no time for any young life. And by the way, do you remember that day we saw the Count leaving a horse on the Canon?"

"What about it?"

"By an extraordinary piece of luck I heard all about it. I was coming back from Bray on my bicycle—I was at the cinema, you know—and I stopped at the pub in Enniskerry for a glass of stout. I'm not the sort of man who listens in to conversation, but I couldn't help hearing what was being said in the snug. The daughter of the sergeant was having a drink with Bradshaw, of all people, and she was telling him how the Count moved a valuable horse out of the way to avoid a London creditor."

"Look here, Loftus. I am not going to listen to a word against the Major. He is a friend of mine and a sportsman. It's no business of yours or mine what he does with his horses. If I had been in your shoes, I'd have gone straight into that snug and told Bradshaw and the sergeant's moll where they got off."

"It wasn't the sergeant's moll. It was his daughter; and she knew what she was talking about. I thought you might be interested. You were always making enquiries about the Count yourself."

"Was I? I wasn't aware of it. One lives in a place like this to be quite sure who everyone is. One bad apple can ruin the barrel; but I count the Major as a friend, a very good friend, and I would thank you to remember it and keep a close hold on that mischievous member of yours."

"What the hell do you mean?"

"Your tongue, Loftus, your eternally wagging tongue. It's the only member I can think of that's likely to lead you into trouble. Now, if you don't mind, I have letters to write."

Not for the first time, Loftus left the Perrys' feeling worse than he went in; but to whom else could he turn? If only, even once, he could score off that self-confident, bumptious, insensitive, common—yes, common—bully, he would die happy. And with that inspiration came : why not a little party *without* the Perrys? Instead he would ask the Coppingers who had been kind enough—say what you like about them—to invite them to their ball. It was a splendid idea, and all that he had to decide upon now was whether to send out the invitations in a casual fashion or formally. The first had its charm; but there was always the danger people would forget or pass it up for some other engagement. After luncheon he would bicycle into Bray, buy invitations and despatch them. Sunday morning at twelve o'clock, cocktails? No, better still, Sunday evening at 6 o'clock, sundowners. That would strike just the right note. For he did feel very often like one who had pitched his tent in a foreign field. At night, to cheer himself up, he had taken to playing 'God Save The Queen' on the gramophone and then drinking her dear little Majesty's health in a cup of Ovaltine before going up to roost.

CHAPTER X

"How wonderfully well-matched they are. How sweet Elizabeth is looking."

Miss Beddington and Ralph Ormsby sat together at a table, neither had until now addressed a word to one another, both had preferred to watch Elizabeth and the Count dancing together.

"He could do with a few more inches," Ralph said.

It was true. Miss Beddington had remarked the fact to herself; but she did not say that sort of thing. Though as graceful as a member of the cat tribe in his movements, and broad of shoulder, the Count was not more than five feet nine. Elizabeth looked rather taller than she was. Dancing together they were of the same height.

But what marked them out from the other dancers was not their physical appearance so much as an aura of gaiety that surrounded them. In this miscellaneous gathering of people, alike only in that all wore evening dress, they seemed to inhabit another world. It was partly Elizabeth's charm of expression. Every time her head inclined towards her partner's, Ralph felt as if an eagle had sunk its beak in his entrails. The Count presented a perfect foil to her champagne quality. He was restrained in all his movements and danced well, if in a mode that belonged to an earlier decade, but this, too, added to the distinction of the couple.

Miss Beddington could not look at the Count without feeling a swimming in her head and sensations elsewhere which she determinedly refused to analyse. She felt as if she was attached to him by a silver cord, and were he to pull on it, but ever so lightly, she would be powerless to resist. At times when his laughing eyes fell on them, she had to hold hard on to her chair in case she should be wafted across the dance floor by the magnetism of that impenetrable gaze.

"Her mother was very handsome, but Elizabeth is far, far prettier," Miss Beddington generously said.

Ralph, who had come in a sulk to torture himself over Elizabeth and felt hopeless in competition with this man (who he knew was a knave), had been quite oblivious of Miss Beddington's presence as a fourth until that moment when he felt a sudden and wholly inexplicable sympathy with her. His parents thought she was a beautiful woman; and the notion had always made him smile as an example of their antediluvian standards. How could a woman be considered beautiful at forty? The very idea was absurd. But now he looked at her, unaware of his scrutiny, and saw for the first time what his parents meant. There was something about her as she sat, her lips very slightly open, her dress ever so much lower than usual, that he had never recognised before in the Miss Beddington who, for so long as he could remember, looked as if she was put away every evening in tissue paper and lavender.

She had been dancing quite a lot, with the Count for the most part—the outing was her contribution to Elizabeth's entertainment—and it was only on his parents' insisting that he must not hurt their dear friend's feelings that Ralph had consented to come.

Elizabeth had been at Cumberland for a week; but except when they met at meals, he had made no effort to talk to her and none to be alone with her. Tonight they had danced together a great deal; and it was impossible for him to disguise his feelings from himself. She had not teased him as she used to do, nor flirted with him, nor sought to discover why he had been so unfriendly. She had behaved as if they were the best of friends and had never had a moment's quarrel. She was giving him a chance to take up their childhood where they left it off; and if he had not responded generously and sensibly to her approach, he had at least dropped the martyred air which had threatened the success of the evening at the start.

The party had dined at Miss Beddington's—a capital dinner—served by Mrs Bartholomew in a new coat for the occasion. There was champagne and brandy and liqueurs, and cigars for the men, very good cigars. Miss Beddington never lapsed through inappropriate economy.

Elizabeth had been astonished at dinner to find that their hostess and the Count appeared to share a passion for English poetry. The Ritzy that she remembered went with bridge and women and champagne. But she had spent her young life discovering new facets to his personality, and she accepted this as but one more. The Count kept on referring to Keats as a poet who exercised a powerful fascination over Miss Beddington and himself—'our bond' he said knowingly; and at each reference to it, she blushed like a schoolgirl and begged him not to 'talk nonsense'.

The introduction of literary topics is usually depressive to an evening's gaiety, but Keats, this evening, seemed charged with aphrodisiacal properties. Ralph, in his martyr mood, neither noticed nor cared. At a small round table he was not called upon to contribute much. Miss Beddington thought he looked 'a duck' in evening dress, and saw the young people in the most romantic light.

With the stark egotism of youth, Ralph had been watching the dancers, unconcerned with Miss Beddington's thoughts or feelings. If asked he would have said the notion of her having any was a biological impossibility. But as he looked at her, wholly absorbed in the couple on the floor, he saw her quite suddenly in a new light. She was feeling something too. Possibly the concentration of his gaze made her eyes turn; when they met his, they went out together towards the pair on the floor. 'I love him', she seemed to say. 'I love her', his eyes said. Then, or a moment later, Miss Beddington put her hand on Ralph's on the table, openly, for all the world to see. It was a gesture, a communication of secret sympathy from one swimmer, out of her depth, to another, struggling against the tide.

The Count spotted them, of course. He had not taken much notice of Ralph during the evening, but his curiosity was aroused by what looked like an affectionate passage between a most unlikely pair. It was wholly out of keeping with Miss Beddington's reserved—not to say prim— bearing; and Ralph had not seemed a likely source from which she could draw affectionate response.

His approach was, therefore, tangential. A clumsier man might have embarked on chaff and provoked resentment. The Count's method was to concentate attention on Ralph and make him the centre of conversation. This achieved, he blew the whole discussion up into the realm of fantasy.

"You must leave the Fox's hole, Ralph. You are meant for better things. Birkenhead was Chancellor of England at forty-seven. If I were a lawyer I would aim at bettering that. You must go to London. Become indispensable to some scheming politician, find someone on his way up, and tack yourself on. Don't be frightened by names. I have met all the top men in England. I never met one that really impressed me, except Churchill, of course. That is the sort of foeman that is worthy of one's steel. And there are no Churchills now. Little men, dogs fighting for their dinner. Not a hero among them. We are only at home with heroes. Isn't that true? Am I not right, Barbara?"

"But why should Ralph go away? Why shouldn't he stay in Ireland? Isn't that what's been wrong with this country : everyone who has something to contribute takes it abroad."

"What is there for Ralph to do here? Unless he can get capital. We mustn't leave him in the Fox's hole, chewing the bones of the old Fox's prey after he has stripped the meat off them. Listen to me; I have the solution to all our problems."

Did Miss Beddington catch a breath? Nobody noticed if she did. The Count was the cynosure of all eyes. He had expanded with his topic. He did seem literally to swell.

171

"Mount Lambert is a sepulchre at the moment, attended by a ghoul. Now, if we could import two first-class sires and do the house up properly, there is no reason why it shouldn't become a successful stud farm. There was a Sir Julian who bred good horses there. He won the Ascot Gold Cup and the Cambridgeshire. Then he took to the bottle."

"That one died before he came in for the place. All the wild Julians die young," Elizabeth said.

"Then you must settle down, Liz. And I cannot think of a better way than to make the place a gold mine. It could be. I'm in a position to get you the very best blood; and I have a filly of my own that I will be sending to the stud as soon as she has had a season on the flat. Wouldn't it be splendid if she were to be mated with a Mount Lambert sire? It would be symbolical."

The Count was carried away. He was among friends; but something jarred like a stone caught in the whirring blades of a lawn mower and interrupted the smoothness of his flow. Ralph had looked up at the reference to the grey filly.

"All fillies at night are grey," the Count said, and left off, his eyes full of squid's ink.

His scheme which promised to solve everybody's problems did not appear to include Miss Beddington in its scope; nor could Ralph see any future in it for him. A cloud might have descended on the evening had a pair who were dancing together not come over to the table at that moment.

"Ah," cried a reedy voice from the dance floor, "the Mile, the League, the half Mile, and the Kilometre."

"A jester approaches," the Count said, his face freezing.

The man approaching them could have been thirty, gone to seed, or fifty, in full flower. He was slim and neatly built, with a profile in which he obviously took a conscious pride. His hair, black trimmed with grey, was brushed back, and looked as if its owner was perpetually heading into a gentle breeze.

"The Coppingers," Ralph explained. He introduced them to the party. Elizabeth was polite and neutral; Miss Beddington polite and interested; the Count impassive. Mrs Coppinger fixed a beam of pure love on everyone. Her husband's light turned inwards.

To arrive at Coppinger's true age one had to consider his wife. One could see that she had once been deliciously pretty, with those round blue eyes and all those curves and dimples—a Boucher for domestic consumption, whose bounty had been spent in producing a family and fussing over them and protecting her husband's profile against the slings and arrows of more outrageous fortunes.

She was almost forty, a contemporary of Miss Beddington; and it was interesting to contrast them. One had never been young and would never be old; the other had had her youth used up so fully that age could take over at any time without anyone noticing the change.

Elizabeth, who had been inclined to gush during her stay, was noticeably cool with the new arrivals; but Bernard Coppinger was a self-secure being, a type which is impervious to his surroundings when intent on his aims. His wife looked from one face to the other, smiling with an indiscriminating friendliness that had the effect of an ultra-violet ray lamp.

Coppinger's eyes clicked into a smile as he took over the conversation. He seemed to have prepared his speech on the way across the floor—it had a ready to fire flavour—but it was impossible to find his meaning in the maze of his manner.

The Count, surveying the speaker through the top of his brandy glass, saw him as a gigantic frog. He nodded to Elizabeth and indicated what he was up to, then to Ralph (who took some time to catch on), then to Miss Beddington.

Bernard Coppinger, looking up, after he had tossed his hair back, and presented himself in left profile, saw himself confronted with four glass balloons through which eight eyes were gleaming. The effect was disconcerting, but he was not to be disconcerted.

"What a good idea—captive balloons in front of each

173

plate at supper, and then at a signal let them all be sent up to the ceiling. We are thinking up gimmicks for the dance. I wanted to give it at Mount Lambert, you know. I've ideas for that place. If you put a factory into the yard and stables, you could use the rest as a culture centre, a place where artists came to write or paint or play, to couple or compose, a sort of inseminating seminary, not seedy in the other sense—a place where the painter can fructify the poet, and the poet fecundate the pianist; and if they do it literally as well as metaphorically, good luck to them. God bless their loving hearts, hearts and other parts. Amen. A permanent party for all parts is how I see it. Of course it will cost a packet to run; but I don't see any difficulty there. American firms with which I have contacts will do a package deal. Dough boys for dodges, delicious as well as dubious. Ars gratia, and gratis we can add for those who dislike the country. But arson, definitely, is out."

"I cannot follow a word your husband is saying." Elizabeth was the first to speak.

"It sounds very interesting," Miss Beddington added, quickly and unconvincingly.

"I don't know what the bawdy house in front will be like, but I don't think Sir Julian will fancy the factory at the back," said the Count.

He had been upset by the cool reception of his stud scheme, and seemed glad of an opportunity to attack a rival proposition. Bernard Coppinger turned his right profile towards the band and shook back his locks again. His wife's smile had eclipsed her face, and stretching far beyond its fleshly boundaries, seemed to spread across the room.

"A factory would give employment on the Mile," he continued. "It would need to be something not requiring great machinery, pumps, fires, or containers—a cottage industry on a large scale, a mansionic lodge. I like the image, what think you?—a mansionic lodge?"

"Are you addressing yourself to me?" the Count enquired.

Bernard Coppinger smiled assent. His smile suggested the chocolate that is made for diabetics. The Count loomed enormous.

"Mount Lambert is a noble house in which noble people should live. It was designed at a time when people's thoughts were in a classic mould. Your suggestion revolts me to the depths of my soul."

"Major Paul doesn't like the idea apparently." Bernard smiled, and turned his face eastward as if inspiration might be expected from that quarter. "What think you?" he said to Ralph.

"I work for Sir Julian's solicitor, Mr Fox. I can't very well discuss any plan for Mount Lambert," he said at length.

The Count nodded his head gravely and sadly.

"O Ralph! Ralph! What a servile condition to be in. The fate of a family in the balance and you must be asked to be excused from giving your opinion! Liz, my dear, how can you sit here and listen to these plans to bring Woolworth's into Arcadia without tearing his hair out in handfuls, if it is his hair?"

"What did you say?"

The gentle blue of the Coppinger eyes had steeled over in the sudden grip of frost.

"Your hair is so charming, I wondered if it was part of your costume or a mere growth like my own."

Miss Beddington could always be counted upon to intervene at moments like this.

"What plans had you for the grounds, Mr Coppinger? I prefer them to the house myself; the house is just a little severe; but the lawn at Mount Lambert—that view of the mountain, and the woods, the walks by the river—there is nothing more beautiful in the county."

"I so agree." Bernard Coppinger put his hands together in the attitude of prayer, and stretched them towards her as if contemplating a header into her lap. "The grounds are so perfect. I walked them with the steward yesterday, Mr

175

Bradshaw, a rugged type, but vastly amusing. At first he regarded me as a natural enemy, and I had to hear all the disadvantages of the house, the leaks, the draughts, the smells, the losses—the lot. Then I said to him, 'Mr Bradshaw, I can see you want to get me a bargain. I shall be careful to offer a very low price. No architect or engineer that I had to pay would ever render me the service you have done.'"

"The scoundrel. I knew he was a scoundrel," Ralph blurted out.

"I don't think so—a dreamer. A man who is disenchanted with his surroundings and impatient with the slow grinding of the mills. I told him my plan; and it was extraordinary how his attitude changed. He became really enthusiastic about the idea of the factory. Apparently he has business interests of his own, and he was anxious to come in on any scheme of a commercial nature. I suggested that we form a company. I shall make my contribution, he is looking into figures; but he hinted that he could invest up to £10,000."

"Bradshaw!"

"You underrate this man."

"I don't underrate him. I want to know where he got all that money."

"Legitimately. By trade. He has two shops in Bray and one nearer to Dublin."

"But he is for ever complaining that he can't live on the salary he gets as steward."

"Neither can he. His sons, apparently, carry on these businesses. He keeps an eye on them. A remarkable man. If only we could inject Belfast people with something to cure them of their accents, we would cherish them. I was hearing so often about 'a grand wee man' and 'a fine wee house' and 'a great wee plan'—at length I had to protest. 'Wee' is a word that I thought I had left behind in the nursery. Whenever he used it I repeated what he said and substituted the adult equivalent. But he stuck to his wee."

"Barbara, this is no place for us. Shall we dance?"

Miss Beddington almost leaped at the Count's invitation. They left the table.

"Don't speak, my dear. Let us close our eyes and drift away. I cannot believe that apparition is real or that we have been listening to a human voice. I am glad the Canon was not here to suffer with us. We must break it to him very gently."

Miss Beddington would have closed her eyes in any case. This was an old-fashioned waltz, and the Count was in his element. How firmly he held her, how decisively he led her through the swirl and sway, turning and tacking; it was like sailing with the breeze over a summer sea; it was like floating on a cloud down the milky way; it was very like a dream, and for nothing would she open her eyes for fear she should wake up.

Bernard Coppinger was talking on in precise and punctuated sentences, decorated with ingenious puns and playful paradoxes—all issuing from the ice box of his imagination previously prepared and ready for display. Mrs Coppinger, with only two to warm, concentrated her beam on them. It was so closely co-ordinated with her husband's flow that it would seem that both were worked off the same battery. But Ralph and Elizabeth had turned away from the glow and were oblivious to the pellucid stream of chat, only a trickle passed through their consciousness. They were watching the dancers on the floor.

Ralph, marvelling at Miss Beddington's entranced expression, wondered if a woman dancing with him would ever look like that. On the Count's pillow, her face could not have worn an expression of greater ecstasy. As for him, he exuded the same confidence as when he danced with Elizabeth; but his bearing subtly suggested the difference between his rôles. Miss Beddington wanted one sort of man, Elizabeth another : the Count supplied both. It wasn't fair; it wasn't fair, Ralph's soul cried out.

His hand reached out and met Elizabeth's under the

table. She gave it a reassuring squeeze, as if she entered into his thoughts.

"I never realised that Barbara was a beauty." She sounded as generous as Barbara when she had watched her playing up to the Count. Ralph turned to reply; but Elizabeth was far away again; and her face, he noticed, with the exquisite precision of pain, had almost an identical expression to that which Miss Beddington's wore when she was doting on the Count. But there was a trace of tears in Elizabeth's eyes; Barbara had been resigned. Ralph dropped the hand that lay lifeless in his.

"So," said Bernard Coppinger. He had come to an end, unaware, perhaps indifferent, that his hearers were not with him—he addressed himself primarily to himself, and regarded anyone who happened to be present as a studio audience.

Bernard Coppinger's close of play, unlike his performance, arrested the attention of Ralph and Elizabeth, lost in their intense and private world. The music stopped at the same time; but the Count and Miss Beddington did not return to the table. On Ralph and Elizabeth was laid the duty of smoking out these intruders on their party.

"And the grounds—what did you say your plan was for the grounds?" Elizabeth asked, as one who had dozed off and was struggling to re-connect with reality.

"Fashion displays, farrangos, fan dances and funiculars."

"Why funiculars?" said Elizabeth, looking in every direction to see where the Count had gone.

"The higher the fewer."

It was, as his wife signalled by rising to it, Coppinger's exit line.

She blew kisses and waved as her smile gradually withdrew and was submerged in the couples who were walking across the dance floor. Coppinger had his own gesture of farewell. It suggested an ice skater, his act over, sliding towards the wings to the applause of discriminating enthusiasts. There was more than a touch of the artist confident of having attained a self-ordained standard of absolute perfection.

"Is it safe to return?"

The Count crept out of the shadows; Miss Beddington, as on tip-toe, following. With a series of discreet gestures, she suggested that Elizabeth should retire with her and leave the men for the moment.

"We are off to the loo," Elizabeth explained.

Ralph, not too happy to be left alone with the Count, suggested a similar expedition; but the Count had a way of not falling in with other people's proposals.

"I will order us some wine," he said. "Hurry back."

When he returned the Count was still on his own, a bottle of champagne sat in a bucket beside him and he appeared to be so lost in thought that he took a moment to recognise Ralph's return. Even then his ebullience had gone. He looked morose. Ralph made furtive glances behind him, hoping to see the womenfolk. Characteristically, the Count, who seemed almost unaware of his presence, caught him out.

"They won't come back for years. I know more about women than most men, but I have never discovered what they *do* on these occasions or why it takes so long to *do* it. Some day I shall follow and find out."

"I think they take the opportunity to compare notes."

"Do you? Well, if they do, you won't come out of it with top marks. Why do you sit with pretty women looking as if you had had a pre-view of eternal damnation? Barbara went to a lot of trouble this evening; but you had to act like a death's head at the feast. Why should they tolerate it? I have no use for soulfulness with a dreary face; and no woman worth knowing likes it either. If you can make women laugh you are half way home with them. Every man is prepared to lay his soul bare for them; and very dingy it looks as a rule."

"I am damned well going to look any way I like. Why should you lecture me on my appearance?"

"Why, indeed? You have not shown yourself to be such a loyal friend to me. Eh? But I see that you are besotten with Elizabeth and I am fool enough to pity you for not having the gumption to get her."

"Little chance you've given me. You monopolise every moment of her time."

"And what do you do? Sit and sulk? That won't win her. All the young men I meet nowadays are the same. They either treat women as if they were ninepins to be knocked down by a casual throw or they get weak at the knees and make burnt offerings of themselves. Women are like horses. I've lived with both all my life. They know instinctively who believes in himself and they accept his mastery; but a funk throws them back on themselves, and they want to be—ridden, I was going to say. That follows in its own place, but before that they want to be mastered; and that will always be true so long as women are women and men are men. I admit there are signs that their rôles may be reversed.

"I learned the secret when I was a very young officer, waiting to go into the ring at a horse-jumping competition. I was standing beside the Colonel's wife; and a voice inside me said you can have her for the taking. I went in and won at the jumping—I could ride in those days—and I collected the Colonel's wife before the week was over. It meant a change of regiment; but I never thought the price too high. If you understand women the mistress is as easy to get as the maid, the duchess as the milliner."

"If it's only seduction one's after, a Don Juan career—"

"Don't be a prig. The principle holds. Do you think you don't have to recommend yourself to any woman you want to impress? Why should Elizabeth go digging for gold when you show her a face of lead?"

"I still maintain that the love that leads to marriage is not like handling a horse."

"Love is a passion, my friend. Marriage is a contract. I am not talking of marriage. If you make yourself indispensable to a woman she will marry you or live with you or do whatever pleases you. If I were a young man I would pursue Elizabeth to the ends of the earth; but if you talk to me of marriage, that over-blown rose grafted on the pansy who was boring us all just now would probably make a far better wife than Elizabeth. Can you see her with five brats squealing round her knees, basting the beef for her husband's dinner, or smiling at a captive audience while he unrolled his wretched rigmarole? I can't. The room is full of hefty wenches who will make admirable wives; and if you conduct yourself circumspectly some of them would marry you. But I thought we were talking of something else."

"Who said I was in love with Elizabeth, anyhow?"

"My dear boy! Don't be disingenuous. You have that starved appearance, and your sulks can only be attributed to one cause. You give yourself away every moment."

"If I am, and I haven't said I am, and if you want to help me, why do you take up all Elizabeth's time?"

The Count took Ralph's shoulder and shook it fiercely.

"Take her away from me. Take her. Take her. I am old enough to be her father. Were I in your shoes—not a bad-looking fellow—I would not have needed to be told this. For God's sake, Ralph, prove yourself a man."

"Now that is exactly what we want," Elizabeth said, leaning over the Count's shoulder to grab a glass. "We met Mrs Coppinger again; she says you are a poppet. Isn't that very sweet of her when you were so bloody rude to that weirdy husband of hers? I said he was a dote and I had a hunch that he had designed her dress. She said he had, and that I must be awfully clever to divine the artist in him. She is going to ask him to design a dress for me. Now you see that I haven't been letting the grass grow under my feet. Shake off the gloom and come and dance with me, Ralph. We shall only be young once."

CHAPTER XI

"MICHAEL WANTS TO see you, Elizabeth. He seems to be very excited about something."

Mrs Ormsby had made one of her lightning raids on her husband's study. Since Elizabeth's arrival, his mysterious morning tasks had been virtually abandoned; and on most days after breakfast, he entertained Elizabeth in the study until the telephone rang, usually to convey an invitation of one kind or other.

This morning Elizabeth was telling the Canon about the Coppingers. He had taken the news badly.

"It is all worse than I feared. I tried to be charitable; I even pooh-poohed the alarmist talk about the changes they were making in Cambridge, but I never suspected that he could be in league with Bradshaw. What can we do? Elizabeth, you must act. Have you seen Mr Fox yet? You know you promised to make an appointment. He must have a great deal to discuss with you as you come of age in October."

"The Coppingers are not so bad. He is a sort of re-inforced pansy, if you know what I mean; he's awfully cold and self-centred and I'd say pretty keen where business was concerned. He may be arty; but I'd be surprised if he didn't make art pay. It took a nerve for a complete stranger to ask Pa for the loan of Mount Lambert, didn't it?"

"From what you tell me, my dear, I think it is very fortunate your father had the good sense to refuse. He might never have got it back."

"At the same time I don't think Pa would refuse if he put up enough money to buy the place. It might be quite feas-ible to live in the front and tin beans or whatever at the back. It's done abroad. It makes more sense than poor Ritzy's stud farm."

"You don't believe in that."

"How could I? Ritzy to my certain knowledge has ruined at least two families whom he persuaded to make over their properties to him for grandiose schemes. He has no idea about money except to get it and to spend it. Between our two selves, Uncle Silverpenny, I'm worried about his ball. It's going to cost a packet. Where's he going to get the lolly from?"

There was nothing the Canon disliked more than minutiae of this kind. When people started to ask questions like that, life became petty and sordid. Look at his own plans for a ball; ruined by calculations suitable only to an actuary's office.

"We don't know about the Major's finances. He may be in funds at the moment. He keeps up quite a magnificent establishment."

"I know; but on what? If you ask me, Ritzy is sitting on a landmine at present. I want to help him; but I don't think the stud-farm is the answer. What I would like to do is to get Mr Fox to go into this Coppinger scheme and see if we could fix Ritzy up in some way. He might be able to keep a few animals in the grounds and take a place on the board of directors. Wouldn't he be impressive?"

The Canon went to the window and looked out at the mountain. The woods in the middle distance belonged to Mount Lambert, the farthest limit of the property. The house, in the trees, to the right, was out of view. His heart was heavy. Elizabeth, without knowing it, was cutting away the line that held him to life. The Lambert Mile had weathered every storm. Like Bruges, thanks to the accidental silting up of the river mouth, it had been cut off from the battles fought and lost on its frontiers. It might be a thousand miles away from Ireland. Now the heir of the Lamberts, the living promise of the future, without any sense of what she was destroying, talked blithely of the destruction of what he had devoted his whole life to preserve. For whom? That was the question. If for Elizabeth, the labour was in vain. Her parents were indifferent. For himself? Surely not. Surely there was more than self-interest behind his ceaseless struggle to preserve the spirit of the past, to resist the enemy at the gate?

Elizabeth sensed his sorrow. Her quickness to catch moods was the sweetest part of her character. She put her arm around his shoulders and shared his contemplation of the view.

"I love the mountain," she said. "Wouldn't it be awful if anyone were to build on it or cut down those trees. They might. They could. But we could prevent it if we woke up."

"Woke up, my dear? Woke up?"

"Yes. Did you ever see *The Cherry Orchard*?"

"Tchekov, you mean?"

"Yes. Don't you remember how the Countess—what was her name?—and her brother just sat there and refused to face the fact that the Cherry Orchard would have to go if they didn't make an effort. The factor, or whoever he was, wanted them to build villas—make a Mile in fact—but they wouldn't listen. In the end, the Cherry Orchard was cut down. I don't want to be like the Russian countess. I've been thinking a lot about this. That Bradshaw man must have his eye on the place like—O what *was* his name?—and if we don't wake up, he will buy it. Pa will sell to him. He is really keen to get rid of it."

The Canon had always been curious about the exact legal position regarding Mount Lambert. He could have asked Ralph, but having pretended to know all Lambert lore, it was a surrender of sovereignty to admit to his son that he hadn't really the least idea how matters stood.

The opportunity had come at last.

"But can he? Aren't there trustees? Where do you come in?"

"The trustees can sell if it is good business and Pa wants them to. I haven't got a say in it. I think there is a plan to

184

break the settlement when I'm twenty-one. Mr Fox is to explain that to me. Pa is very vague. He's not awfully straight, you know, where business is concerned."

"You mustn't say that."

"I wouldn't say it to anyone else, but really he isn't. The Lamberts are always either bad or mean. Pa's father was bad; he is mean. I suppose I'm destined to be bad. It is nicer than being mean, don't you think, if you had to choose?"

The Canon was saved from having to answer this by his wife's appearance in the doorway.

"I had better go and see what Michael wants. I have seen very little of him these holidays," Elizabeth said. Ritzy had been taking up so much of her time that she had neglected almost everyone. Tonight was the Perrys' party, to which she had gathered she should not look forward. That would start off other distractions, and she was glad to take this opportunity for a talk with Michael. Rather an ordeal always because he was so concerned, so devoted, and so inarticulate.

He was waiting outside the hall door, agitated, embarrassed and pleased—full of good-natured importance.

"Hallo there," Elizabeth said from the top of the steps. "I hear you want to see me about something, and I want to see you, we haven't had a proper chat since I came, and you must take me over the house. You are my agent, you know."

Michael gibbered for a few moments before he gained control of his speech.

"There's something there I want to show you," he said at length.

"Wait two ticks and I'll put on a stronger pair of shoes."

Michael would bring her by one of the innumerable short cuts which involved a certain amount of trespassing, wall-climbing, ditch-hopping and bush-beating; but it avoided the walk along the Mile and the long avenue up to Mount Lambert.

185

Michael led the way across the back of Miss Beddington's grounds and then through a dried-up stream at the foot of Clarence's garden into the Sussex wood; from there stepping-stones across the river—very low just now—and a clamber up the bank led them into the grounds of Mount Lambert where they traversed a broken section of the wall. They crossed the back avenue and a field before they came to a path leading into the trees. To the left was Bradshaw's house, to the right the deserted cottage.

Elizabeth had no idea what Michael was planning for her. The path brought back nostalgic memories of earlier holidays, and when she saw the slated roof of the cottage she remembered it as the place where she had trysts with Ralph three years ago.

"Michael, this is marvellous. Did you do it all yourself? What are you going to use it for?"

Michael, fluttering like a bird after a shower, was feeling in his pocket. A key was produced, and with the excitement of a child giving a present he watched Elizabeth's face when he opened the door and invited her to look in. The panelling had been completed. A hideous piece of linoleum covered the floor, a table in the middle of the principal room was laid out with a miniature tea-set. There were three lodging-house chairs with prim backs standing round the table, and over the fireplace hung the miniature. To add to the general effect, curtains of butter muslin were hung on the newly-glazed windows, and some wild flowers wilted in a jam pot on the kitchen dresser.

"It's for you, miss. It's yours. I saw how you used to come here and I said to myself that when you came back I'd have it ship-shape for you."

"It isn't mine, Michael. You were perfectly sweet: but don't you see I just found it when I was playing here as a child with, with—the others. You know the way children like to play house."

"It's yours, miss. Won't it all be yours some day? I will write and tell Sir Julian I did it up for you. That Bradshaw would like to get his hands on it, I'm sure. I seen him poking round, wondering what I was up to; but I never pay any heed to him. I only answer to one of the family or Mr Fox or the Canon."

"Do write, Michael. I shall write too and say what a marvellous job you've made of it. I must come and stay here. There's no bed, I suppose."

Michael blushed deeply, but whether at the idea of a bed or at his failure to supply one, she couldn't be sure. To put him at his ease, she went to the fireplace and examined the miniature.

"Do you like that, miss?"

"It's very nice, indeed. Who is it? It has quite a look of Pa, but he never wore a uniform."

"It must be his daddy, your grandfather. He was killed in the First War. You do like it?"

Elizabeth could not honestly say that it had more than a mild family interest for her, but she played up.

"I think it is absolutely beautiful and so interesting. I never saw a photograph of my grandfather at that age."

"Well I'll give it to you, miss. I found it at the lodge after me mammy died (R.I.P.) and I thought it would look nice here. I'm glad you like it."

"I have a funny feeling that I have seen it before. It's familiar in some way. It reminds me of some other picture. I must say you are awfully kind. But you must use the place when I'm not here? I mean it would seem rather hoggish of me to keep it when I'm away for so much of the time."

Michael shook his head firmly.

"It's for you, and nobody else. Look-at." He showed her how he had mended the shutters so that the house could be properly sealed up.

"If you leave me a key I can come and light fires in it," he said.

"We must have a tea-party here some day. You and me and the Ormsbys and Miss Beddington. No one else. We are the salt of the earth, Michael, aren't we? Don't you feel it?

187

Perhaps Major Paul could come too. What do you say? although I think of him as one of my friends abroad, not here. He isn't part of Mount Lambert as we are."

"The Major is a nice gentleman. I think he has his eye on the place but. I seen him walking the fields and measuring."

"He wants us to make a stud-farm here and put him in charge of it. What do you think of that? You could look after the garden then and Bradshaw could go off and attend to all his other businesses."

Michael's face lit up at this.

"If Sir Julian and the family were still in it, that would be a great thing. I wouldn't like to see the place given over to the Major entirely. He's the sort of man would be here today and gone tomorrow. It wouldn't do."

"Well, that's a bargain then. Shake hands on it."

Shyly Michael put his hand out. It was red and so calloused that it had lost whatever shape it originally had; but as a horny palm closed on Elizabeth's little one, he looked up. It was the first time that she had ever looked Michael in the eyes; he habitually hung his head.

"My God!"

Michael looked as if he was going to cry.

"You reminded me of someone else," she explained. "I thought for a moment I had seen a ghost."

A look of relief came at once into his face. He thought that she had been upset by something he had done.

"Them's the very words old Mrs Nugent used one time when she was visiting me mammy (R.I.P.). I was sitting in the corner of the kitchen, and it was winter time. I got up to tend the lamp and when she saw my face Mrs Nugent let a yell out of her, just like you did then. She said I had a great look of the Lamberts; but I don't think she was ever quite right in the head. It was a fancy that took her."

"Very probably."

Elizabeth was embarrassed by the conversation, and she

188

turned it off by suggesting that they should go up and inspect Mount Lambert.

"Bradshaw keeps the keys. He wouldn't care for the likes of me to be getting in."

"You will get in if I want you to get in. Come along."

Bradshaw was out; but his wife, after a feeble greeting to Elizabeth and an uneasy look at Michael, found the keys.

"I will leave them back," Elizabeth promised.

The way to the house led sideways from Bradshaw's lodge, skirting the walled garden, by a path known as the Yew Walk. They passed the elm planted by Mr Gladstone when he paid a visit, and went round to the back of the house to get in. The front door was double-locked and chained.

The kitchen had not been altered much in a hundred years, the passages smelt of resin. Elizabeth pushed a door covered with green baize and they found themselves under the great staircase.

It made a curve under a fine Venetian window at the back of the hall, on each side of which stood Corinthian columns.

"Won't it be a marvellous place for a ball?" Elizabeth said.

She wandered through the drawing-rooms. They looked across a lawn at the mountain view which the Ormsbys had from the back of Cumberland Lodge. On the other side of the house there was a library, the shelves with busts of the great Greeks on top of them were still there; but the books had been sold by Julian. Behind the library, the dining-room looked out on the woods. Behind that again a billiard-room had been constructed in the manner of a Gothic hall, an excrescence reflecting the taste of those Lamberts for whom Gladstone had planted the elm.

They went upstairs to the bedrooms, the principal room had still its four-poster bed, which nobody had the temerity to buy.

"I wonder how many Lamberts began and ended their

lives in that," Elizabeth said, but regretted it at once when she saw Michael shivering with embarrassment. They looked at five bedrooms and one rather dreary little bathroom, added as a concession to the modern taste for plumbing when Julian was a child. Upstairs the house was divided into two enormous nurseries.

"No Lambert ever had more than two children. They must have found it lonely up here," Elizabeth said. "But they had plenty of space for exercise. No wonder they ran wild." Michael said nothing, only screwed his hands together.

"I wonder how the Major is going to cope with his guests," she said as they were going downstairs. "It's like a barrack upstairs. Everyone will be making for the four-poster bed. He will have to install some furniture. Wasn't it awful of Pa to sell up, and at the worst possible time, too? Lovely things sold for a song."

She was talking to herself. Michael, however, in his own way had obviously had a red-letter day. He insisted on going back to Cumberland with Elizabeth, and when she thanked him for the hundredth time for all he had done to the cottage, his face, growing redder with every word, threatened to explode with suppressed emotion.

"You like it?" he kept on demanding, "you like it?" She wondered desperately what to give him; any reward that was in money or its equivalent would have hurt him beyond all telling. Suddenly she thought of something—a photograph of her parents and herself taken by some very famous press photographer on a visit to Majorca. She felt quite regal when she wrote "For Michael, with grateful thanks, Elizabeth" across the corner as she knew it was done in the circles where photographs are given away to admirers.

Michael's pleasure knew no bounds. When he went so far as to go in to show it to Angela—an unprecedented step for him—he was clearly beside himself.

CHAPTER XII

THE ORMSBYS WERE dreading the Perrys' party,
but the Canon forbade the family to say so. Ralph had
refused so many invitations that he had been dropped of
late; but on this occasion—the Mile's Elizabethan age—
bygones were magnanimously overlooked, and Ralph was
included.

Miss Beddington who shared the Ormsbys' antipathy to
the Perry style always went with them. She came in from
next door through a friendly gate that long association between the occupants of Cumberland and Clarence had
established. As it was a fine evening—what weather Elizabeth was having!—they walked along the road to Sussex.

A boy suffering from adenoids had been employed to take
charge of cars for the evening, a task which, judging by the
confusion over which a certain amount of bad language
could be distinctly heard, he was not discharging to general
satisfaction. Lights blazed in every window in the house—
under the Perrys' care it had become the most flashy of the
Lodges—the open hall door showed wall-to-wall carpeting
within and other indications of no expense spared.

The majority of the guests had already arrived, and a din
proceeded from the drawing-room where they were standing, talking in groups. Perry rushed forward to greet the
new arrivals with a nicely graded effusiveness that left him
something in hand to give Elizabeth a very special welcome.
No one in the room could doubt that she was the guest of
the evening.

Ralph received only token recognition, a sign that he had
not been taken back fully into favour and would have to
work his passage. Any hope that he had of sticking to Elizabeth vanished at once. "You'd think they had won you in a

raffle," he muttered gloomily as she was made the centre of a little court with the host acting as a sort of chamberlain.

The Ormsbys and Miss Beddington retreated as usual into a corner, but Ralph was seized upon by a group of Perry's friends in financial circles who were glad to see a familiar face.

Loftus, absent temporarily, made a noisy entrance with a bottle. The office of butler had fallen on him again; but as always he was making sure that nobody would be under any misapprehension about his standing by calling out, "Can't get anyone to drink up, cousin."

It was like all Perry parties; but on a larger scale; and this was of interest to the Ormsbys who kept saying to Miss Beddington, "Never saw so many unfamiliar faces. Do you see anyone you know?"

Elizabeth had now been assimilated, the Perrys continued to bring people up to meet her; but outside Mile circles she was merely an attractive-looking girl. Perry's financial friends were not impressed by her status. Not one of them was on a board that lacked a retired revolutionary, a lord, or, at a pinch, a baronet.

An observer might have noticed that Perry was showing signs of anxiety, glancing towards the door, snapping at his wife, and pointedly ignoring guests who had nothing to offer except hunger and thirst.

There were other lions, and they had not appeared, and it was getting late.

One had arrived at last; that was very apparent. Perry swooped and Mrs Perry came across the room at a canter to greet the Count. Everyone turned to look. To the men in the city he was obviously somebody—they knew the look— but who? To the Milers his coming was extremely significant; he had snubbed the Perrys so thoroughly in the past : this was a diplomatic triumph of the first water. No wonder Perry looked pleased. It was hard to believe that a few days ago he had sworn to expel from the neighbourhood the guest whom he was now embracing.

The Count, looking more than his height, wore an expression of indulgent amusement; but when his host put an arm round his shoulder to bring him into the financial circle, he extricated himself; and, making off on his own for the corner where the Ormsbys and Miss Beddington were watching the party, he kissed Miss Beddington on both cheeks.

The result was remarkable. Nobody had taken any notice of the quiet group in the corner. They looked frumpish; but now everyone was asking who the handsome woman was. The Captain, of no interest to anybody, plying the bottle, was alive to all that was happening; and this phenomenon was not lost on him. He, too, had the entrée; he was damn well going to show he had.

"Drink up. Drink up," he cried and put his short arm round Miss Beddington's waist. It seemed to be almost level with his shoulder.

"I am doing very well," she said and smiled very sweetly, but at the same time she leaned back so that the Captain's arm was pressed rather painfully against the window-frame. When she eased the pressure he was glad to extricate himself.

"What about you, Count? What are you having?" he said.

But the Count's eyes had gone black. Dropping his voice—a device which added to its emphasis—he said, "I never gave you permission to call me by that name that I can recall, did I?"

Loftus was so alarmed, he nearly dropped the tray he was carrying.

"Did I?"

"I'm sure I'm sorry. Everyone..."

"Everyone? Who is everyone? You are nobody. And may I warn you that if I catch you again putting your monkey's paw on any lady in my presence, I will thrash the life out of you."

Loftus turned puce; but words would not come. He must

either hit this brute with a bottle or go away. As nobody had heard the unpleasant and humiliating exchange, it was probably better to go away and think out a scheme of reprisal. The decision was made easier by his adversary having turned his back on him to renew his conversation with Miss Beddington.

Fighting down the urge to shout "Bankrupt. Spy. Nazi. Jew. Impostor" and all the other things that Perry had called his assailant, the Captain withdrew.

He met Perry looking anxious again, and complained about the way he had been treated.

"I've told you to keep your hands off women. They don't like being mauled," he said.

"A mere friendly gesture. I've seen you . . ."

"Loftus, do you mind, I'm rather busy. And I did hope you'd make an effort to help out. Just push the bottle round like a good fellow and don't pick quarrels with the guests. Ah!" The last exclamation greeted the arrival of the Coppingers, of no particular interest to the city end—Bernard was a familiar figure in business circles—but of overwhelming interest to the Mile. Once they had been identified—the reaction would have interested a naturalist—there was an immediate migration of all Milers to the Canon's corner. It became a Rorke's Drift, in which the beleaguered band clung together, to resist to the death.

Mrs Coppinger made a dive at Elizabeth and began to mother her in a score of little ways. Bernard Coppinger paused as an experienced actor will to add emphasis to his entry. Then he descended on the city group, picking out one of their number as a mark, and began a long and complicated monologue which he preceded with the question, "Has it ever occurred to you that if income tax were to be based on the payer's personal appearance it would yield more and present none of the difficulties of collection that beset the present system? We would all like to prove that we had to pay on an enormous assessment if our faces were our fortunes."

The impression created was of a mechanical toy that had been wound up on the way to the party and was now released for the benefit of the guests. On and on went the dissertation between dashes of quickly drawn breath. Nobody was ever quite able to follow Bernard: the result was a strained concentration as if he had dropped something into a well and they were waiting for the splash.

Perry had champagne in the study to be produced at an appropriate moment. This was known to Loftus in his capacity as High Steward. He loved champagne. He very seldom drank any nowadays; and he knew Perry was inclined to go easy when filling his glass.

An idea occurred to him: Mrs Brown was rather isolated; her Raymond had made for the city end, recognising members of his various charitable boards; she had dithered and was now rather cut off; at that moment she was the only person in the room who would have positively welcomed the Captain's advances. She caught his eye. He winked, then nodded. She took the suggestion and came over to him at the door.

"Herbert wants us to shift the crowd a bit. Let's go into the library. There's fizz in there."

That decided her. Not so much that she wanted champagne, but where it was was a privileged quarter.

"Don't you think we should wait?"

"I'm in charge. This is Liberty Hall. Hold up your glass."

After the first bottle, the Captain realised, what had never struck him or anyone before, that Mrs Browne was a desirable woman. The leathery texture of her skin brought back the memory of nights in the tropics. Lying back in the chair her thighs had a certain magnificence, like the entrance to the War Office. If her little eyes lacked mischief, they had a rodent gleam; he watched them as if he was held up by traffic lights.

"Here. Have another swig."

He opened a second bottle. This was consumed as to

three-quarters by himself and one quarter by Mrs Browne. Neither spoke at all, and both gave the impression of drinking against the clock.

"My God, you are a lovely woman. Did anyone ever tell you so?"

"He is going to make a nuisance of himself in a minute" was Mrs Browne's answer; but she communicated it to herself.

"I wouldn't open another," was what she said to Loftus who had taken steps in that direction.

Perry entered at that moment, having been looking for his 'cousin' to order him to attend to his duties; he came in to hear Mrs Browne's remark. His inhospitable expression confirmed that he supported her view.

"Damn it all, Loftus, I think it was a bit thick to come in here and pinch all the champagne."

"Not all, Herbert. I opened a bottle for Mabel here."

"Oh, please!"

Mrs Browne, furious with the Captain for leading her into this trap, had no desire to go in any further.

"Don't you deserve a drink, just as much as any of the rest of them? We are all friends here. To hell with that bunch of pansies and pawnbrokers out there."

"You're drunk, Loftus."

"I resent that, Herbert. I resent that."

"I am very sorry about this, Herbert. I was given to understand that everyone was coming in," Mrs Browne said.

The sight of her looking so plain and the two empty bottles beside her, exasperated Perry.

"You're drunk, too," he said.

"Herbert, how could you? I shall ask Raymond to leave at once, at once."

"He is at liberty to go whenever he pleases."

Mrs Browne, in tears, marched out to seek her husband. Perry, rather sorry now, followed. The Captain put the bottles out of sight and then brought up the rear.

Raymond Browne was enjoying himself. The financial set were a group with which he was always anxious to improve acquaintance. He met some of them on his boards; and always hoped that, struck by his abilities, somebody else might someday invite him on to a board which paid its directors. Bernard Coppinger was never exuberant, but he showed all the good-will of which he was capable to this plump, little man who was such a wonderfully attentive audience.

Raymond, encouraged, seized a moment when Coppinger was thinking of something else to say to welcome him as a neighbour. At that moment Mrs Browne caught his sleeve.

"What is the matter, Mabel? Can't you leave me alone? If you don't like the party, why don't you go home? I'm enjoying myself—for once."

"Herbert has grossly insulted me."

"My God, he hasn't—"

For a wild moment Raymond wondered whether Perry had made a pass at her. He believed it to be impossible; but he was always faintly hoping that he would catch her in the wrong and acquire for nothing a permanent privilege ticket to philander without remorse.

"He said I was drunk."

"Are you? You do seem to have laid in to something."

"Certainly not. That little pig, Loftus, was throwing champagne about. Unfortunately Herbert caught us together."

"He *what*? Oh, I see. I'll have a word with Herbert. You know what he's like when he's fussy. I'm sure he never meant a thing. Keep away from Loftus. He's no use to anyone. Oh! Hell!" Looking round he saw that Coppinger had seized the opportunity to slip away.

Perry was fussing about; one anxiety followed upon another. All his lions had arrived, but they were not roaring as he had planned. He could hardly conceal his vexation with the Count for ignoring all efforts to put him into circulation and insisting on talking to Miss Beddington. It was a sort of sabotage. Efforts to mix the different elements were not wholly successful, largely because Perry didn't know any of his guests very well.

Ralph, not included in his host's deployments, was free to roam at will. He had seen Elizabeth surrounded, but this was a sort of protection against the Count, and Ralph was pleased to see the latter's preoccupation with Miss Beddington. Of course they were much more of an age than the Count and Elizabeth; it should have been natural enough, but, somehow, it was impossible to reconcile the Count's reminiscences of masked ladies and anonymous copulations with Miss Beddington's lavender and rose-water aura.

Suddenly the Count looked across the room and met Ralph's eyes. There was a challenge in his glance which as much as said 'I am giving you a chance, can you make use of it?' As if in conspiracy with that challenge, Elizabeth slipped away from Mrs Coppinger's benevolent patronage, and, as she passed Ralph, said "I am escaping."

She went into the library and out through the french window into the garden. He followed.

It was an evening of great beauty; breathless, the trees at the end of the garden were black against the star-filled sky. The scent of stock and roses filled the air. In the distance could faintly be heard the river as it tumbled over the weir. Elizabeth walked quickly, anxious to put a distance between her and the house, from which the roar of voices followed them.

The garden was on two levels: lawn with flower-beds round the house, then steps down into a fruit and vegetable garden. Behind that a field which sloped down to the river.

Elizabeth led the way to a little gate at the end of the garden."

"Your feet will get wet," Ralph said.

"Take my shoes."

Barefooted she led the way down a track in the grass that led to the stream. She said nothing to Ralph. He began to wonder if she had meant him to follow. She was unpredictable.

She continued to walk along the path until it came to the river's edge. There she jumped on a rock and stood looking, Ralph thought, like a naiad. After a while she leaped on to another stone, this time it was wide enough for two to stand on; Ralph came across and joined her.

She looked exquisite but intangible. He felt heavy and stupid, at a loss for anything to say.

She was the first to speak. "What a bloody awful lot of people!"

"The Perrys' parties are always rather ghastly."

"I'd run away if I were a man. I couldn't settle down among that crew. All they can talk about is their cars and their trips abroad."

"I don't suppose they are very different from people everywhere."

"There are so many exciting places, so much to do."

"But if you come back to Mount Lambert..."

"Oh, I couldn't for long, you know. I could never settle there."

"Everyone here hopes you will. I wish..."

"What do you wish?"

"Oh, it's no use. I'm bound hand and foot."

"I wouldn't be, if I were a man. Look at Ritzy. He moves about."

"But he is settling here."

"Ritzy. Not on your life. This is one of his schemes. They last for about two years. Ritzy will be off again on his travels as soon as he finds he can't get Mount Lambert. He's pressurising me like hell at the moment. But, of course, I can't do anything. It's up to Pa and the trustees; and they know old Ritzy too well: he is here one moment, gone the next, and then he pops up somewhere else. Always on the top of the wave, too. That's the extraordinary thing."

"He's an awful blackguard, really."

"By Lambert Mile standards. I'd prefer his standards to Perry standards or Browne standards. How can you compare them?"

"Oh, I know you find us all awfully dull, but, be fair, if I tried to behave like your friend Ritzy I'd find myself in jail."

"Stop talking about Ritzy. Leave him alone. He's not to be judged by stuffy standards. Anyone who adds so much to life is entitled to his own whack in exchange. Did you see him in that crowded room? How ineffectual he made them all look, all except Uncle Silverpenny, of course. In a perfect world Ritzy would be king and Uncle archbishop."

"No laws and no prayers. It would be an interesting experiment."

"There you go, Mr Snoot. Why can't you be mad, bad and dangerous to know? Why must you be so solid and good?"

"I'm sorry. I don't feel good in the least. I ..." But before he could describe his feelings Elizabeth had run ahead to the edge of the river and leaped from the bank on to a flat rock where she stood looking like—"Botticelli's Venus", Ralph told her.

"I'm rather over-dressed for that part. I wish you could see me as myself. You've no idea what a strain it is for a girl always to be only an idea in a man's mind."

"I thought you looked lovely."

"Thank you very much. But say that next time and don't go on about Botticelli or Rossetti or someone. That's what's such a comfort about Ritzy. He makes you feel a woman, not just a piece of china that somebody wants to kiss."

Ralph was beside her now, about to put his arms round her; but she had this way of making him feel inadequate. So he sulked instead.

Elizabeth didn't appear to notice. There was something about her which was new to him tonight, as if she was preoccupied and excited. Suddenly she turned to him with a look in her eyes that he knew well. Since their earliest days it meant only one thing. She was going to suggest something unlawful. It was always she who had taken the initiative when they got into trouble.

"Wouldn't it be fun to bathe now?"

"Here?"

"Why not?"

"Like this?"

"It's pretty dark."

It was a dare. The last of many. And she always expected him to refuse. He went to the bank and gingerly took off his clothes. When he turned round Elizabeth was standing waist-deep in the water. He clambered over the stones at the edge.

"It gets quite deep there," she said.

He slid in off the stone and began to swim towards her. They stretched out their hands to one another. He pulled her towards him, as wet and cold as a fish, and kissed her. She kissed him, laughed and slid out of his grasp.

"It's cold," she shivered. "I'm going back."

She was quicker than he at crossing the stones. He slid about and had ignominiously to crawl out on his hands and and knees. When he looked up, Bernard Coppinger was standing with his profile turned in Elizabeth's direction.

"Hello," she said. "We've been bathing. It's rather cold, though."

The Brownes who had followed Bernard now appeared on the scene. They pretended not to see and competed in describing the lie of the land to Coppinger.

"Have you a handkerchief that I could use as a towel?" Elizabeth said to the profile.

"Oh yes. By all means."

Coppinger produced a square of silk, and with her teeth chattering Elizabeth did her best to rub some of the wet off.

The Brownes continued to pretend that only they and Bernard were present.

"I've squeezed it out; but it doesn't help much, I'm afraid."

Coppinger took back the handkerchief; then he turned his profile away, as if allying himself by this gesture with the Brownes. Elizabeth and Ralph made their way back to the house.

"Bad for business," she said. "I'm sorry about that. I let you in for it. I must say it was worth anything to see the Brownes' faces. I wonder if they will cancel their tennis tournament on Saturday. I do hope so. That will be something, anyhow."

Ralph shivered, but he was unable to see anything except Elizabeth standing on the rock and the whiteness of her coming towards him in the water.

He met the Count's eyes as soon as he came back into the room. Were they curious? Or mocking? He couldn't make out.

"Before you disappear," Ralph said to Elizabeth, "will you come out for the day with me on Saturday. I'm tied up during the week."

"Saturday is the Brownes' American tournament."

"Damn the Brownes and their tournament."

"I know; but we said we'd go, unless, of course, they put us off now as unsuitable chums for Syl."

"They won't; they'll talk. That's all. Sunday then?"

"Let me think."

Was she looking across at the Count? Ralph thought so. A suicidal desire to cancel the invitation before it was refused, or left in the air to await the Count's pleasure, came up and was killed just in time.

"I think that will be fine. Where shall we go?"

"Wherever you like."

"No. No. You're the man. You must decide. I hate being asked to make suggestions about how I am to be entertained."

"I'll think of something."

The kiss in the river, the undressing and bathing naked—

it all seemed suddenly remote; of no significance, apparently, to her.

As always when he had been with Elizabeth, he was miserable; whatever self-assurance he had was undermined by her elusiveness and a sense she gave him of comparing him with someone else and finding him wanting.

CHAPTER XIII

"I'm afraid Michael won't approve of my furnishings," Elizabeth said.

The doll's house arrangements had been radically altered, a mattress covered with a rug on which there were variously coloured cushions was laid out in front of the fireplace, which Elizabeth had banked up with an armful of greenery.

The Count in whose lap her head lay looked about him.

"That miniature puzzles me," he said.

"It's my grandfather. Michael gave it to me."

"Where did he get it?"

"I think his mother had it."

"Does that suggest something to you?"

"You mean—she must have pinched it."

"No. Not at all. He gave it to her, and she put it away in some hiding place. Michael only discovered it after she died. Take it down. Do you not see a resemblance?"

"To Michael?"

"Yes. The eyes and the forehead. This is a proud young officer; Michael has gone round the world hanging his head; but dress him up and give him a few glasses of champagne, and I swear he will look very like that miniature. But don't let him come between us. Come back to me."

Elizabeth pretended not to hear.

"Now I understand. Grandfather landed Mrs Molloy with Michael. He said he was born the year Grandfather went to the war. He only got married on his last leave. Pa was a posthumous child. So Michael is my uncle. Isn't it awful?"

"You don't like to have an uncle a peasant?"

"You know I don't mean that. It's awful to think of Pa just sitting around doing nothing and my doing whatever I like really, neither of us ever lifting a finger; and all on the strength of Lambert money to which Michael is as well entitled as we are."

"There I can't agree. Bastards have never made those claims for themselves. Long ago they swarmed on an estate like this, and nobody was particularly worried about them. Think of Tolstoy; that pious old prophet. His bastard was the coachman on the estate, and drove his half-brothers and sisters whenever they went out in their droshky; and his mother used to wash their kitchen floor."

"I don't want to think about Tolstoy. I'm thinking of us. I'm going in tomorrow to see Mr Fox and I'm going to tell him that Michael is to get half my share of the estate, and I'm going to ask Pa to recognise him and let him have half his share. But Pa won't, I bet."

"Why should he? I'm sure provision was made at the time. The coachman married Michael's mother. They have had a free house, and you'll probably find that some money was paid to keep the child, to sweeten the obliging coachman who, I suppose, regarded it all as part of his duty."

"What sort of provision? Look at Michael. He wasn't trained for anything. He milks the Canon's cow, cuts wood and mooches round Mount Lambert. I wonder does he guess?"

"Possibly. And doesn't resent it in the least. But he will if you start putting ideas into his head. Come back to me. Look who I have waiting for you."

"I'm not coming near you. I just can't bear you today. You're part of the awful selfishness that has always surrounded me. You are every bit as bad as my family. My grandfather puts a girl in the soup, and my father leaves his brother in it, and we expect to be allowed to live in peace and comfort. And you think that's a fine thing; well you aren't going to wheedle me into furthering any of your plans. And that's that. And you can tell your friend so, with my warmest regards."

This spirited speech seemed to amuse the Count. He got on his feet with extraordinary agility for a heavy man and putting his arms round Elizabeth closed her mouth with a kiss. She struggled but without avail. And then, as if in a French farce, a knock sounded on the door.

Each felt the other stiffen; each held his breath; each waited for the second knock. It came. They exchanged glances. The curtains Michael had supplied were drawn, but a peeping tom would probably find an opening to pry. The Count signalled to Elizabeth to go into the small room behind the cottage fireplace. Then he went to the door, unlocked and pulled it open so fast that Bradshaw who had been looking through the key-hole had barely time to stand upright.

"What do you want?"

Bradshaw did not cower under the Count's attack. His active little eyes were taking in the scene; and he waited to answer until he had taken in as much as he could of the room when there was such a burly figure in the door-way. But the Count allowed him to see that he was, to all appearances, alone.

"I was just checking up, Major. This wee house is part of the property, you know. I'm responsible for it. Mr Fox didn't tell me he had let you have the use of it."

"Miss Lambert asked me to help her with the decoration. She is using it as a summer house."

"Mr Fox didn't tell me about that either. A great wee job you've done on the place." He stepped sideways to peer in.

"Well, I'm telling you now, and Miss Lambert will tell you."

"You're welcome fine so far as I am concerned—more than welcome; but I must take my orders from Mr Fox. Miss Lambert has no more right than yourself to take over any of the cottages."

"I shall write to Sir Julian today and let him know about this. Do you mean to say that you won't allow Miss Lambert to use this cottage without an order from Mr Fox?"

"It's not me. Miss Lambert can use the whole estate. That's fine with me, you understand. But I have my orders, and my orders are not to let anybody on to the property without a letter from Mr Fox."

"Very well. Miss Lambert is seeing Mr Fox tomorrow and she will tell him. There are other matters, too, that he will be interested to hear about the estate. I believe you are supposed to be in whole time employment. I'm interested because I expect that I shall be taking Mount Lambert over at the beginning of next year. I shall be going in to see Mr Fox one of these days. I shall want to examine the estate accounts. We will be seeing quite a lot of one another. You know that Michael Molloy rebuilt this cottage, don't you? And may I ask for whom he rebuilt it?"

"Michael is it? Poor Michael. I wouldn't be taking any notice of him if I were you."

"May I inform you that he rebuilt the cottage and furnished it for Miss Lambert. She has always used it when she was over here on holidays."

Bradshaw made no answer to this. He peered in again, then looked the Count over, and began to whistle, slightly out of tune.

"I shan't keep you. I am sure you are busy," the Count said at last.

"I'm thinking I'll have to ask you to give me the key of this wee cottage until I get word from Mr Fox. Miss Lambert may have the use of it if he says so; but not on Michael's say so: and I wouldn't be doing my duty, Major, if I let you stay here."

"Are you daring to ask me to leave?"

"I must. I don't want to lose my job."

The Count laughed at this.

"If you want to retain your job at Mount Lambert you will need to change your tune, my friend."

Bradshaw made no answer. He continued to whistle; his hat pushed back from his forehead; his attitude suggesting that he had time to kill.

"If you don't go away I shall report you to Sir Julian."

Bradshaw smiled. Once he had come across his bank manager in a country lane with his typist. It had greatly helped his over-draft problem. History was repeating itself.

"I don't like to be a tale-bearer, Bradshaw; but I'm informed by Mr Coppinger that you ran down the house to him when he came to inspect it, and then offered to put £10,000 into a company if there was a chance of buying it. I think it's my duty to let Sir Julian know the character of the man he employs as his steward."

"I've talked to Mr Fox about that. He has sent on the offer to Sir Julian and expects an answer very soon. Don't be worrying yourself about that, Major."

"I am not worrying, my friend. But you may have cause to worry very soon. I am not a vindictive man; but I can tell you nobody has made an enemy of me and has not lived to regret it. You have never lived among the Arabs, Mr Bradshaw, have you?"

"Arabs, is it?"

"What's going on?"

Elizabeth came to the door. Bradshaw made a feeble effort to salute her by pushing his hat a fraction of an inch further back off his forehead.

"Mr Bradshaw wants the key of your cottage. I was telling him I had come over to help you decorate it. He wants to turn you out."

"I didn't say a word about Miss Lambert, Major. You never let on she was here."

Elizabeth looked wonderfully imperious. "What do you mean?"

"The Major never said there was anyone inside. If he had said you were, miss, it would have been different. I'll get in touch with Mr Fox and tell him the position. I'm sure it will be all right. Why didn't you tell me herself was inside, Major?"

"Major Paul has my full permission to go anywhere he likes about the place, Bradshaw."

"Whatever you say yourself, miss. All I know is I was told not to let anyone in to the property. I can't make exceptions for any gentleman, even if he comes from the Mile, unless I get instructions."

"Well you have them now. Any of my friends are welcome to come here; and I'm not going to have them asked a lot of questions."

"Oh, they are very welcome. I didn't understand, that's all."

He gave another of his comprehensive glances round the room, smiling; then, still smiling, and whistling out of tune, he went away, but not without pushing his hat back a little further on his head in token of farewell.

"That is a devil," the Count said. "I would be very glad to put a bullet in him, but he doesn't deserve such a good, clean death."

"Did you hear what he said about Coppinger?"

"Bluff."

"I wonder. And he will make capital out of today. It won't help to further your plans when the parents hear you have seduced their daughter. Mummy *will* be pleased."

"Elizabeth. You have no delicacy."

"Oh, come away. I've got to hate this rat-trap."

She locked the door and started to walk a few paces ahead of the Count, but suddenly she stopped and said, "wait there". She went back to the cottage and returned after a second.

"What was it?"

"Nothing," she said.

"Be careful of nothing."

"Never fear."

CHAPTER XIV

W HEN R ALPH KNOCKED on Mr Fox's door there was as usual no reply. This might mean that his employer was immersed in his papers; he might equally well be doing *The Times* cross-word or carrying on a conversation in baby-talk with the sparrows, who shared his morning and afternoon refreshment. A second knock always produced a scream; so he decided on this occasion to enter unbidden. The chair at the desk was empty, nobody was talking to the sparrows at the window. Ralph did not want to be found in here—reticence was almost a mania with his employer. No one was allowed into his office, the door of which he kept locked. It was better to meet him on the landing; but just as he was shutting the door, Ralph heard a noise in the further corner of the room where law papers were piled up on a large table, stacked on chairs and lying in bundles on the floor.

Round one of these came the tonsure on Mr Fox's rather unkempt head. He was on his hands and knees.

"Can I help you, sir?"

Mr Fox did not look up.

"The mice have got out. Someone must have gone to the cupboard. The door of the cage is open. You look over there. They may be hiding behind the encyclopedias."

Ralph went to the far corner of the room where the over-flow of the book case formed a barricade behind which bundles in red and green tape lay in profusion. A colony of mice could hide here in perfect safety. With no great enthusiasm he started to poke the bundle.

The very shiny seat of Mr Fox's trousers disappeared into the bundles in the corner under his personal investigation.

Ralph lifted up the papers as if they were sheaves of

wheat, but his methods were not approved. Mr Fox wailed at him : "Don't do that. Don't do that. You are putting the papers out of order. I shall never be able to find anything now. You are not looking. We have got to find the mice. They'll eat up the papers if they are left loose."

"Why not get a cat? The housekeeper has one."

"They are my pet mice—Sadlier and Keogh—I wouldn't let any harm come to them. I do wish you would try to help."

'Bloody old fool' was Ralph's unspoken comment; but he knelt down in the dust and prowled through the bundles. From time to time Mr Fox called on his pet mice by name. Sometimes he groaned. Coming round a pile of steel boxes on his hands and knees, going at a fair pace, he met Ralph head-on. The knock hurt; but Ralph's being the larger and harder head, it disabled Mr Fox. He sat down, holding his head, looking like Blake's drawing of Job.

"I'm awfully sorry, sir."

Ralph went over to the basin behind the screen, dipped the towel in cold water and applied it to Mr Fox's forehead. The injured man moaned; a single sound managed to convey both the extent of his physical affliction, his plight at the loss of his mice, and his despair at his assistant's bungling incompetence. A slight variation in tone indicated an addition to the message. Ralph looked around, straining to keep pace with the demand on his intelligence. He saw nothing but he heard quite distinctly a rustling sound.

"There. Over there," Mr Fox whispered. "They are in Haughey v. Colley."

Ralph had no idea where the papers in this case lay but he had heard the rustle and he crept across the room in that direction.

A weighty bundle tied up in green tape was labelled 'In re Lynch, Haughey v. Colley'. The papers were rather loose as if they had been put together in a hurry, and Ralph saw a pair of pink eyes looking at him out of the end of a brief. The eyes withdrew at once; but he leaped on the bundle

and carried it over to the open cupboard, in which he saw a
mouse cage, musical instruments, a tailor's dummy, a battle
helmet, a court sword and two flags.

"Well done! Well done!"

Mr Fox had forgotten his injuries. His pale eyes glowed
with pure pleasure.

Ralph shook the bundle and two mice slid out into the
cupboard where Mr Fox's fluttering fingers grasped them.

"Naughty fellows. Naughty, naughty fellows. Naughty
Sadlier, naughty Keogh," he said.

Gently he returned them to their cage and then put in
cheese. Then he shut up the cupboard and returned to his
desk. Ralph noticed a gradual swelling on the top of his
forehead; but he seemed to have forgotten this; he also
seemed to have forgotten his good humour.

Melancholy once again claimed him for her own. Dejection hung about him like wet garments.

"Major Paul has been here," he said. "I believe you
know the gentleman."

"He lives on the Mile. He and my father are friends."

"I want to put you on your guard. I am afraid Major
Paul has over-reached himself, and I can't see how he can
survive for very much longer. The position is embarrassing.
He bought an Alfa Romeo from Mr Bechstein, a client of
mine, and he hasn't paid a penny of what he owes for it. I
have checked, and so far as I can discover, he owes at present at least forty thousand pounds to various creditors. I
think I am in duty bound to inform Sir Julian, although
Lady Lambert was the active party in making the arrangements. I wonder if you would tactfully convey to your
father what the position is. I am very much concerned
about the proposed ball at Mount Lambert. It will certainly
be followed by law actions for payment of the caterers, the
band and anyone else who is employed. I don't think the
Lamberts will like this. In fact I expect I shall be told to
withdraw permission for the use of the house."

Ralph said nothing. As always his sympathies went over

to the Count when he was on the run. He was also thinking of the reaction of the Mile to the news. It would be the end of the Count. His pride could not stand it.

"Couldn't the Lamberts put up the money? The dance is for Elizabeth. It seems rather hard on the Count—Major Paul, I mean—that he should be ruined over it."

"The Lamberts must be the best judges of what they should do for their daughter. They know her better than we do. She is coming in to see me this afternoon, and I want to hear from you before I talk to her how much she knows about the Major."

"Everything, I expect."

What Mr Fox understood by 'everything', he did not elucidate, nor did he ask Ralph to. It was part of his technique not to appear to need information; to ask for it implied someone else had knowledge he was without; and like most influential people he had learnt that information came unsought from less secure individuals seeking to make themselves important.

Now came that awkward moment in all interviews with Mr Fox. Ralph never knew how to say 'good-bye'. He was undecided whether to excuse himself and, perhaps, be snubbed, or wait on to see if there was more to discuss. The risk in doing that was to be dismissed with contumely. And it was even so. A telephone call produced a series of wails, one of which was not aimed at the receiver, but at Ralph.

"Can't you see I have work to do?"

When he got back to his room he found that his knees were covered with dust, his face and hands were filthy. No wonder Mr Fox looked so grubby. How much of the time, behind the locked door, did he spend on his hands and knees?

His agonised shrieks on the telephone were occasioned by the information that Mr Redwood Bradshaw wanted to see him. In the ordinary course he would have refused a demand for immediate access to his presence; but today there was something providential about the visit. Bradshaw was certain to add to his stock of information; it might help him when he was talking to Elizabeth, it would certainly add to the dossier on Major Paul. Mr Fox screamed because Mr Bradshaw's descent on him was symptomatic of the way in which the world oppressed him with its cares. Why could nobody solve their own problems? Why lay the whole burden on him? But he was even more upset when he heard of people consulting other lawyers. There was no peace on earth for him; and so he wailed—not wishing to confide in anyone—at his condition.

Mr Fox had shrouded his office in awe. Even clients were inclined to drop their voices when they entered the portals. Typists lost colour when summoned to his room from which proceeded a baa, not unlike a sheep's, whenever his cryptic orders were not at once translated into action.

All this was lost on Mr Redwood Bradshaw who did not absorb atmospheres in spite of his urge to play different rôles in different places. Impervious to the encircling gloom he took on the character of a good fellow here as much as in any other of his ports of call.

The young lady at the reception desk did not allow Bradshaw's 'Is he in?' to interrupt a minute of her nail varnishing. The tone of the question was wrong and the visitor would have to rephrase it before she was going to condescend to reply.

"Is the old man in?"

For emphasis he jerked his head towards the ceiling.

"Who do you want to see, please?"

Her grammar had not been brought to the same perfection as her nails, but her dignity was overpowering. Bradshaw was not to be impressed by refinements of speech or manner.

"I want to see the boss."

"Is it Mr Fox?"

He winked. She had a large bosom. He liked that.

"Have you an appointment?"

He looked genuinely surprised. He had never made an

appointment in his life. If he wanted something for nothing he was prepared to wait; if he came on someone's else's business—as on this occasion—he did not stand on ceremony.

"Tell him Mr Bradshaw of Mount Lambert wants to see him."

The word Lambert did the trick; a call was put through to Mr Fox's secretary (the only person who had the courage to interrupt him) to say that Mr Bradshaw was asking for an audience.

The baa that sounded over the house telephone amused Bradshaw very much. He invited the receptionist to share his glee with a double wink, one aimed at the ceiling, the other at her bosom, which prevented him from seeing her expression of disdain.

"Will you take a seat, please."

"I haven't time, love. Tell him if he can't see me, I'll write to Sir Julian."

Once again he had dropped a name at the right moment; Mr Fox was interrupted again and the proud girl, to her surprise, after a long baa, was told to send Mr Bradshaw up.

"Mr Fox will see you in a moment," she said severely. "Please sit down."

Bradshaw ignored the invitation; his hat firmly on his head, whistling out of tune, he walked up and down taking note of whatever was to be seen, the names of clients on steel boxes, addresses on envelopes, as well as gleaning such facts as are displayed on trade calendars.

It was a war of nerves; and the clerk was the first to capitulate. Bradshaw was told to go up when he produced a pen-knife and started to pare his nails to the tune of 'The Protestant Boys'.

Ralph was still overawed by the business of knocking and entering his chief's domain; Bradshaw had no inhibitions, he opened the door and walked in, ignoring the shocked and disapproving stare that greeted his entry. Neither did he wait to be invited to sit down, nor did he remove his hat.

"There's a hanger on the door if you would care to take your hat off."

"I only dropped in for a moment. It will do where it is."

Mr Fox's habitual expression was one of grief; but now he flushed with anger.

None of this was wasted on Bradshaw, who aimed under the skin when dealing with social superiors.

Settled in his chair, he said, "How's tricks?"

Mr Fox refused to say, and continued to look angry. Bradshaw decided to get down to business. "A few things I wanted to be clear about. First, this dance. I'm not going to be responsible for getting the house ready. Second, I don't think the floors are safe; but, maybe, that is not my business. Third, what about this cottage that Miss Lambert and the Count are staying in? Is it all right to leave them a key?"

"What cottage? What are you talking about? Who is the Count?"

Rage and curiosity informed Mr Fox's manner, the latter having slightly the edge on the first.

"The Count is what they all call Major Paul."

"You said he was living in a cottage with Miss Lambert. Miss Lambert is staying with Canon Ormsby."

"So she may say; but I'm telling you what I've seen with my own eyes. I noticed that Michael Molloy was doing the wee cottage up. I didn't interfere. Michael is a law unto himself and I supposed he had your permission. Then one night I came across himself and the Count looking over the cottage. I said to myself, 'Watch this, Bradshaw'. The Count has been sniffing round the place ever since he came to live on the Mile. I know he wants to take it over; but where the money is to come from is another question."

"I don't want to discuss Major Paul's private affairs with anybody."

216

"Quite right. You have enough on your plate as it is, I daresay; but how you manage to get anything done with all this jumble of papers is a mystery to me."

"I don't want any impertinence."

"I was just wondering how you managed, that's all. No offence."

To show his independence Mr Bradshaw looked around him with an air of comprehensive appraisal, whistling as he did so.

"I want to know on what you base the very serious statement that Major Paul and Miss Lambert are sharing a cottage."

"I suppose that is what you would call Major Paul's private affairs."

"I am not concerned with the Major, but Miss Lambert is very much my concern."

Bradshaw seemed to brood over this before admitting its justice, then he said.

"I was looking round the place yesterday and I noticed something about the cottage that was different. There were curtains in the window for one thing. The door was locked; but I heard noises inside, so I knocked. After a time the Count—the Major, that is—came to the door and started to talk to me in that stuck-up way he has—nothing like that impresses me. I stood my ground and said the cottage belonged to the estate and I wanted the key. He tried to get rid of me; but I wouldn't go. I wanted to find out what his little game was. I didn't think Sir Julian would fancy letting out a cottage on his demesne as a 'knocking shop'."

"Knocking shop?"

"A kip."

"Go on with your story."

"We were likely to be there arguing all night when Miss Lambert comes to the door and tells me to go about my business. The Count is helping her to decorate the place is how she put it. I never heard it called that before, and I've travelled round quite a lot."

"I'd advise you to bridle your tongue and not to be making low insinuations."

"I'm not insinuating anything."

"Did you see them there at any other time?"

"No."

"And what time was it when you had this conversation?"

"About tea-time."

"I suppose Miss Lambert uses the cottage for entertaining. Major Paul is a family friend."

"Nobody told me about entertaining. Was I to let this go on and not to report it?"

"Reporting is one thing, drawing conclusions is another. If you are the means of taking Miss Lambert's character away it won't recommend you to your employers. And as I am on that topic I think I should tell you that Sir Julian is questioning the amount of petrol the estate is using. According to the accounts there were very few sales last year, but the petrol consumption was doubled."

"Petrol has become so expensive you'd be better off running a car on champagne."

"Maybe. But it hasn't doubled its price in the last twelve months."

It was now Bradshaw's turn to get angry.

"If this is all the thanks I'm to get for working for a pittance for the Lamberts, watching their interests as if they were my own, I'd better go. Let them get someone else. I'm only wasting my time. *Insinuations* indeed! Is my character not to be protected against insinuation?"

"I'm sure you will be able to explain the petrol bill to the auditors. I only mentioned it."

The telephone on Mr Fox's desk rang. He groaned and picked it up.

"I will see her now," he said; and then, turning to Bradshaw, "Miss Lambert is on her way up."

Bradshaw did not wait; with a salute of his first finger, he moved out and was going down the back stairs as Elizabeth came up the front.

Mr Fox had a special manner for Elizabeth, rather deferential and angularly avuncular. He rose to meet her, flapping his long hands. A visit to his office was part of every holiday. He used to have a box of chocolates for her.

But today he seemed more distrait than usual, and she noticed that he stared at her rather sadly as if he had heard that she was suffering from some fatal disease while he sprinkled crumbs on the window-sill and plaintively clutched at the sparrows.

Everyone, except Bradshaw, waited for Mr Fox to begin; but today when he turned away from the window, Elizabeth could not wait while he folded and unfolded his hands and bleated gently. She burst in at once.

"Mr Fox, you know everything about the family. Tell me about Michael Molloy. Why is nothing being done for him? He is my father's brother and about a month older and he isn't even allowed to be the steward on the place. That awful man, Bradshaw—"

Mr Fox blushed. Puritan that he was, the idea of discussing such a matter with a young girl was for him unthinkable.

"I don't know who has been talking to you. Michael Molloy is the son of the coachman at Mount Lambert, a very loyal servant, and his mother was the late Lady Lambert's personal maid. Naturally the family looked after him. He's not very strong in the head, poor fellow. He is allowed more or less to do what he likes, and he has that lodge for nothing. It would be a great pity if anyone were to put ideas into his head. There are always scandals and stories about old families. Take my advice and don't let such things enter your pretty head."

"I'm not a child; look at that. Have you seen that?"

The lawyer recognised immediately the miniature that Michael had left with him.

"Where did you get this?"

"Michael gave it to me. He said it was my grandfather, and he was sure I'd like to have it. It is my grandfather, but it's his father."

"Why do you say that?"

"Look at it. It's the spitting image of Michael if you dressed him up."

"There may be a resemblance; but I wouldn't set too much store on that."

"Now, come off it! You are holding out on me. Tell me the truth. Anyhow I have made up my mind; Pa wants me to join in some deed or other when I'm twenty-one; well, I want to say now, once and for ever, that I join in nothing unless we go shares with Michael, fifty-fifty."

"Elizabeth, I beg of you. Be advised by me. Michael wouldn't know what to do if you gave him that amount. He would spend it in the pubs or give it away. You can't reverse the order of things. He is a workman, a very decent and rather simple-minded one. You can always keep an eye on him and help him; but to do what you say would be a form of cruelty. Even if the story were true, he is quite reconciled to his lot and, in law, he is entitled to nothing. No injustice has been done him."

"That's cant, if you don't mind my saying so. Who knows who their father was if it comes to that?"

"I certainly hope I do. I would deal very summarily with anyone who cast a doubt on it."

"I'm not talking about you. I'm sure you are O.K. But there are lots of people who sleep around, and there must be a great many cuckoos in the nests. I'm sure you are always coming across them. Anyhow, my mind is made up."

Mr Fox was accustomed to getting his own way. He had not expected to have any trouble with Elizabeth. On the contrary, he had rather looked forward to explaining her position to her and, practically, holding her hand while she signed the necessary papers. He was accustomed to being a legend and a court of appeal whose judgements were never questioned. The suggestion made by Bradshaw had shocked him; but he preferred not to believe it true. Now Elizabeth was showing herself to be excessively modern, with that irritating combination, so characteristic of the present-day young, of taking a high moral tone about everything except morals.

He would have liked to have made a very idyllic occasion of Elizabeth's first legal transaction. All that side of him which expressed itself in cat-worship and sparrow-feeding and mice-keeping and making the cleverest puns and doing exquisite sketches at the end of letters—all that he wanted to bring out for Elizabeth's delectation, instead he found himself having to be—not cross, exactly, but firm. He was going to get no fun at all out of this transaction. And he had looked forward to it. Life was hard.

"I think I had better make things quite clear, Elizabeth. You are at the moment what is called a tenant in tail. That means you have no right to anything until your father dies. When he dies you have a life estate and your heir becomes the tenant in tail. The way to break this is in joining in a deed when you are twenty-one. If Sir Julian doesn't see eye-to-eye with you he won't break the entail, and all you can do is to try to raise money on your prospects. You won't get very much. Your father is still comparatively young and might outlive you. Of course the trustees can always sell the place, but they would have to hold the proceeds on the same trusts. I hope I make myself clear."

"How would you feel if I were to give the story to the papers with photographs? Can't you see one of the Sunday rags jumping at it? A human document. And how the sins of the rich would be lapped up. Michael would become famous. He would be asked to give his views on the population explosion and the future of the United Nations. And I'd get quite a lot of lolly for the story."

"You would never do anything so infamous, my dear."

"Oh, wouldn't I? You don't know me. Besides, who is the infamous one? I'd be a heroine in the eyes of Sunday readers. Is the story dirty enough? I'm rather looking forward to the campaign. I feel like Mrs Pankhurst."

Mr Fox got out of his chair and began to walk up and down behind Elizabeth.

"Would you please not talk to me from behind my back. If you want a walk, let's go out and take a stroll in the park. It's a perfectly gorgeous afternoon."

This was the first remark that had been made since the interview began that fitted into Mr Fox's picture. To his own amazement, instead of being cross with the first person who had ever had the courage to stop him in his tracks, he became almost boyish.

"I haven't had a walk for years. I'll take you round the park."

He bleated down the telephone to say he wouldn't be back for half an hour and then went to the cupboard in which he kept his white mice and took out a very soft hat.

Elizabeth was delighted with the success of her plan; but once in the park Mr Fox took over and she felt like a child out for a Sunday stroll with her father. He told her the history of the various houses that looked in over the tree tops. He was a mine of reminiscence. Whenever she attempted to turn the conversation towards the topic that engaged her mind, he went off at a tangent. He made jokes; he was playful, she could see that he had a picture of himself as a delightful old gentleman. He wanted to know what she read, but was more concerned to tell her about his own reading. Nevertheless, his pleasure in showing her what a whimsical person he was never convinced her that underneath he was at all quixotic. He was seeking to win her confidence, she thought, by showing a loveable inside.

The ducks in the pond gave him a wonderful opportunity. He had crumbs in his pocket to feed them with. He called them by names he had invented. He made up little stories about them.

"It's one of his turns. He does it with everyone," she told herself.

She was piqued that he was so insistent on charming her when she had suggested the outing to give herself the chance to charm him.

They were on the path that led back to the office and she had not yet got a word in about Michael when she saw the Count sitting on a bench staring at them as they approached.

Mr Fox saw him, too; she knew that by the way he broke off suddenly in the middle of an anecdote about Sir Jonah Barrington.

The Count continued to stare; and she was wondering whether to stop or to wink—not being sure what the relations between the two men were—when she realised that she was being cut. He looked through them.

Mr Fox had attempted a salute of a vaguely episcopal character.

"That was Major Paul, wasn't it?"

Elizabeth didn't answer. Then she said, "Would you mind waiting? I must see him."

The Count's back was turned, but she put her hand on his shoulder.

"Ritzy! What's the matter? I'm not going to be cut by you. Why are you so cross?"

He kept his basilisk stare. She shook him.

"Ritzy! Ritzy! What have I done?"

"You are plotting with my enemies."

"Nonsense. I am trying to twist Mr Fox round my little finger. But I find it very difficult. He thinks I'm Alice in Wonderland."

"He is my enemy. You are plotting with him."

"If you must know I'm trying to persuade him that Michael Molloy is entitled to share in Mount Lambert; and I can't get him even to discuss it."

"I am not interested in Michael Molloy. I told you that was folly. Fox is trying to sell Mount Lambert to Coppinger and Bradshaw. Are you going to allow it?"

"He can't sell it. He's only the family solicitor."

"I tell you he is. He is a very dangerous man."

"But listen, Ritzy; try to listen to reason. How could we ever put your scheme into practice?"

"Keep them from doing anything until you are twenty-one. Then you and I can plan something. I thought we were comrades, Liz. I never let down a comrade."

"I'll do what I can," she said. "I'd better go, Brer Fox is waiting."

The Count continued to look as if he had frozen into marble; and Elizabeth wondered what she was going to say to Mr Fox who, she noticed at once, had resumed his office expression.

"What is the matter with Major Paul? I don't trust that gentleman, and I am sorry that you are so much in his company."

"He is an old family friend."

"That doesn't alter my opinion."

"Well, if you must know, he says that you are trying to sell Mount Lambert to that awful creature Coppinger."

"My dear child, I can't sell Mount Lambert to anyone."

"Well, trying to persuade the trustees to sell it."

"The plain truth is that your father has been trying to sell the place for years, and nobody has made a realistic offer until now. Mr Coppinger has offered £40,000. I think it would be folly to refuse it."

"If Michael doesn't get half of that you know what I shall do."

"Has it occurred to you, young lady, that Michael might not thank you for telling the public that his mother had a love child, that he is illegitimate? Do you realise what that may mean to him? He will not want to be pointed at in the neighbourhood where he has lived since he was born. So far as I know Michael is quite happy with his lot. You want to attract publicity to him, to make him ashamed of his mother, to disown his father. You are like all the young people of today, you don't mind who suffers so long as you cut a figure and make a scene."

"I am not cutting a figure or making a scene, I don't like injustice."

But she saw that the lawyer had a point. It was curious

224

how the old always found right reasons for not doing the right thing.

"I'll write to Pa myself."

"By all means."

It was impossible now to resume the conversation on a whimsical level. For a time they walked in silence. When they reached the gate and the parting of their ways, Mr Fox took her hand.

"I have known you since you were a very little girl, Elizabeth. I would like to think you regarded me as a devoted friend. I've suggested to your father that if this deal goes through he puts £10,000 at once into trust for you. It will give you a little independence. Think over what I said about Michael. He will always have his house and he has about a thousand pounds in gold that his mother kept for him. Later on, if he needs help, you will be able to give it."

His hand was clammy; his eyes when she looked into them were fish-like : she felt no comfort but only an acute physical distaste from what she knew was a sincere and kind profession of friendship. She had wanted to seek help for Ritzy; this odd creature was the only source from which it was likely to come; but she knew that what she wanted was hopeless. She had no faith in Ritzy's plans for Mount Lambert; but she was prepared to sacrifice her share to help him, to sacrifice it knowing that like all Ritzy's schemes it would run aground. But how was she to explain this, to convince this strange hermit that she wanted to take the risk. She couldn't justify it in reason. Only a woman would understand. This man wanted to help her, the other to use her; yet she could hardly wait to get away from Mr Fox and back to Ritzy. The lawyer read her thoughts.

"Do be careful, Elizabeth. I know Major Paul."

"I don't think anyone knows him."

"I know enough to think him a most undesirable associate for you."

"Undesirable? Bad, you mean?"

"Mad."

"I never thought of that. It's quite an idea. What a clever person you are."

Mr Fox returned to his office with his self-esteem restored. Elizabeth made a short detour and then went back to look for the Count. But the bench was deserted. She sat down and watched the procession go by, mothers with their prams, calling out to children who had fallen behind, workers on their way home from offices, and the mysterious retinue who seem to belong to nothing and nobody and yet whom someone must support.

A man and woman went past with a new baby in a pram, a nice-looking couple, very proud of their child. Elizabeth felt a pang of self-pity. If only she could love someone respectable and uncomplicated like Ralph. Was it his madness that drew her to Ritzy, of whom she disapproved in her mind, but felt drawn to irresistibly? Was she also a little mad?

CHAPTER XV

THE TELEPHONE RANG incessantly that Sunday morning; and Elizabeth talked at great length to her callers. Telephones have this effect on young and old; they obliterate the sense of time. Middle-age is wary of the medium and distrusts a voice without a face.

When Elizabeth had finished with her last caller, she came out to find Ralph sitting in dejection at the wheel of his car. He had been waiting for half an hour; and glimpses of Elizabeth pirouetting on her heels and taking side-long glances at herself in the looking-glass did nothing to alleviate his pain. She spotted his ill-humour at once and set about trying to coax him out of it. Her apologies were accepted in grim silence; but she decided to pretend not to notice.

As they passed the Brownes' house, the memory of the previous afternoon provided a hopeful distraction. The tennis tournament had been very funny in the way only the Brownes could be funny, through their "sheer insensitive bloody awfulness", as Elizabeth said.

The Count had not appeared and sent no excuse which meant that there were uneven numbers. His absence left Bernard Coppinger in complete control of the proceedings. Partnered by Sylvia, he played a dazzling game and they won first prize. Mrs Browne and the parson from Bray came second. Mr Browne and the parson's wife, who had been a games mistress, third.

This was Mrs Browne's idea of a successful entertainment.

Elizabeth had been partnered by Loftus who hadn't played for years and was rather lame. Ralph, who was reasonably good, had found Mrs Perry an overwhelming handicap. The Count was to have played with Miss Beddington; but when her partner did not turn up, she was scratched. It was a pity as she was rather proficient and had been looking forward to the game.

"I do think Mrs Browne should have stood down at her own party." Elizabeth said, noticing that Ralph's profile looked less severe.

"She did say to Barbara, 'If you would like to take my place you are more than welcome; but I have a feeling that you are glad enough of the excuse to drop out.' She knows Barbara."

"Barbara spent the afternoon helping with the tea. You know I have a mean suspicion that Mrs B. was determined Syl was going to put her old chum in the shade."

"After the river episode you were already in the shade. So was I. I wasn't offered strawberries."

"And when I was going Mrs Browne said, 'It was very sweet of you to bother to come. I'm sure you are used to more exciting entertainments than our little tournament.' "

There had been a lot to laugh at, and Elizabeth skilfully recalled it, and in due course Ralph forgot that he had a grievance.

"I don't think you have as much to complain about as I have : you at least had old Loftus who must have played in India. I don't suppose Mrs Perry had ever held a racquet in her hand before."

"You were given her because you are in disgrace."

"What about you?"

"I am neither an eligible young man nor a solicitor; and I was brought up abroad, and I am a Lambert, and the party was by the way of being given for me. You can't bracket us together on the strength of a solitary bathe."

"I'll never live it down."

"Of course you will. Secretly everyone is envious of you. I shouldn't be surprised if we caught Mrs Browne and the Captain at it before the summer is out. Didn't you enjoy our match against Herbert Perry and Mrs Coppinger? Wasn't it a lark when Mrs Coppinger couldn't stop apologising and he got sulkier and sulkier? Did you see Loftus lash a ball into Perry's stomach at the net—he had to retire until after tea—and they both argued with the umpire about every decision. I don't know what got into them. I thought they were as thick as thieves."

The tennis party was still yielding ore as Ralph drove into the mountains. He stopped at the most picturesque spot he could find, where a valley stream was lined with willows, and proposed they should lunch there.

"I don't suppose you want to take a dip," Elizabeth said; Ralph did not seem to hear, and as he had on his intense expression, she decided not to repeat the flippancy. She could cope with anything she thought except intensity at the moment. How self-conscious he looked unpacking the lunch basket; but he had really done things in style with proper napkins, family silver, and a bottle of Moselle. There was smoked salmon and chicken and salad and strawberries and cream. Elizabeth looked and sounded appreciative of his efforts; it was not her fault that the salad dressing had been left out, the salt and sugar got into each other's receptacles, the cream spilled in opening, or that the cork went into the bottle when Ralph tried to draw it. She made nothing of these misadventures and showed herself most ingenious in washing the salt off the strawberries; but she could see that Ralph took it all as a set-back in whatever campaign he had devised. There was anti-climax in the air.

"I'm feeling quite cold; are you?" she said. A wind had certainly sprung up; but Ralph, as he rose to his feet, couldn't have told whether it was without or within.

They drove over the mountain roads, explored each of the valleys, sometimes in sun, sometimes in gloom; they stopped for drinks at a thatched pub; at length they found themselves on a long road which ran across the face of the hills, looking east to the sea.

"Let's stop and enjoy this," she said.

Ralph pulled the car in to the side of the road; she got out and jumped up on a wall.

"Look. A field of red poppies."

She let herself down, hanging by her finger-tips, and then dropped into the field below. Ralph followed.

He took off his coat and spread it out for her to sit on; but she had already thrown herself down, her hands behind her head, her eyes closed, sucking a blade of grass. He sat beside her and looked at her. What a perfect face she had. It was gentle and delicately shaped; but her eyes were always laughing when she looked at him. It was impossible to cut a figure under that glance. It seemed to say that she knew him far too well ever to be impressed, ever to be moved, ever to be deeply interested in anything he could say or do.

"I wonder how Ritzy is getting on?" she said, unwisely. The Count was at that moment passing through Ralph's mind. "Take her," he had said.

"Are you in love with him?"

"With whom?"

"The Count."

"Love is a big word."

"Would you marry him, then?"

"He hasn't asked me to."

"But would you if he did?"

"He won't. He will never marry anyone."

"Then what am I to think?"

"About what?"

"You know."

"Honestly, I don't."

"About you and him."

"Don't think about us."

"I can't help it."

"Aren't you spoiling a lovely day for both of us? Let's enjoy it. You are awfully inclined to go biting off your nose to spite your face. It's foolish."

He wanted to say, 'How can I enjoy anything in my state

of mind?', but the Count's face loomed up before him and he remembered his order to take Elizabeth. But how was it done? The Count had given an example when Elizabeth was with him; they were laughing all the time. Ralph wished he could make her laugh.

He had tried to impress her by driving very fast; but she begged him to slow down. He had even found himself, to his disgust, boasting about his successes on the Rugby field; and she had said, making him feel like a small boy:

"Men look funny in shorts."

He lay back and gazed at her. She still looked remote; but he had seen her bathing, seen her naked. What held him back from seizing her in his arms? Why did he not tell her he adored her? What was this awful curse that hung over him which meant that he could only express his feelings by sulkiness and ill-temper?

Elizabeth was not to blame today. She pretended not to notice his glooms. She had been gentle and amusing and appreciative except when he talked about football.

"There is nowhere in the world so lovely as this," she said, looking lovely as she said it.

"O God! I adore you, Elizabeth."

She put her hand over his mouth. He kissed her and she kissed him back. He covered her face with kisses.

She did not resist him; but whenever he tried to say anything she put her hand over his mouth. The sun and the wine had made her ever so little drunk. She had begun to wish that she hadn't taken that gin in the thatched pub. She didn't recognise the man who was trying without success to slip her dress off her shoulder; he was becoming more insistent. Baffled by her frock, he had changed direction. The moment of decision had come. It had gone. But even then the almost extinguished voice of reason made its last request.

"Please . . . it's too risky . . . I'm afraid . . . unless you . . ."

He botched it of course, and lay beside her, while she

stroked his hair and comforted him who should have comforted her.

How sweet and defenceless she looked at that last second. He had felt a rush of pity even when more urgent feelings swept him past all other considerations than to have her—half have her. What a will o' the wisp it was.

"It was all right. I mean you didn't?"

"No. No. Honestly. You needn't worry."

"It would be the end if . . ."

"I promise. I've wanted you so much. I love you."

"Please . . . Please . . ."

"I must tell you I love you. I can't just . . ."

"Be happy. Just be happy."

"But doesn't it . . . I mean . . . Surely it isn't just that?"

"Questions! Questions! I tried to make you happy. It's not my fault if— Oh, it's no use! Why must you bring the weight of the world on me?"

She sat up and started to pull her clothes on. She looked cross.

"Don't you love me?"

"There you go."

"But surely you wouldn't—just to please someone—I mean . . ."

I don't let everyone who wants to make love to me, if that's what you mean."

He looked at the place where they had lain. He still retained in his nostrils the sharp smell of earth, his first sensation when he came back to life. She had let him take her. He had possessed her. She was his . . .

But nobody could look as if she belonged less to anyone than the girl who was now settling her stockings, with as business-like an air as if she were wrapping up a parcel. Then she took up her bag and looked at her face in the compact mirror. Satisfied on that point, she stood up and patted herself; then she smiled on him. She had not been hostile, merely abstracted. She took his hand and they made their way back to the car.

"Don't start again."

"Let me just kiss you."

"Once. Just once. Chastely."

"I adore you."

"You are very sweet."

"Do you love me?"

"I'm awfully fond of you."

"I'm asking you if you love me."

"Don't ask me that."

"And yet you ..."

"I knew you'd say that. How mean only men can be. They beg and beg; and then ..."

"Then what?"

"Oh, then nothing. Come on. Let's go home."

On the way home she rested her head on his shoulder and chatted away about life in Majorca, very gaily, unaware of his mounting gloom, or flouting it. When they came within the precincts of the Mile she sat up.

"Hell's delight! We have forgotten the Captain's sundowner."

"He won't notice in the crush."

"Oh, he'll notice all right. People always do. But, perhaps, he won't mind. I'm sure the Brownes have told on us by now."

The Canon, hearing the car on the drive, had hastened out on the steps to welcome the return of the travellers. It was what he expected when he was away from home.

"Elizabeth, are you back? No mishaps, I hope. How did the day go? Penny! Penny! Where are you? Hurry. Elizabeth and Ralph have come home."

CHAPTER XVI

Loftus stayed away from church. He had so much on his mind; he was also afraid that the Perrys might be there and he would weaken and ask them to join his select little party. He spent some time examining the sky, licking his finger to test the direction of the wind, then indoors, tapping the barometer. Everything indicated another fine day. It was important because the sundowner on the lawn with the mountain view was infinitely to be preferred to a gathering in his sitting-room. Wales, there was no getting away from the fact, was a come-down after the other villas on the Mile. Having been built for a stable the architect had had no consideration of views or the direction of the sun. Like so many houses of its type it looked its best from outside. Moreover, the furniture, suggestive of a frontier post, provided a contrast which might have been exploited if the presence of too much dust and rubbish did not immediately leap to the least attentive eye.

With luck his visitors would not see the house at all. The hall had a door at either end. Both could be left open revealing the table with its hospitable bottles and glasses as a lure at the furthest reach.

"Let me see," he said aloud, and proceeded to count the number of seats he would require. A garden bench would account for three. He had two camp chairs. Why not a rug with cushions on it for the rest? The dog had left a lot of his hair on the rug, but a brisk brushing dealt with most of that.

Drinks? He had laid in a bottle of whiskey. The Canon and Mrs Ormsby always stuck to sherry. It would probably do Miss Beddington. If anyone asked for gin there was a third of a bottle. But gin raised the question of something to put in it. He would have to bicycle as far as the newsagent and get lime juice. The young people would just have to take whatever was going. The Captain set his face against cocktails. Members of the old school had given him the example; and he had made it a point of principle; not that he really objected to them, but it saved a great deal of fuss and trouble not to provide them.

Would he be able to get olives or those horribly salty potato chips at this late hour? Or would he stand on principle here as well? A sundowner was a sundowner—a drink, or maybe more than a drink, not a meal. Why not stand on that firm ground? After all the whole purpose of the exercise was to lend an authentic touch to a week that was full of synthetic entertainment.

Rather fun to run up a Union Jack on the flagpole! It wouldn't be seen from the road, and it would give just that final touch.

His tropical uniform had put up a brave resistance to the moths. Age which increases the corpulence of most men had taken flesh off the Captain: the suit hung somewhat limply. He played with the idea of wearing a solar topee. Was it going too far? The Canon and Miss Beddington never made one feel uncomfortable, but would the young people think he was an old fool? Or admire his spirit? After all if he was wearing the uniform he might as well go the whole hog—unless it was raining. That would rule it out.

Everything was now settled and the telephone rang. Loftus, all a-flutter, went as fast as his limp allowed to answer it. The Count's basso profondo filled the little house: he was sorry but he had to go abroad unexpectedly and he would not be present this evening.

Loftus tried to say something and choked.

The telephone was replaced. He had quite forgotten that he had invited the scoundrel, and it was anyhow astonishing that he should regard the invitation as still open after his violent behaviour at the Perrys' infernal party.

The reminder of that hateful and humiliating evening

greatly reduced his spirits, he even went so far as to eye the bottle of whiskey; but decided to keep it intact for the party and consoled himself with a bottle of stout.

He was half way through it when the telephone rang. Bernard Coppinger's voice was saying :

"No sundowner tonight for Sahib. Sahib listen to Muezzin. Sahib sorry, Salaams." And the telephone was replaced on the receiver.

"Fellow is mad," the Captain said to his own instrument.

Some time later Mrs Ormsby rang up to say that the Canon had been called upon to take an evening service and the idea of a sundowner beforehand struck him as incongruous in the circumstances. He hoped the Captain would understand.

Late in the afternoon, Mrs Bartholomew, Miss Beddington's invaluable maid, called to say that her mistress had been adversely affected by something she had eaten at the Brownes' tournament and was quite unable to leave home. She sent a little nosegay of wild flowers as a contribution to the party.

That left only the youngsters—Ralph and Elizabeth.

The Captain had heard all about their goings on, but he had decided to take the opposite side to the Brownes who were making heavy weather about it. It was no business of his, he decided. And if it came to a show-down he was going to back the Lambert-Ormsby against the Browne-Perry axis. The story did provoke lewd ideas in his mind, and he felt an intense jealousy of Ralph. His own arm had been crushed because he laid it on Miss Beddington's fully-clothed waist; Mrs Browne had proved impervious even under the influence of champagne to his gallantry, why should this surly young pup have a damn fine-looking girl like that bathing in the buff with him? Life was monstrously unfair.

With only two to entertain he decided to anticipate the party and poured himself out a really good whiskey. It mellowed him. Was it not rather a lark to have the scandalous young pair here? Put him pretty well in the picture. He would use it as a score next time Herbert Perry tried to come it over him with some impertinence.

At six o'clock he started to fuss. At quarter past he was pacing up and down the drive. At half-past six he decided to haul down the flag. It looked silly, perhaps, when there were only to be three of them. At a quarter to seven he hung up his topee. At seven he rang up the Ormsbys and was told the young people had gone out earlier in the day but would probably be home for a cold supper.

A car on the road sent the Captain hot foot to the window; he recognised Ralph at the wheel and a girl beside him. The car drove on without Ralph even looking in the direction of Wales.

"Is that you, Herbert? Loftus speaking. I was wondering if you and the missus would like to drop round for a quick-one before dinner? What's that? Oh, no. Just ourselves. I thought . . . If you had nothing better to do. Don't if it's a bother. Oh! You can. Good show!"

He would just have time, he calculated, to change out of his tropical uniform before Herbert arrived.

CHAPTER XVII

The Count was away for a week. He called on Mr
Tartan Young and after a frigid reception, re-established
their former genial relations to such effect that Mr Young
pressed him to join a yachting party to the Greek islands in
September. The Count deferred his decision. Only on one
matter did they fail to reach agreement : Mr Young was not
interested in investing capital in an Irish stud-farm.

The Baroness Hoherleden was staying in a retreat near
Davos with an Italian adviser on art matters, considerably
younger than herself. Graciousness itself, she did not manage, however, to disguise from the Count that she was
preoccupied and could not attend to any matter requiring
business calculations at the moment. Moreover, she would
require an expert's appraisal before she bought Mount
Lambert. Perhaps, the Count would consult her lawyer.
They had lunch together on the terrace of the villa; but the
Count was not asked to stay. He decided that the Italian
was a charlatan and endeavoured unsuccessfully to get the
Baroness to share his opinion.

From Zurich he took a plane to Paris, and drew a blank.
Then he went to Majorca and saw the Lamberts. Julian
told him that the trustees were definitely selling to Coppinger. When the Count expressed himself forcibly about this,
Julian lost his temper and accused him of seducing his
daughter.

The Count had several answers to this charge but preferred to say that he severed their friendship from that
moment.

Julian took this calmly. His wife was not more co-opera-
tive. She refused to take any interest in Mount Lambert
and confined the conversation to the subject of Elizabeth.

Solicitude for her daughter was alloyed with a certain pique. There had been an understanding between herself and Ritzy since Elizabeth was a child. In her annoyance she used schoolgirl expressions: Ritzy was a snake in the grass, etc.

He made a bold throw. He had loved her for years. Now she was accusing him on some worthless gossip of having taken up with Elizabeth. Very well, then: would she come away with him openly and tell Julian to divorce her?

In vain she protested that this was not the issue. What was going on in Ireland? What was he up to with Elizabeth?

The Count stood firm: he wanted an answer. She gave it, and he returned to Ireland alone.

A large correspondence awaited him through which he flicked with his usual expertise. An envelope with Mr Fox's seal on the back was extracted and read at once.

Having studied it with care, the Count put it in his pocket and set off for the Canon's. He found him in the throes of composition but more than willing to talk.

"Welcome back, Major, we have been very lifeless without you. Elizabeth went for a tour of the west, but we expect her back this afternoon."

Speculation about the Count's absence had been rife. The Captain had put it about that he had gone for good; but nobody ever paid any attention to his theories. After all, his ball, the event of the year, was only a week off. Those in the know were aware that the sale of Mount Lambert was what had sent the Count away. Coppinger made no secret of the fact that he intended to buy Mount Lambert. The connection with Bradshaw he kept to himself. The Canon heard everything but kept his own counsel. Incurable optimism persuaded him that whatever was to be was right. He could not see why the Count could not carry on perfectly well at Kent in his splendid establishment. Elizabeth's feelings were unknown as she had quite suddenly decided to explore Connemara, returning in time for the great entertainments. She sent facetious and affectionate post-cards from the West to everyone.

After the brilliance and scandal of the week before, it was a breathing time, and the Count's return was like the rise of the curtain after an interval.

He looked at his most dramatic when he found himself with the Canon, Mrs Ormsby having retired to leave the men alone.

The Count refused a seat, preferring to stand. His pose reminded the Canon of a performance of *Coriolanus* that had impressed him greatly in his youth.

"I am in trouble," the Count said. It was a quite unexpected beginning for which the declamatory attitude seemed entirely inappropriate, and the Canon's heart sank. For a craven moment he feared that he was going to be asked for a loan of money. He was ashamed of himself at once; but by then the danger had already passed.

"I come to you as the only man I can put my trust in. The Lamberts have let me down. For the first time in my life I have to admit defeat."

"If I can help in any way. I ..." The Canon trailed off. He hoped he had redeemed himself.

The Count shook his head and smiled. "Here is the friend who will do that."

He took a revolver out of his pocket and laid it on the mantelpiece.

If he had aimed it at the Canon he could not have startled him more.

"Give me that. What are you talking about? I forbid you to touch that revolver. This is no way to behave."

The Canon had leaped to his feet, but he hesitated to seize the revolver, never having handled a weapon and suspecting that it might go off at any moment. The Count put the revolver back.

"Don't worry, my dear friend. I wanted to show you that I shall take my own exit in my own time."

"But I am dreadfully worried. Whatever makes you so

240

desperate. There is no trouble in life which cannot be faced with courage."

"I shall never lack courage, my friend. You have heard that Coppinger and Bradshaw are to get Mount Lambert—beauty and the beast. I cannot raise the money to beat them. The world has shrunk. The heroic scale has gone. We now operate on ground level. I want you to do me one small service."

"Of course. Gladly."

"Take my grey filly into your stable. The pirates are abroad again."

The Canon, who had geared himself up to making almost any sacrifice, found what was required of him peculiarly unpleasant.

"Say 'no' if I ask too much. Be man enough to say 'no'. I may not understand—it is outside my code—but I shall know where I am."

"I would do anything in reason to help you, Major, only—forgive me if I am being too blunt—this strikes me as being an attempt to evade the law; and in my position . . ."

"Say no more. I understand. I am on my own."

He brushed aside the Canon's attempt to detain him and stalked out of the house with the same majesty that he came. At the gate, however, he paused and consulted his watch. Then he set off for Molloy's lodge.

Michael's mother had warned him that the Count was in communication with the devil, and this filled him with a certain awe; but he liked what he knew of the Count and admired his autocratic manner.

Nobody ever heard what the Count said to Michael when they sat down together, nor did anyone except themselves know of the meeting. As soon as the Count left Michael and returned home, Michael went to the field where he kept his horse and harnessed it to his cart.

The Count proceeded towards Miss Beddington's. It was his practice to stand outside the house and whistle "Sur le pont d'Avignon . . ."

241

Miss Beddington was always at the door to sing, "On y danse, on y danse". Today his visit was totally unexpected: so he had to knock. Mrs Bartholomew answered the door, and went off to fetch her mistress, who was in the garden.

"He's here," she simply said.

Miss Beddington flushed at once and became agitated; none of which was lost on Mrs Bartholomew.

"I put him in the drawing-room."

"I'm in such a mess," Miss Beddington wailed; but she looked rather becoming.

When she came into the drawing-room, the Count took her by both hands and looked at her so searchingly with his black eyes that she felt a dreadful surmise, he had come to say good-bye. She, too, had heard the week's rumours; but she had refused to believe them until now.

"What is it?" she said at last.

"I am in trouble. Will you help me?"

"Anything I can do. Of course."

"My enemies are closing in. I must go on my travels again. Any moment they will have taken all my belongings. But they won't take me."

"But how could they—take you, I mean?"

"I have powerful enemies."

"Tell me what I can do."

"Believe in me."

"I do."

"Silence my traducers."

"I won't let anyone run you down in my presence, if that's what you mean; but that goes for any friend of mine."

"I owe you money."

"Please forget about it."

"You gave it to me for the ball."

"What does it matter? I only wish it had been more."

"Why are you such an angel to me?"

"Because ... oh, because ..."

"You are the noblest woman I have ever met."

"Nonsense. Any woman who..."

"Who what?"

"Any woman wants to help a man if she...if she is a friend of his."

"I have certain things in my house, my lares and penates, things that I don't want the dirty hands of bailiffs to seize, may I leave them here with you? Some day I'll come back, but if I don't they are yours. There's a drawing Cocteau made of me I'd like you to have in any case."

She pressed his hand. If she tried to speak, she would only cry.

"I must go now."

He stared at her, his eyes going black because he was thinking, thinking whether to leave this matter where it so satisfactorily was, or take it further. He had not the least desire for Miss Beddington; but did she not deserve a demonstration of affection? Would it not be something for her to live on? He was sure that no man had ever had this effect on her before or would ever again; for where was his like in the world? On the other hand there were practical difficulties: he was in a hurry; that estimable woman in the kitchen was unlikely to stay there for whatever time it took. There were telephone calls and rings at the door to be allowed for. While he debated these considerations, his eyes became increasingly mysterious and impenetrable.

She read into them feelings of unfathomable depth. She was too agitated to think consecutively. All she wanted was to give, give, give. Herself and all she had was his for the asking, for the taking.

When he took the handkerchief—a rather crushed one—out of her shirt pocket and pressed it to his lips; when he turned and with head thrown back walked out of the door, stopping at the gate to bow his head—Renunciation—before striding on head erect—Resolution—to face the worst his enemies might have in store for him, she believed that he had exercised self-restraint on a scale that was surely godlike.

243

It was fortunate for Miss Beddington, too sad to cry, that he had been able to think for both of them.

Michael's cart was in the yard; and it was noted by several persons on the Mile that enough hay to feed a regiment of horses passed from Kent to Clarence that day.

Pictures, looking-glasses, silver, glass, china were piled high on Miss Beddington's tables and in her already crowded rooms. As the evening drew on larger objects were found under the hay—tables and chairs.

While Miss Beddington to all appearances was laying in a superfluity of hay, the Count brooded over the fate of his horses. Michael offered to take them; but Bradshaw would soon see them if they were anywhere at Mount Lambert. Miss Beddington's coach-house and stable, now a garage and turf-shed, were not a suitable harbour for valuable thoroughbreds. There was nobody else whom the Count could trust. Ralph's connection with Mr Fox made the Canon an unsuitable bailee even if he could be persuaded to overcome his objections.

In the end the Count was reduced to doing what anyone else would have had to do in his plight : he rang up a large horse-dealing concern and asked them to send for the animals and dispose of them on his behalf. They promised to send out a box at the first opportunity.

There remained but one other matter to dispose of. He rang Ralph up on the telephone. "Is that you Ralph? I want you to do something for me. I have just heard that my sister's husband died suddenly. They lived in the Bahamas. Yes. It is very sad. In the circumstances I cannot very well give a ball. I want you to get a card printed at once and sent out to my guests. I will draft it and leave the names with you; can you manage this for me, dear boy? And how is Elizabeth?"

Everything that could be done had been done. There remained the question of rewarding Michael who was hard at work until midnight.

He pondered this. His total in cash was fifty pounds. This

would have to keep him until he got to Switzerland, where he believed he could rely on the Baroness to have seen through her Italian admirer by the time he arrived.

If the sale of the horses went through there would be plenty for everybody; but there was a very real danger that Mr Fox would get wind of the sales and proceed for a court order to seize the purchase money for creditors.

The Count emptied his pockets : a revolver, a fountain-pen, a leather wallet, a gold watch. He must not leave on a low note; there was nothing for it but to give Michael the watch.

He would see him in the morning. Meanwhile he settled himself in one of the few remaining chairs, with a bottle of brandy beside him, to sit out the night.

CHAPTER XVIII

NEVER HAD THERE been a summer like this summer, sun-lit days and star-crowded nights; it had reached the stage when the faithful were being asked to pray for rain—and then the rains came.

They started before anyone had woken up, on a Sunday, and came down in fine sheets that the wind caught and curled and twisted as if they were curtains. One by one the inhabitants of the Mile, aroused by the unaccountable din, looked through misty window panes at the soggy scene without, the wild trees and the innumerable sudden streams, and decided not to go to church. This threatened the grape-vine communication on the Mile which depended on Sabbath observance, there being no postal service on that day, no link between house and house. Michael's massive hay lift had excited general curiosity, and Miss Beddington might be expected to throw some light on it. But not today.

Never in fact had there been such drama on the Mile, but it had not been communicated. There had been a break-down in the machinery.

The Canon was taking evening service again, six miles away; and he enlisted Ralph to drive him. Ralph had been morose and listless all week on account, his parents supposed, of Elizabeth's absence. She was coming home on Monday.

The Canon spent the day brooding over his sermon. At lunch Ralph let drop the information that the Count's ball had been cancelled. The Canon took the news very badly.

"We should have persevered. I knew that we should have carried out my plan," he moaned.

Mrs Ormsby refused to join in the lamentation. She had wondered how the Count was going to meet the crippling expense and she assumed he was glad of the excuse to avoid it.

"Glad? Did you say glad? Our good friend has lost someone close and dear to him, and yet you say that he is glad."

"It's the first I ever heard of his having relations. He never mentions them. I can't believe it is a great tragedy, but it does give him an excuse to get out of a great deal of expense."

The Canon threw up his hands. He had fed his imagination with this ball which had become confused with the scene at Versailles so movingly described by Edmund Burke in a hackneyed passage. Elizabeth, in the Canon's version, was Marie Antoinette, on whose account ten thousand swords were leaping from their scabbards.

The saddest occasions found their solace for him in the exercise of literary composition. He played with the idea of introducing the Count's bereavement to his sermon this evening; but discarded it because nobody in the wayside church—particularly if the rain hadn't stopped—would recognise the allusion. Instead he took his pen and wrote:

My dear Major,

Ralph has told me in strictest confidence of the awful blow which Providence has seen fit to deal you at a time when one might in all humility have expected His sovereign hand to be stayed. But there are mysteries which neither of us is in a position to unravel; and if only your lost dear one could come back I am sure all would be made clear and we should bow cheerfully to His purpose.

Ralph is uncertain as to whether your loss is a sister or a sister's husband. I was going to say I trusted that it was the less close of these, and then was abashed by my effrontery in assuming I knew of the state of your relations with either.

There are many instances in my own experience of connections formed by marriage which became as precious

247

and valuable even as those depending on a blood-tie. When our boy marries, as someday I suppose he will, if we are spared to know her, my wife and I hope that his wife will be as dear to us as if she were our own daughter. As I say—writing under the handicap of uncertain knowledge as to the exact nature of your loss—whether it is your sister or her husband may be for you but a choice of evils.

I hope I am not intruding on a sorrow which I know you will bear with that fortitude which is one of the many admirable facets of your character; but I cannot let the opportunity pass without assuring you of my own and my wife's and my son's very sincere regret and affectionate sympathy with you at this stark moment.

When the shock and pain that you must now be suffering have subsided a little, you may be able to tell us something of this dear sister (or brother-in-law) whom we grieve for on your account.

The decision to cancel the ball was, of course, inevitable; and we must see it in proportion and weigh it against the magnitude of your personal loss; but it will bring home in a poignant way to all your good friends in the neighbourhood what shadows we are, what shadows we pursue.

Your affectionate friend,

Oliver Ormsby.

P.S. Elizabeth comes home on Monday, and if you would like to take pot-luck with us any evening we should be delighted. It may help in this sad time to get away and be with friends.

The Canon derived a good deal of innocent enjoyment in the writing of this letter; and when it was read over and addressed he fussed about the best way to get it safely and expeditiously into the Count's hands. Ideally—if there were not something disreputable in the plan—he would like to drop it in the letterbox and then post himself at a window to observe the manner of its reception; but as with all literary artists he realised that this sort of pleasure is known only to the orator, the actor and the instrumentalist. A writer's reward is his own satisfaction.

But he did want the Count to get the letter quickly, so he decided to leave it in on the way to church. Refusing Ralph's offer to act as postman, he got out of the car and put the letter himself into the brass-edged slit in the door. Then he knocked. The knock produced a hollow echo, a most dismal and discouraging sound. Anxious and curious, he knocked again. Again it was as if he had disturbed a tomb.

Although it was still raining heavily he ventured to peer through the lunette at the side of the door. The hall which had been so sumptuously furnished was almost empty. Looking round to make sure he was not under observation, he picked his way across the lawn and peeped in through the window of the dining-room. The large table was still there, and an elaborate side-board, otherwise the room was bare. Through the drawing-room window he could see a sofa and a high winged-chair—nothing else. Absorbed in his quest, and unmindful now of anything else but the mystery of these clearances, he went round to the back of the house and looked in through the kitchen window.

Seated in a chair, with a revolver lying on a table, the Count met his enquiring gaze with a blank stare.

"Ralph, Ralph," the Canon called out in horror. "Ralph."

But Ralph on the roadside, chafing at the delay, could not hear. At last his father came at his nearest approximation to a run to tell him what he had seen.

"We had better go in to the house first; then we can decide what to do," Ralph said.

The Canon led the way to the yard.

"Look for yourself," he said when they approached the

window. He found that he was averse from facing the horror again.

Ralph looked in.

"Well?"

"I can't see anything."

Impatiently his father pushed him aside and nerved himself to look. The chair was there and the table : there was a bottle and a glass on the table, but no revolver. And the chair was empty.

"You will be late for your service."

The Canon, humiliated, followed his son back to the car.

"I could have sworn I saw him. I am prepared to swear it."

So great was his surprise that he forgot the lesser mystery, still to be explained : why was the house empty? But he had to defer analysis until he had disposed of his sermon.

The Coppingers were at church. Bernard had no religious beliefs, but he liked to play the organ when the organist was away, and this evening he was in luck.

The Canon was bursting to discuss his recent adventure; but in the few minutes conversation after service it seemed somehow too involved for a passing mention. He did say that the Count's ball was off; and he noticed that Coppinger pricked up his ears at that.

As soon as the Ormsbys came home, the Canon called a council of war to discuss the situation. It was only after he had endured a certain amount of ridicule from his son that he recalled the reason for his inspection of the back premises.

"Well tell me then, if you are so sceptical, where has all the furniture gone? The hall is bare and there are only a few pieces in the other rooms."

"I hope the bailiffs haven't been in. It would explain why he decided to call off the dance."

"The bailiffs?"

"I'm afraid the Count is in pretty low water. Mr Fox doesn't tell me anything; but I see most of the correspondence. I knew the end was near. Besides I was told that his servants went to the Coppingers last week. A friend of mine who was at dinner there recognised the man."

"I am sorry. I am deeply distressed."

The Canon spoke sincerely; he had insulated himself early in life against its shocks by participating very mildly in adventures of the spirit. But in so far as he felt anything, he felt this. Nor was his feeling quite disinterested; he had allowed the Count to form a part in a little world that was complete. Now it was imperfect. There was a jagged edge, as if a Dresden figure had lost a hand or a toe.

Mrs Ormsby never cared for the Count and was not surprised at his fate; but she had more natural warmth than her husband, and her sympathies took a more practical form than prose effusions.

"Why not ring him up and see if he is all right? He likes you, dear, and I think it's the least you could do."

"Penny! What a good idea. Why did I never think of it?"

He rushed in nervous haste now to the telephone and made a sad muddle of dialling, but at last got the number. All three held their breath, listening to the telephone ringing in that empty house; then a voice filled the whole room.

"Major Paul speaking. Who is that wants him?"

An expression of childish delight illuminated the Canon's face. He turned eagerly to the others nodding unnecessary reassurance.

"He is all right."

He repeated it for the benefit of each of them and then put back the receiver.

"Gracious! I should have said something, shouldn't I? Anyhow, the great thing is that the dear fellow is alive and well. I could have sworn..."

But the dismay on his son's face arrested the Canon. His imagination had played him tricks again, or so his family were convinced. They saw him living with one foot at most on the earth, in a world of fantasy. But to him it was only a matter of values, of interpretation. The Count's welfare, for example, was of great importance to him because he supported traditional values on the Mile. Miss Beddington had spoken of his resemblance to the Bartolomeo Colleoni statue in Venice. The parallel was very close. To the Canon, the Doge of the Mile, the Count was an invaluable condottiere, a strong right-arm against the enemies of that precious redoubt. His personal peculiarities were his own concern. The others seemed to forget that they had a common cause with him. If he went they would soon notice the difference. The barbarian was already at the gate. At any moment he could be in the citadel.

At this point in his reflections the Canon remembered that, in deference to Ralph, he had failed the Count by refusing to hide his horse. That was prudent but unworthy; was it too late to offer now? He glanced uneasily at his son to whom he had taught Christian morality from the cradle. "Be just and fear not" had been a regular text, and he had liked to enlarge on the happiness which was the inevitable reward of a clear conscience. It would take no little casuistry to reconcile joining in the Count's conspiracy with these lessons of the past. "Render unto Caesar" was binding on all; the Count made a point of withholding from Caesar, being in all matters a law unto himself. "The greatest of these is charity"—would that carry the day? Would it justify participation in a scheme to cheat creditors? But... He had no certain knowledge that the Count was under any legal obligations. One should discount denigratory rumours. All he had requested was a roof for his horse. If he had asked for similar accommodation for himself it would have been granted with a heart and a half, and no questions asked. Why strain at the horse if one were prepared to swallow the owner?

He wished to be open but had to resort to furtiveness. Of course he could assert himelf, take the horse and refuse to discuss the matter. Ralph would resent that as disloyal to him, compromising him with his employer, but it would be quite feasible if only Angela were not there.

"I wish Elizabeth were back," he said aloud; but did not explain that it was her help he required at the moment. Why had she gone away so suddenly?

"She will be here tomorrow," Mrs Ormsby said. "I must say I miss her too."

CHAPTER XIX

THE WORST OF the rain was over on Monday; but
the sky was full of clouds; the wind had settled in the south-
west, and there were going to be interminable showers. At
one moment the mountain looked so near that one might
throw a stone and hit it, at another it was miles away and
swathed in mist. The grape-vine was in operation again. By
half-past ten o'clock it was known to everybody on the Mile
that the Count's dance was off. It was also known that he
was incommunicado and without servants. It was known
that Bernard Coppinger had bought Mount Lambert for a
sum that was variously estimated at figures between £10,000
and £100,000. It was known that Miss Beddington was
unwell and was refusing callers. It was known that Elizabeth was returning; and it was left an open question whether she had been banished by the Canon as a result of
information that had reached him of a certain scandalous
episode in the river during the Perrys' party.

All this shared knowledge kept everyone busy. The
Canon retired as usual to his study. He had never had so
many anxieties pressing on him at once. Ralph had refused
to discuss Mount Lambert at breakfast. Ever since he had
gone into Mr Fox's office he had adopted a pedantic reticence about such public questions.

More than once the Canon resolved to call on the Count
and offer assistance; but what if he was presented with a
request for £1,000? The Count dealt in sums of that magnitude and would show contempt for offers of less. This consideration ultimately prevailed and brought the Canon back
to his chair.

A glimpse of Michael Molloy through the window suggested another plan. He opened the window and beckoned to Michael who was on his way to the yard with the milk.

"I want you to run a message for me. I understand that Major Paul is short of staff at the moment. Will you slip over to him and say I shall be only too pleased to look after any of his livestock for the time being. You won't mind lending a hand, Michael, will you? I think we all want to give the Major as much help as we can."

Michael, as always, raised no difficulty, but he hung on instead of going about his business, and it was clear that he had something he wanted to say. He required to be rescued from these positions.

"Is there anything on your mind, Michael?"

"Is it true, Canon, that the ball is off."

"I'm afraid so. The Major has suffered a loss in his family."

"I'm sorry to hear that."

Still Michael didn't go.

"Is there anything else?"

"I heard Angela say that Mount Lambert is sold to Mr Coppinger."

"I heard that, too. I'm afraid it is the case. But you won't be disturbed, Michael. I heard my son say that whoever bought it would have to let you have your house and your field."

"I wasn't minding about myself. Does Miss Elizabeth know?"

"I don't suppose so. She has been in the West. But she will hear when she comes back today."

Michael remained silent.

"Is there anything else?"

"Could you not get on to Sir Julian, Canon, and stop this? The place must go to Miss Elizabeth. Sir Julian will listen to you."

"I'll certainly write, Michael, though it's not really my business. I'll say how upset we all are and mention you."

"Do that, Canon. Do that."

Michael looked relieved and waited no longer.

"One for Coppinger; one for Bradshaw; one for Fox; and the last for myself."

The Count arranged the ammunition in his revolver, and then took up the telephone. Each time he dialled he was met with a vague noise which was all too familiar. The telephone had been cut off again. He wanted to urge haste on the horse-dealers because his antennae told him that today was the last day. Fox's men would certainly come. Otherwise the Count had no desire to communicate with the outside world. He had made arrangements with Michael to call when passing for messages. In the last few days he had established a perfect understanding with Michael; the Canon's defection and Elizabeth's mysterious disappearance left him no other ally. Miss Beddington had done her bit.

He could only pace up and down, taking a glass of brandy at intervals, waiting to see who would arrive first. At half past eleven he saw Michael riding up the road very fast on his bicycle; and he went down to meet him. He had a bulky parcel on the carrier which he pushed into the Count's arms as if it were a damp baby.

The Count looked annoyed. He was on a razor's edge, and he had no patience to deal with well-intentioned distractions of the kind Michael was likely to offer.

"Look."

Not concealing his irritation the Count tore open the package and found inside a bag. In the bag there was a large heap of sovereigns.

His first impression was that Michael had carried out a burglary.

"You can take it. It's mine. Ask Mr Fox. He'll tell you. It will pay for the ball for Miss Elizabeth."

Michael perfectly understood that if lack of funds was the reason for cancelling the party, the Count, as a gentleman, would have had to devise another explanation. The Count said nothing. His fingers ran through the gold as if they were sifting sand. There were tears in his eyes. Moses had struck the rock. Seizing him with one hand, with the other he stuffed the money roughly into Michael's various pockets. Then he clapped him on the back.

"Too late, comrade. Hang on to them. God bless you."

While this scene was in progress there were sounds outside on the gravel; and Michael was deprived of an opportunity to argue by a knock on the door.

"At last," the Count said, and went to answer it.

There were two men at the door. They looked like clerks. One said, "Are you Major Christian Paul?"

When the Count said he was, he was given what the man explained was an execution order over his goods. He and his assistant would make an inventory of them and remain on the premises. The amount due on the order, as well as costs, was £1,579.18.4.

The Count was no stranger to legal proceedings. Another man might huff and bluff. He wasted no time on that.

"I am going up to my study," he said; then, to Michael, "I want to give you a note for Miss Elizabeth."

Then he went to his study and locked the door.

Later in the day, the horse-box arrived. The Count did not appear; but after a conversation between the Sheriff's men and the driver the horse-box returned to Dublin empty.

Another council of war was called at the Canon's house when it was known that the Sheriff's men were in possession at Kent and that the Count had locked himself into his room.

Miss Beddington came over to see the Canon in dignified distress: she had a solution to offer: they must find out how much the Count's debt was and pay it at once; it was the only way to get 'those dreadful men out of his house'. The Canon blenched, but he was not going to let Miss Beddington make the sacrifice alone. He would certainly join. His objection that the Count's pride would be hurt was swept aside by Barbara. But they had to find out how much was involved.

Mrs Ormsby listened to these proposals with alarm. It was all very well for Barbara, who (and at her age) was notoriously 'mad about the Count'; but it was really pushing the loyalty of the Mile to an absurdity if any part of her own capital, their only means of support, should be siphoned off in this way. While the conversation was in progress she bethought herself of ringing up Ralph to inform him what was in the wind. He was able to tell her not only the amount of the present debt but to warn her that it was only a drop in the ocean. Bankruptcy was the Count's certain fate. He had survived it twice, and would, no doubt, again.

Fortified by this information, Mrs Ormsby marched in to the study where the two idealists were hatching their relief schemes.

"This nonsense has got to stop," was the way in which Mrs Ormsby prefaced her bulletin.

The Canon's head bowed before the storm; as so often in his life his wife was rescuing him from the consequences of his good-nature. She acted as an unfailing goal-keeper of their fortune, guaranteed to save the free kicks that he so liberally gave away. Under his gentle anguish there was a relief which he was careful to conceal. He even put up some half-hearted counter-proposal.

But Barbara Beddington was in love. Prudence which had marked her whole life until lately had become disgusting to her. She was wasting time, she told herself. She would have to act on her own. £1,500 was about a tenth of her fortune; but she was quite prepared to sacrifice it. Her cheque-book was in her bag; and she was going to call at Kent and pay off the Court messengers. That was her simple plan. Presumably they waited long enough in the house of their victims to enable them to look for last-minute help before they emptied the house of its contents. (Miss Beddington had not told the Ormsbys that she was housing the Count's valuables.)

Mrs Ormsby had argued that the Count's best policy was

to clear out. Barbara heard this as a sentence of doom. He had taken leave of her; but while she held his furniture she could reasonably hope that he would return; and Mrs Ormsby's suggestions were arrows in her heart. At length she excused herself, going just as Elizabeth arrived. The sight of the girl seemed to unnerve her completely.

"What is the matter with Barbara?" Elizabeth asked, looking after the retreating figure. Miss Beddington had rushed past her in tears.

Mrs Ormsby gave Elizabeth an account of recent events. She listened to it stone-faced; and then said she wanted to see Michael. It seemed quite irrelevant—she was the most unpredictable girl—and Mrs Ormsby explained that Michael wouldn't appear until later in the day. That did not satisfy her. She *must* see Michael. She would go at once to his lodge.

She was away for about an hour, and returned looking preoccupied and mysterious.

The Canon had been looking forward enormously to having Elizabeth with them again. He could not understand why she had gone off to Connemara. Distressed as he was by his neighbour's troubles, now that he was honourably relieved from being involved in them—the arrival of the bailiffs had put an end to any prospect of stabling horses—the Canon was looking forward to a lowering of tension, to hearing of Elizabeth's adventures in the West. He never liked to be racked for long; and his instinctive aim in life was to avoid the fate of Lear in the last act: he had no appetite for tragedy. But Elizabeth was tongue-tied at dinner. Ralph had not come home. Mrs Ormsby was preoccupied. The Canon opened up several themes, but got no encouragement. He was reduced in the end to silence. It was a miserable occasion.

They were about to rise from the table when a frantic knocking at the door was followed by the appearance of a flustered Angela to say that Mrs Bartholomew had come over for help.

This very superior woman was standing in the hall, frightened and rather incoherent. Miss Beddington had come home from calling on the Count in a state of complete collapse. Mrs Ormsby went with her at once. The Canon accompanied them for part of the way and returned to find that Elizabeth had gone up to her room.

On leaving Cumberland Miss Beddington went straight to Kent. Nothing was going to put her off. Voices were counselling caution; she needed every penny of her capital; the amount she was giving away would bring only temporary respite; she was throwing money down the drain to demonstrate the sincerity of her feelings; her money was a symbol of her own surrender; with it she was throwing herself at him. If she waited her resolution might cool. She must act at once.

Kent looked forlorn as she approached. The grandest of the lodges, today it had a deserted air. As she came down the drive her excitement as a deliverer gave way to gloomy apprehension : she had come to save; but she felt now that there was nothing left to save. She knew the Count's study. A glimpse of his face at the window would provide the link with reality that she needed—she seemed to be acting in a dream—but the windows shared the abandoned air that had descended on the house and grounds. A battered Morris, belonging presumably to the agents of the Law, only added to the general feeling of desertion. She hesitated at the door; and as she did so the weight of impending catastrophe settled on her heart. She wanted to shriek for help.

A shot rang out.

She turned and ran, ran from the house, falling once, pursued by the shapeless form of a living fear. Mrs Bartholomew found her prostrate, in the hall.

CHAPTER XX

Mrs Ormsby's first action was to ring for the doctor. Miss Beddington was plainly suffering from shock. Her condition concerned the Canon's practical wife directly; the reason for it was a secondary consideration. Only when Miss Beddington was in bed with the curtains drawn and reluctantly consuming brandy, Mrs Ormsby took in the fact that the Count had shot himself.

She heard the news with remarkable fortitude; but, then, she had never cared for the Count, and there was something comfortingly final about his latest exploit. That was her first sensation; her second was shame at her first. Her third, an amalgam of excitement, curiosity and compassion. Miss Beddington's hopelessly subjective account had blurred the issue; only the shot had been decisive. She was not able to give any further particulars. Had the shot been fatal? One gave him credit for that, a perfectionist in all matters requiring taste of skill. But shouldn't somebody do something practical at such a moment? Ring the Guards, for instance. Mrs Ormsby decided to pass the responsibility over to Ralph who had been of inestimable assistance earlier in the day.

The doctor came, found the patient had received the right treatment, gave her a sedative and congratulated Mrs Ormsby on her efficiency. Mrs Bartholomew could be left in charge; and Mrs Ormsby returned to Cumberland.

The Canon was walking up and down, flapping his hands; he, too, had turned to Ralph, and was waiting for his report. Elizabeth had not come down and was short with Mrs Ormsby when she went up to enquire. She was tired and had gone to bed and wanted to be left alone.

"She is upset, poor child," the Canon said, "and it takes

her in her own way. I have tried to pray; but I find it difficult. One is thrown back on one's resources at these times,
and they are inadequate. While you were away with Barbara I found myself rehanging the Rowlandsons—a sudden
compulsion. I could not have explained it. I wish Ralph
would hurry. I want to hear the whole story. What an
exposure of my inadequacy that a friend should be on the
verge of self-slaughter and that he should not have turned to
me for sympathy. I thought he was only acting from bravado when he produced his gun the other day. But it gives a
very curious complexion to that apparition I saw through
the window. Was it a glimpse into the future? Are we
vouchsafed such things? Should I have acted then? Ralph
was unsympathetic. The young are so summary. He thinks I
am a fool."

"No dear. Of course not," said Mrs Ormsby, who was
knitting.

The crunch of tyres and the glare of head-lights brought
the Ormsbys to the door to greet their son. They had both
assumed the attitude of people who are about to hear the
details of a tragedy. On Mrs Ormsby it sat awkwardly: it
was habitual with the Canon whose sensibilities were in a
constant state of siege. The contrast between their unnatural
gravity and their son's nonchalance—he was grinning
broadly—was ludicrous.

"He shot the grey horse and turned the mad one out. It's
going to be the devil to catch," was Ralph's first remark.

"Who cares about the horses? Have you seen him?" Mrs
Ormsby demanded.

"He's gone."

"But Barbara said he shot himself."

"Barbara is talking through her hat."

CHAPTER XXI

ON THE MORNING after the Count's disappearance the breakfast tables on the Mile were as lively as the Stock Exchange during a boom, not only was there the news from Kent, subtly varied in each house, but the post had brought a letter from Bernard Coppinger to say that the ball planned for his own house would now take place at Mount Lambert.

Miss Beddington had been given the good news about the Count the night before. The Canon had called in person at midnight; the Coppingers' letter was, in her eyes, dastardly. She knew that Bernard Coppinger had had the effrontery to ask for Mount Lambert before. This meant that he was cashing in on the Count's disaster. It did not strike her that Coppinger was now the owner of the house.

The Brownes were delighted at the news. Syl had wanted to come out at Mount Lambert, and the Coppingers had included her in their first invitation. The Count had pointedly excluded her until one day, on a whim, he decided to recant.

Since the Count's financial failure the Brownes had written him off. So had the Perrys. Herbert Perry regarded bankruptcy as the most anti-social of all malfeasances beginning with the letter B. The Captain had been in splendid form since the Count's troubles began. He had even dreamed that he was dancing on Herbert Perry's face. The Coppingers' card pleased him no end because he rarely received letters from anyone.

The Canon shared Miss Beddington's view; but he saw further. This meant that the Coppingers had bought Mount Lambert. He was grieved, for himself and for Elizabeth (still in her room) and for Michael (milking the cow) unaware that his world had come to an end. The Canon went out to break the news to him. Michael listened and then, to his employer's surprise, asked for Coppinger's letter. He was wonderfully calm.

Elizabeth, who seemed to be a hundred miles away, shrugged her shoulders when in due course she was told.

All day trucks and vans were seen going up the road to Mount Lambert. Bernard was himself in charge of operations, it was said. To hope to prepare the house in two days was certainly to ask for a miracle; but he liked a challenge of that kind. Expense was no object; and already the newspapers had been tipped off. *The Irish Times* announced to its readers that Saturday would carry a feature by Bernard himself of which the intriguing title was "Operation Ball". It would be illustrated by photographs of the dance in progress as well as containing his own account of what it was like to acquire one's dream house and condition it for such a grand occasion in forty-eight hours. It was a scoop for the paper which the Sundays would copy, trying to pretend they had been let in on the story too.

The ball distracted attention from the Count's disappearance; but that would undoubtedly be the main topic of conversation at the dance. Miss Beddington sent her excuses to the Coppingers. The Canon was perplexed in the extreme; direct action always intimidated him. Ralph had no compunction. He was going. So was Elizabeth (Miss Beddington was shocked by this). In the end the Canon decided not to go but to send a long letter of apology by Ralph. He would plead his age and his wife's reluctance to take part in festive occasions.

CHAPTER XXII

THE LAST WORKMEN had left Mount Lambert at six o'clock. The dancing floor was polished. The supper table was laid. Theatrical improvisations gave the house an inhabited appearance. Bernard Coppinger surveyed the scene with understandable complacency before he went home to get himself ready. He had planned a special costume.

His pleasure was not increased by the appearance of Bradshaw in the doorway.

"Come to look round," he explained. He did so, whistling rather loudly, and it occurred to Coppinger that he was expressing his right to be included in the party. Was he not a substantial shareholder in the property?

The idea of inviting him had not occurred to Bernard; but he was a man who marched with the times and he was too indifferent to everyone to distinguish very much between people. That the Milers would be outraged by Bradshaw's appearance did not occur to him. That Bradshaw and Mrs Bradshaw would look incongruous did; but that was their own affair. Bourgeois society had its doom pronounced by the brothers Goncourt. The message had not taken a hundred years to reach the ears of Bernard Coppinger. He was the means selected by Providence to pass it on to the Mile.

His eyes clicked into a smile.

"If you and the missus would like to come you'd be very welcome. I didn't know whether you went to dances."

"My old one can't put a foot under her."

Bernard clicked off his smile. Bradshaw stopped whistling. He had gained his point. He would hang round and watch the fun. There would be plenty to do and to see. He had been recognised as an equal. That was all he wanted. By not giving a conclusive answer to Bernard he had given a hint that he was getting no more than his right. He would let himself be seen during the evening. It meant shaving and putting on his Sunday suit; but it was a red-letter day.

Ralph was in a state of acute but suppressed excitement on the day of the ball. The Count's adventures had upset the pattern of life; and this was the first time Ralph would have an opportunity to be alone with Elizabeth since their mountain drive. She had sent him post-cards from the West, but given him no idea where he stood with her. The Count's disappearance was from his point of view an unmitigated blessing : even if Elizabeth had been upset by it, he stood a better chance of coming to an understanding with her now. She was probably piqued.

The ball began at ten o'clock. Elizabeth dined with the Ormsbys; Ralph stayed late in the office and came back at nine to change. When he came down he was irritated to hear that Elizabeth had slipped in to see how Barbara Beddington was, and had not returned by ten. It was a most eccentric time to choose to pay a visit. On edge, Ralph drove round to Clarence and, inexcusably, put his hand on the horn. Some minutes later he rang the house bell and Mrs Bartholomew answered it.

"I've come for Miss Lambert."

"She isn't here, Mr Ralph. She came over at tea-time. Would you like to see Miss Beddington?"

Ralph had no desire to see Miss Beddington : he drove home, bumping his car on the gate-post in his hurry to look for an explanation of Elizabeth's behaviour. The headlights of the car lit up the Canon and his wife and Angela standing on the steps, staring in the direction of Mount Lambert. The trees hid the house from view, but sheets of flame rose over their tops and danced like fountains in the evening sky.

266

CHAPTER XXIII

E<small>LIZABETH'S DRESS CAUGHT</small> in the brambles as she made her way by Michael's short-cut. The weekend rain had left the path very muddy in places, and she lost her shoes more than once. She had to take care crossing the back avenue in case any cars were coming that way. She must not be seen. It was unlikely that Bradshaw would be snooping round this part of the estate tonight.

Inside her cottage she had a change of clothes and a small suitcase. She kept looking at her watch. At five minutes to ten she locked up the cottage and took the path that led past Bradshaw's house. This was unnerving; but she had the cover of trees. From there to Michael's lodge was a minute's walk. She knocked three times on the window. After a short delay the door opened and the Count came out. He said nothing, but walked across the haggard to the barn. Elizabeth followed. The Count started to pull at the hay, and after a few seconds the bonnet of his Alfa Romeo peeped out from under it. He opened the door and Elizabeth got in beside him.

A car was turning in the gate; the Count let it pass and then drove out and turned to the left, away from the Mile. The road made a half-circle and then ran steeply up-hill. At the top, the Count pulled up.

"Look down, Elizabeth. I want you to see this."

She could see nothing but the black outline of the mountain against the sky. Underneath them the trees were a dark lake.

But she waited and watched. Someone had lit a bonfire in the trees. It made a pool of flame. Then another appeared beside it. Another and another and another. Now the whole forest looked as if it was on fire.

"Mount Lambert gives its answer to Mr Coppinger," the Count said.

They watched. Then the Count started the car, and it rolled down towards the city. Elizabeth said nothing. Not for the first time had she put her stake on a wild chance; but never had she burnt her boats so completely. The first exhilaration had passed; she was a little frightened; a little lonely.

The Count was in tremendous form. He sang his favourite song, unmindful what tender associations it had for a woman whom he had left on the Mile.

"Sur le pont d'Avignon
On y danse, on y danse."

They drove to the airport. The plane was going to London, where they would change for Switzerland.

They had ten minutes to wait. The Count had no small change. He borrowed pennies from Elizabeth and bought a post-card which he addressed to a Mr Bechstein telling him that his Alfa Romeo was in the car park of the airport and could be collected on payment of a few shillings. The key was with the attendant.

"I would not feel happy if Mr Bechstein did not get back his car," the Count explained. "I am sensitive on points like this. I suppose I am a fool; but when you betray your code the time has come to throw in your chips."

They did not discuss their plans. Michael had given Elizabeth the Count's note and they had met in Michael's lodge. He had told her everything then. "I will settle with Coppinger. You will see. Fox thinks he has trapped me. His clients won't get a penny. I shot the grey filly. If I can't keep her, she will not win or breed for any of Fox's crew. I think that settles my account with Fox. I sent a case of champagne to the little Captain. I had hit him too hard, and he has no sting.

"I could have married nice Barbara, but the boredom would have been terrible, and I would have spent all her money. I leave her a beautiful dream. The Canon failed me; but he is not a bad man. I understand him. The others are not worth our consideration. Michael will be all right. He had that money he tried to give me. Noble little fellow. He has his field and his lodge. He wants no more. Moreover he has been my chosen instrument to revenge the Lamberts. He will save their honour. He is a happy man.

"I told Ralph to take you away from me if he could; but I fear that he is as ineffective as his father and as prosaic as his mother. What do you want, Liz? What can I give you? I do not promise love. I don't know what that word means. I will not marry. I am old enough to be your father. But I am a good comrade. Ask any of the men who fought with me in the Legion. Will you be my comrade?"

"O cut it out, Ritzy. You know I can't live without you."

EPILOGUE

THE FIRE AT Mount Lambert broke out just before the first guests arrived. The house was completely gutted. Fortunately no lives were lost. The suddenness of the fire and the astonishing speed with which it spread made it look deliberate from the start. Its thoroughness made investigation difficult. One of the workmen had remarked a smell like petrol during the day but had not given it a second thought. The Insurance Company's investigators found that all the petrol kept in the yard had been used up. Descriptions of how the fire started confirmed the impression, which was finally arrived at, that someone had soaked the attic storey in petrol and set it alight on the evening of the dance. The fact that Bradshaw was found to have such a substantial interest in the premises (they were fully insured) and that the petrol used was under his control, made the Insurance Company very suspicious. They made enquiries about him; but discovered nothing worse than a reputation for extreme shrewdness in business.

Bernard Coppinger was upset. Nobody had ever seen him in that condition before. But if he had no ball to describe in the newspaper, he had a wonderful fire; and his prose was highly coloured enough to match the occasion. If he had to abandon the idea of an artists' playground, he did very well by selling building lots. There are a hundred new houses at Mount Lambert; and they are very much in demand by young couples who want something a little out of the ordinary. Bradshaw moved into Kent. The Count's carpets are in safe custody up the road; and Bradshaw prefers linoleum : being in the business, he got his at a considerable reduction. Bradshaw is flourishing, and seems to derive satisfaction from his business association with Coppinger. He rings him up at his office and at home at all hours, invariably beginning "How's tricks?" On Sundays and holidays when the Coppingers are entertaining, Bradshaw frequently drops in. When he is left out of the 'crack', he whistles.

The Count when last heard of was in some mysterious African army; he had high rank and was successful in training native recruits who believed him to have occult powers. Elizabeth was stranded in an African town and, it was said, showed signs of extreme boredom. The Ormsbys and Miss Beddington have often spoken of leaving the Mile; but they take no steps to put the plan into execution. Ralph Ormsby was employed by Bernard Coppinger to look after his interests at the time of the fire. He managed the task so efficiently that he was given all the Coppinger business, including the Mount Lambert housing development. He is doing well and Mr Fox has hinted at a partnership. Michael Molloy has become odder than ever. He never talks to anyone now; but he is seen walking about, rubbing his hands together. He is constantly laughing to himself as if he were enjoying some delightful secret. He is putting on weight.